HE TOOK HER BODY
AND STOLE HER SOUL

He said against her mouth, "I want you, Leah." They made love in her bed, the student papers hastily brushed to the floor, Ben's clothing, Leah's nightgown, strewn across the floor. He was wonderful. He was tender, solicitous, "The perfect lover," she thought, gasping with sheer pleasure . . . "Ah, no," she said aloud. "Ah, please *yes.*"

She had fleetingly wondered, as her nightgown fell, "Why does he want to make love now?" and had now been able to answer. "And what if it doesn't work with me?"

But the moments of doubt were lost, dismissed . . .

Other Avon Books by
Shirley Schoonover

MOUNTAIN OF WINTER
WINTER DREAM

A SEASON OF HARD DESIRES

SHIRLEY SCHOONOVER

DISCARDED

NORMANDALE COMMUNITY COLLEGE
LIBRARY
9700 FRANCE AVENUE SOUTH
BLOOMINGTON, MN 55431-4399

JUN 1 5 2006

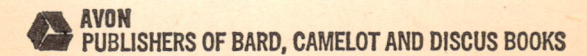

AVON
PUBLISHERS OF BARD, CAMELOT AND DISCUS BOOKS

Dedicated to Ron, Robin and Noel,
the three people I love most.

A SEASON OF HARD DESIRES is an original publication of Avon Books. This work has never before appeared in book form.

All of the characters in this book are fictitious and any resemblance to actual persons living or dead is therefore coincidental.

AVON BOOKS
A division of
The Hearst Corporation
959 Eighth Avenue
New York, New York 10019

Copyright © 1981 by Shirley Schoonover
Published by arrangement with the author
Library of Congress Catalog Card Number: 80-69893
ISBN: 0-380-77149-7

All rights reserved, which includes the right to reproduce this book or portions thereof in any form whatsoever except as provided by the U.S. Copyright Law. For information address Sterling Lord Agency, 660 Madison Avenue, New York, New York 10021

First Avon Printing, June, 1981

AVON TRADEMARK REG. U.S. PAT. OFF. AND IN OTHER COUNTRIES, MARCA REGISTRADA, HECHO EN U.S.A.

Printed in the U.S.A.

10 9 8 7 6 5 4 3 2 1

ೞ The Lightning Struck ೞ Tower

FIRST it had been the matchbooks. No, no, Leah thought, coming up out of the dream. It had been the thread she'd been following through the labyrinth. A bloody thread, a red line traced on road maps. Vacations and trips he'd taken without her. Orion. "No, Ben," she said aloud. She'd rolled in her sleep, coming up through the watery light, the sea creature of her dream, moving through the deeps of her dreams, now moving into the shallows of wakefulness. "We have to talk," she said aloud. She sat up in the narrow Icelandic daybed and lit a cigarette. "Four o'clock." The casement cloth in the open window shifted, holding the wind like a shroud, and the apparitions in the corner slouched farther into shadow. Ben would still be asleep in the master bedroom, withdrawn to his side of the big bed, his back turned to the center. "But we have to talk," she said. She smoked the cigarette and waited for the day to begin.

Before she could talk properly to Ben over breakfast, the telephone rang. It was Zulu. "Hi!" Zulu's low voice grated. "I know Ben's going out of town again. Wanna have dinner with me tonight? I haven't seen much of you this summer and when school starts I won't be able to get you away from your students and books. Hah?"

Ben took his coffee cup and cigarette to the dining room, shrugging at her as he closed the door.

"I guess so. I'll call you later, okay?"

"Whyn't I just come by around seven. If you don't wanna go out I'll go on by myself. Come on, you can't mope around that big house all alone."

"I'll see you at seven," Leah surrendered.

"Okay!"

Leah put the receiver back into its wall cradle and followed Ben into the dining room with the coffeepot.

"Ready for more?" she asked him.

"No, thanks. I have to finish packing." He flipped the newspaper open to the editorial page and glanced at it. "I'll take this along for the crossword, all right?"

"Fine. Ben, we've let the summer get away from us and we still haven't really talked."

"Mmm." He took out the crossword page, folded it, then let his eyes meet hers for a moment. "I don't think this is the appropriate time, do you? Not when I'm on my way out of town."

"I know. But we waited until summer because you said we should. School and final exams for me to finish. You had the histology lab class to close up. And . . . I couldn't seem to find a . . . an appropriate time this summer. And we don't even sleep in the same bed now so I can't catch that split second that might be appropriate. . . ."

"It wasn't my idea for you to move into the study."

"That's it. I couldn't stay in the same bed. There's something between us, some . . . thing . . . between us. A coldness . . ." She was searching for a more descriptive or less damning word, but he interrupted.

"When I get back. That will be better for both of us. You'll be rested. My head will be clear of this seminar thing."

She didn't answer. She let the moment move from a pause to a loud-drawn-out declaration of silence.

He tapped his fingers on the white tablecloth, then let his hand go flat. "I don't want to talk *now*." She suddenly knew why novelists described eyes "obsidian": Ben's were bright, clear, hard.

"Ben. We have to talk now. It's August. In three weeks it will be September and all the excuses and reasons for not talking will again become all too available. . . ." She meant to go on, but he glared her into silence. "There," she said. "That's precisely what I want to talk about. Somehow I feel so damned helpless. Stared down into being quiet. We have problems, and I don't know what they are and you won't let me ask about them."

He stood up. "Not now, Leah." He walked out of the dining room and the door slapped shut behind him.

She sat for a moment staring at the empty space he had

left in the room. Then she picked up the coffeepot, carried it back to the kitchen, and followed Ben to the bedroom.

He had laid his open suitcase on the luggage bench and was folding slacks into it.

Psi, the Siamese, climbed up into the suitcase and lay down on the slacks, washing his face vigorously, purring with huge approval. Ben picked him up and set him on the bed. He smiled at the cat, then at Leah. "He's grown some more, hasn't he? He weighs a ton."

"He had a potbelly this winter, remember?" She perched on the foot of the bed.

"Let go of that." Ben pulled a rolled-up pair of socks out of the cat's jaws, pausing to rough its stomach. The cat bit his hand, not breaking the skin but laying ears back in mock ferocity. "You'll be all right, won't you?" Ben asked.

"Oh, me, you mean. Yes," Leah said. Something in his tone startled her. There had been another level of meaning in it. It reminded her of the dream, something from the labyrinth. She tried to catch the thread from the dream. She closed her eyes, thinking: If I can find it out, pry it out to look at it, confront this *one* thing, I can . . . I can . . . But it eluded her. She looked at Ben.

He was looking at her, which was not startling in itself, but with such a rocketry of changing expressions that she couldn't trace any one configuration: affection, impatience, concern, anger, what? She was muted by shock, felt her face and lips form a question that she couldn't articulate.

He looked at his wristwatch. "I'm about ready to go. I can pick up a shirt if I run into laundry or cleaning problems," he said, then made his remark doubly irrelevant by adding: "But I hardly think I'd have cleaning problems at the Beverly Hilton." He closed the suitcase and locked it. "I can take a cab to the airport if you'd rather."

"No. I want to take you out. I'm used to the traffic by now. Anyway, I can take your car—it's got better pickup than Sassy."

"You should get that clutch looked at. Thirty thousand is a lot of miles on a Pinto. Well, I'm set." He adjusted his necktie and pulled his suit jacket on, shooting his shirt cuffs and shrugging his shoulders for fit.

Leah, tying a wraparound skirt over her shorts,

watched him, half smiling, aware of her bone-marrow response to him. He is so damned sexy, she thought. I *had* to love someone like him. She looked at the cat lying in the middle of the bed. Is lubricious a word? That's how I feel. Lubricious, my heart's lump, you Ben, you lover. Aloud she said: "I'm ready. Let me just lock the doors and grab my shoulder bag."

She watched Ben put his suitcase into the trunk of his black Ford LTD. She walked around to the driver's side and, unlocking the door, saw on the floor of the back seat, in that meticulously kept, spotless car, a crumpled beer can.

Leah backed the car out of the driveway and drove along Dickon Avenue. It always takes that first block or so, she thought, for me to be accustomed to driving Ben's big Ford.

It was not until they were out on the freeway that she thought again about the beer can. Another knot in the thread that led me ever deeper into the maze, she thought. Too much is beginning to happen to me. She was learning too much; she couldn't osmose it all, not all at once. Matchbooks, maps, knots, threads, too many answers, she thought. What's the question that eludes me? She looked at Ben.

Part of her attention still on maneuvering the LTD through the freeway traffic, she studied Ben's left profile —the handsome brow, the slightly hooded eye the color of lantern light now by day, the lean face, the straight (not Roman, but almost Roman) nose, the long upper lip— that philtrum where she had kissed a thousand times and died in breathing the air from his lips, the deep-cut cleft chin, the strong jaw where she had rested her own face. She looked at him: his elegantly long bones, the manicured doctor's hands, the faint hairs on the tops of his hands and wrists, his flat belly, and those long sexy thighs. She looked at him, yearned, and falteringly said, "We really do need to talk. I love you. But there is something going on . . . or not going on . . . that I don't understand." She looked back at the freeway.

"I assumed you knew," he said. "There's been someone all along."

She didn't hear the last few words. Hysterical deafness, she thought. The air scorched her skin. Lightning struck.

Or something struck; she heard it strike. And suddenly, nauseatingly, she did hear him, but only as she heard the other sound: the *crack* of her fist against his jaw.

"Oh, Ben! I'm sorry!" she said. Left hand on the steering wheel, she tried to touch him with the right hand.

He flinched, his eyes looking as stunned as she felt. "Uh-oh." He warded her hand away, shaking his head. He looked frightened of her, angry, wary.

"Oh, my god! What can I do?" She tried to touch him again, but he glared lethally at the hand she held out. "No, I won't touch you. I didn't *mean* to. What can I do? Are you hurt?"

He held his jaw with his left hand, still glaring at her. A tear formed in the corner of one eye. He brushed it away in a fury. He was shaking with rage.

"Tell me what you want me to do." She prayed: Oh, *please*, Ben, tell me what to do. She heard the panic in her voice, she tried to calm herself. "What can I do? I did hurt you? Do you want to go to the hospital? Yes?" Half mad from the storm of feelings, she looked for an exit sign, found one, and turned off the freeway. "Do you want Saint Luke's West? Yes?" When she saw him nod, she located herself mentally and turned back toward the city. "Do you want emergency? Should I call anyone special?" Timidly: "Do you think it's broken?"

He shook his head. He continued to glare at her over his askew, half-opened mouth, warding her off with his left hand.

"I'll go in with you and then I'll wait. Is that what you want?"

He nodded.

They drove the rest of the way in silence, Leah cringing away from Ben, from her hysterical guilt.

Saint Luke's West was where Ben had his office and laboratory and where he taught histo-pathology, where he conducted his research, now focused on choriocarcinoma. Leah parked the car in the doctors' parking lot and followed Ben into the hospital. She let him walk ahead through the tiled corridor to the emergency sector. The receiving nurse glanced up and recognized Ben.

"Doctor Calloway!" She bobbed to her feet and came around the counter. "What can I do for you? Nothing serious? What happened to your jaw? Oh. I'll buzz Doctor

Pollack for you." She turned to speak into a desk microphone. "Now, let's get you into Room One and take a look at you." She glanced at Leah. "Hello, Miz Calloway. How did it happen? Is he in much pain?"

Leah blushed. "It was . . . an accident. I think he must be in pain."

"Well, you sit down out here. I'll let you know how he is right away. Here comes Doctor Pollack. He'll get this put right." She had taken Ben's elbow and ushered him into the emergency room, moving with a speedy competence that was soothing to Leah.

Leah found a cigarette, stuck it into the Water Pik filter and lit it, inhaling mightily. The hospital air conditioning chilled her. She could feel her shirt drying as she sat there; she shivered. He can't go to California now. Her heart, which had been reviving, sank. Oh, God. I can't . . . cannot face him. I hit him. Oh, Jesus. Don't let his jaw be broken. She looked at the door of Emergency Room One. Doctor Pollack had closed it behind him. She couldn't hear a murmur. She paced down the corridor a few steps, knees slippery in their sockets. She sat down suddenly and put her face into her hands. I cannot face him. Not that silent reproach, that glare.

The nurse came out of the room. Seeing Leah, she came over and put an arm around her. "It will be fine!" Pat-pat went the hand on Leah's shoulder. "Don't cry, Miz Calloway. I know how upsetting it is when someone you love is hurt. But he'll be all right. Can I bring you anything?" Pat-pat.

Leah sighed, groaned, shook her head.

"I told Doctor Calloway you'd be out here worrying. So I came out to tell you he'll be fine. Doctor Pollack ordered X-rays just to be sure. And then when the X-rays are done I'm sure you can take Doctor Calloway home."

The door opened and Ben strode down the corridor. He did not glance at Leah.

The X-rays had agreed with Doctor Pollack: a dislocated jaw. Which Doctor Pollack set tidily in place.

"It feels perfect," Ben said, shaking Doctor Pollack's hand and smiling widely at him.

Ben stopped at the reception counter on the way out of the hospital. "Thank you, too, Mrs. D. You're certainly on top of everything. Our patients are fortunate to have you to attend to them." He shook both her hands and hugged her, still smiling.

"Oh, thank you," the nurse said. She glowed.

"Thank you," Leah said, too. She followed Ben out of the hospital; the nurse was still at his side. She ushered them through the sliding glass doors and waved.

Ben's smile Cheshired out of sight. He went to the passenger side of the car and got in.

Leah got in behind the steering wheel, glanced at Ben, and turned the ignition key. "D'you want to go home?" she asked hesitantly.

"No. Can I trust you to keep your hands on the steering wheel? Sorry. I shouldn't have said that. I'll go on to California. I certainly don't have anything more to say right now."

Leah nodded. She concentrated on driving the LTD through the traffic to the freeway and then on to the airport. She parked the car in the short-term parking lot after a split second of argument with herself: I'll let him out at the passenger dock. No, I'll go in and get him checked in. I'll park the car and wave good-bye to him. Then I'll start the motor and commit suicide right damn here. Oh, God, I'm going crazy. I'll help him with his suitcase and then I'll go home.

Ben took the car keys from her and unlocked the trunk, taking his suitcase and briefcase without waiting for her to help. He handed her the keys and, back rigid, strode to the escalator.

"Wait, Ben. Don't you want me to come and help you check in?" She slammed the trunk door and trotted after him.

"It's up to you." He continued up the escalator.

"Oh, Ben, don't you want to talk to me? A later flight? Could you . . . wait until tomorrow?"

"And risk another contretemps? No."

She felt the guilt accumulating around her in layers: a papier-mâché of guilt; she felt it first soft, then hardening into an unmanageable shape around her. "Wait, Ben. No, I don't mean another . . . ugly reaction thing. But we could have a carefully thought-out exchange . . . ?"

"That would take time. And we don't have the time right now." He stepped off the escalator and moved away across the gleaming marble floor of the airport terminal.

She darted after him. "Ben, don't you see? This has become a pattern with us?" She ignored the heads turning to look at her. "You go off in some direction, even at home, and I follow trying to . . . understand or explain." She caught up with him and touched his sleeve.

He looked at her admonishingly, and she let her hand fall. He asked, "Are you going to make a scene here? Now?"

And all the scenes she'd ever made dumped on her head. She shook her head. "No. No, of course not." But then a laugh, unbidden, bubbled to her lips. And the sea-creature self turned, came surging back: resolute. "I should make a scene," she heard herself say. "I should. And then maybe, *maybe* we'd talk, because it seems the only time we do talk is when I've gone too far and we're both scared. Or we're scared at different times about what, *what* is happening to us."

"You forget." He stopped walking to look directly at her; but he held his suitcase between them. *"I didn't hit you."*

"TWA Flight Number Five Seven Nine for Los Angeles is now boarding. Repeat TWA Number Five Seven Nine now loading," the public address system said.

Ben shrugged. "You see." He walked past Leah to the ticket counter. "I'm Doctor Calloway. I have confirmed reservations on Five Seven Nine. I'm checking in now. Smoking section near a window, please."

"Your tickets, sir." The attendant stamped Ben's tickets and repocketed them in the folder. "Have a nice flight, sir."

Suitcase checked through, Ben walked to the down escalator and began the descent.

Leah followed, tears shooting out of her eyes. Nails, she thought. Bullets. Rivers. Tacks. My tears never come like Camille's. My heart is being torn out and I go machine-gunning tears. And Ben knows that. That's the other reason he's rushing ahead of me. Not just that he's furious beyond words. But that I cry so . . . so burlesque! "Ben!" she said aloud, blowing her nose, gulping. "I'm not crying. I'm not making a scene." She struggled to contain herself, the tears, the sobs. "Stoic. See, I'm learning from you. To be stoic." She rubbed her face with a frazzled tissue, and when he turned around, she knew that she had, for once, managed to dam the overflow of emotions and fluids that Ben so dreaded.

He had made his mind up about something. Leah could see that. "Leah," he said kindly. "We may be past talking. I don't know."

"Will you call me? Shall I call you?"

"No. Don't. You always rush into things. You know that. It's not a fault, really. But . . . let's both think. No more assumptions. All right?"

Leah, about to hug him, paused. The sea self resolved; she stood back from Ben and nodded. "All right." She stepped back farther, serious, concentrating, seeing him; seeing something about him and herself that made her take one more step back, to gain a clearer view.

"I suppose you'll hate me now," Ben said.

Surprised, Leah said, "No! How could I?" But the sea self thought: Now he wants to talk. One foot on the airplane. Why does he feel safe now? And the sea self, the gentle sea mammal of Leah, shook her head. I don't hate you. I guess you are right. We should both think. Sort things out. God knows, all the demons and cacodemons are set loose now. She smiled at him.

He didn't reach for her. She knew he wouldn't; he had taken a posture now and would not, or could not, relinquish it. But I do that too, she thought.

She took two more steps away from him. She waved, smiled, and turned away. She glanced back and saw him go through the metal detector. He did not look back.

᛫ The Magus ᛫

THAT was the Lightning Struck Tower. I turn the card around and hear again that lightning *crack* as my fist hit Ben's jaw. And now, at four o'clock in the morning, sleepless, I stop pacing and sit at my desk with the Tarot, laying out a pattern of cards, seeking the clues, the blood knots in the thread that lead me through the labyrinth. The Lightning Struck Tower, and I can almost smell the scorched air, hear the thunder, as the bricks come tumbling down and the tiny people are thrown from the tower and fall forever, endlessly, caught as they are in a sudden, inexplicable convulsion of fate. They hang in midair, arms outstretched, unable to control their direction, their arms always reaching out for balance or for the comfort of another hand that will at least touch them.

I put the card down and light a cigarette. And, unable to sit still, pace the length of my study to the open window, where the casement cloth whispers in the predawn wind. What *had* wakened me? The sea changing, I think. But the sea is part of a continent away, so it is the wind making sea sounds in the trees. And I had surfaced to those sounds, moving through the deeps of sleep to this skyless beach of wakefulness. A cigarette. What had I been dreaming? Of the sea, where I had lain silent and safe, one eye gazing up through the water weeds. The weeds so thick and green that even in the dream I knew it was the Sargasso. It hadn't been a nightmare, not with sea horses and my sea self browsing in the green quiet. No, I had to waken to the daymare.

The wind moves again. Sea-sounding yet, and now it stirs the curtains so that the metaphor changes: they move like shrouds against the white wall of my study. Those shrouds now the wrappings of the dead. The shadows move into the corner of my study where the apparition stands. "I will not look at you," I say aloud. My nightgown clings to my legs. The room closes in on me, I feel it on the back of my neck; across my bare shoulders something draws cobwebs.

Outside, the grass springs up black under my feet, sparkling under the sky like the sea; I walk on the wetness. Something gleams in the wet. I expect seashells, almost, but find toadstools: the Angel of Death, cocks up, thumbing up through the grass. Thumbs or cocks, I step around them and look at the sky. No lightning, not now.

Orion swings in his eternal pattern, aloof, distant beyond imagining: Ben. Ben is like Orion; I have known that, known it without admitting that I knew. Orion moves west and south now; so too does Ben in California. They stalk the night sky, ice-eyed constellations cutting such promises in the air that my bones would rise from the dust to follow.

I sigh at Orion, turn back to the house, pace over the glittering wet lawn. I come from a long line of nightwalkers, my grandmother told me that: of her mother walking by candlelight, by firelight in the Finnish tupa that stood across the lake from Olavinlinna, of Finnish women who walked the castle walls when the mists smoked from the lake and the yarrow and thistle drifted by moonglow, my great-grandmother waited for her red-haired husband who came by moonfall with the unlawfully caught deer or the snared ermine, that red-haired husband who farmed the forests of Savonlinna and played the kantele but who was gone, gone, and she was left alone by firelight to sing hunting songs to the daughter, Henriika, who became my grandmother; and she walked the slanting floor of the sod house built in Minnesota, the uncut land she came to as a bride, her damask tablecloths brought to set a table on the grasslands, the lakes moraine region that groaned and heaved in winter under her feet and wrenched the timbers of the house she helped to build, that house haunted by the earth beneath it, heaving in waves that moved and groaned and foamed up boulders, house-sized boulders, from the belly of an ice age not yet past; grandmother walked those heaving floors with a milk glass nightlight, watching through the ice-burned patterns on the windows for the husband whose voice she heard long past his death, his too early death at forty, and she was left with eight children and the paisleyed walls of the big house and the photographs of stern, staring, somewhat frightened-looking aunts and uncles under domed glass frames; she walked through the spaces made by ticking clocks and the caught breath of untimely death again when her oldest son fell into the November lake, staggered home to fall on the porch and die in her arms, the ice of his clothes crackling around him; she walked, it seemed then, to exorcise the ghosts of her life. And my mother walked from one moonlit room to another, adjusting the crocheted antimacassar, the starched and foaming doilies, the crooked lampshades, brushing crumbs from tables, wiping up the moonlight in a dream she'd had, dreaming always of the twin sons who died: she kept their pictures and baby clothes in a cedar chest, that chest opened at night when sleep emptied from her as mysterious life had emptied from them; I'd hear the thump of the cedar-chest lid at night, hear her pace to the kitchen table to play solitaire, cheating the devil, pursing her lips in concentration, tutting with disappointment or kissing the air when she won. A fact of life: they didn't sleep, those women, couldn't rest in bed, but must pace the distances around and around the earth. The night was not night if my grandmother did not pace slowly through her house, the nightlight haloing her approach, making the shadows run ahead of her; it was not night if my mother did not make the hall floor creak, if she did not tweak a curtain or mouse along the stairs, if she did not, finally, sit down and slap the cards together in a whisper, the dim light of a twenty-five-watt bulb making a fingerplay of shadows on the table that predicted her daytimes: "Hearts, clubs, spades and there's a tear for you," she'd murmur. She'd say, "Unfaithful lover in the cards for you, lost causes for me." And the cards chuckled in her hands, the hearts love, the spades death or grief, the clubs work, the diamonds success or money or your heart's deepest wish come true. And she'd get a letter in the mail that week or the next to fulfill the prophecy. She was not surprised by disaster: forest fire, drought, early frost, a wet spring, all had been seen in the slide of the cards. A birth, a love affair, a death, she'd listen and nod to herself, the secrets gleaming in her eyes, the satisfied look of knowing all beforehand dimpling her cheeks. And the night was not night if she did not lay out the patterns, the mazes of fortunes, cheating the Devil, casting glances at that past that could not change, taking the sting away from the future because, she thought, it could not surprise her.

I hear the clock strike the quarter hour as I walk back into the house. Too early to begin the day: yet I am not able to sleep. If this were autumn and school were in session, I'd have student papers to read, lecture notes to work over. But no, I have nothing but my thoughts and the quiet house; even the shadows are still. The long living room is breathless, the casement cloth motionless at the windows. The dining room is my least favorite room: I have spilt wine there too often, have heard impatient fingers tapping on the damasked table. The kitchen hums to itself, the refrigerator clicking ice cubes endlessly, the electric clock chuttering tinnily, the white Formica counter tops unusually clean, gleaming. "Unusually" because I scrub and polish only when I am upset. And today, yesterday, the day of the Lightning Struck Tower, I hauled the refrigerator and electric range away from the walls, scrubbed, waxed and polished under them, threw the kitchen curtains into the washing machine, washed the windows inside and out, pulled the cupboards apart, emptied drawers, washed every spoon, fork, knife, ladle, pot, pan, paring knife, breaed pan, cookie sheet, Jell-O mold, skillet, ornamental platter and bowl in a fury of penitence and rage. And agony.

Ben.

I turn away from the kitchen, slipping through the side door to the backyard. There Psi comes disapprovingly out of the deep black shade of the pines and sits on the flat stones of the walk. He washes one ear, then stares at me. "Hungry?" I asked him. He follows me into the laundry room, leaps to the top of the dryer, and waits while I dole out his cat food. He eats ravenously, then looks up at me and margles. "Don't talk with your mouth full," I say to him.

I pad along the hall to the master bedroom. The king-sized bed looms white: the Polar Ice Cap of beds; it is uninhabitable now. "Ben," I say aloud. "I won't think about that now." And close the door quickly lest the cold escape with me.

I go back to my study, light another cigarette and look

at the pattern I have laid out, the Tarot cards face down, the labyrinth.

I turn up the next card. The Magus. The Juggler. A quirked eyebrow, a cleft chin, five bells on his cape, the serpent of wisdom at his waist, he's stepping off a precipice, smiling backward over his shoulder. I know this card: foolish idealism. He blithely steps off the precipice, his eyes filled with fantasies. So who does *that* remind me of? And on his back a bundle, his karma, the sum total of his experience. That is all he has—or I have, from forty years of living, a small bundle of experiences and one foot over the precipice. But I look at him again. His face is knowing, as if he has the answer to many riddles. But he is mute, won't talk, won't tell.

Who do I know that has the same kind of etched line in the chin? Who is as enigmatic with silences and riddling looks? Ah yes, Ben. And when he does talk, he deafens me with answers I do not want, cannot yet accommodate. "I assumed you knew," he said. Like the Magus, he has been the juggler of what I knew. A juggler of my fantasies; a juggler of the light and the dark, so skillful that I followed always the misdirection and missed the actuality.

"But, Leah," I say aloud. Cautioning myself, a sword in my own hand, I am the Queen of Swords, and prone to anger. And I see myself, the Sword Queen, running down this maze of cards, tracking the Magus, hearing his bells, searching for him, for whatever lies behind the riddle of *why*. And what would I do if I ever did solve it? "Don't run with that sword," I say aloud. You already have done enough. Don't add Medea to the cast of characters. Prone to impulsive acts, I warn myself. Prone to leap. And I remember another Leah here in the maze, when I went moaning over the moors in search of Heathcliff, unaware that the moors *were* Heathcliff, that I was climbing on the glass mountain even as I searched those obsidian eyes, kissed that mouth, climbed the iceberg and, in my proneness to leap, fell off the precipice with the nightmare sound of my first . . . Oh! if I could have been deep underwater at that moment, my sea-creature self dominant and sounding for the bottom of the Sargasso and my protective weeds.

"Better if I had thrown myself off a cliff," I say. Another prone. Prone to leap, prone to look the other way, I am also prone to self-pity. It is no nature's error that I am part sea creature, for I wallow well, roll about in the thick rich bubbling mud of self-pity. But, at forty, I know that. And know that a good mudbath can be salutary, healthful, and it feels so good. So I take a turn through the nose-drip and the quiver-cheeks with one eye on the clock and hope I have not allotted myself too much time in the tar pits where my griefs and woes are cooking.

I haul out a box of tissue and go to it, sozzling away with the sob and the whimper that I feel I need. I am a good crier. I involve all of me, rocking back and forth, howling and sobbing; a sweat begins, tears shoot out of my eyes. My lungs heave, bellowing the air in and out; the tears soften, turn fruity and ripe—plums, pears, over-ripe and squelching. I roar. The muscles in my neck swell with the effort, I grind my molars. I feel my eyelids swelling. The tears niagara luxuriously. I throw my head back and howl, then I bang my head down on the desk and weep face down for a moment. I stand up, taking the box of tissues with me, pace the hallway, elbowing the apparitions to one side: "I have no energy for you," I wail. The bedroom door is half open and I rush in to throw myself on the bed. But I stop. Bawling and snuffling, I glare at the bed. Three years old and not even the comfy, worn indentations a bed-bed would have; no, it is the Polar Ice Cap. It broadcasts self-containment and stoicism, not lending itself to the roiled sheets of lamentation. Certainly not to the bitten, tear-stained pillow. I hiccup.

And from under the self-pity, its bosom ballerina comes: resentment. I resent the stoicism and self-containment; I resent the tear-drying response this chaste bed elicits from me, the Pavlovian stiffening of my upper lip the moment I cross the threshold of this room. But that's self-pity for you, it skin-ties dishonest rages and valid angers like Siamese twins. Sighing, blowing my nose, I walk back to my study.

The rage of self-pity weakens. But I know that it clings to what I would now have, a clarity of vision. And hindsight does not always come pure. I look at the Magus, dancing there at the precipice. He carries with him his own destiny, the seeds for what he will become. Does he look backward so that he can know better how to go forward? And how far back must I go to know my own destiny? And even as I sit brooding over the Tarot, I realize that too much can happen in one split second; too many patterns, threads, too many rages and griefs can come together to be contained by reason. Does Ben look back, as I do? I dodge, I dodge. I wanted Ben to go to California, not to look at me, not to finish his sentence; not to confront me with what was worse than the truth about him: the truth about me. And I hear that coughing from the shadows, from the center of the maze.

The Page of Cups

THE Page of Cups smiled up at Leah. A flower-decked cap on his head, blond curls, blue eyes, he gleamed, a sun child, a child of sudden squalls; he was to Leah a mystery and a toy. He appeared out of the sunshine when he was five and Leah was six, to stay on the farm; he came swaggering out of the tall grasses behind the farmhouse, eyes belligerent, fists doubled, scabby-kneed, apple-faced, a temper tantrum on the boil. He and Leah were immediately intimate enemies. They slept spooned together in the same bed, he smelled of goats, butted her in the dark, whimpered in fright at the great dreams that billowed and swayed over their heads. They went to the outhouse together, where they read the same pages of the Sears and Monkey Ward wish books, wiped their butts simultaneously, and hauled their pants up with the same snap and grin. They fought each other to a foaming, bawling, blatting, falling-down impasse almost every day, then examined each other tenderly for cuts and bruises; Leah found in him a lifelong love. They were friends. They made faces behind their hands in church, farted in unison in the choir, crawled under the audience's benches and looked up together at the fat knees and thighs of the minister at the altar and his wife in the organ loft.

Joel had tender places in his psyche, and when those places hurt he needed a cozy place to cuddle. And so they found a place under the willow tree and tucked in there for the tears and the consolings. And they talked.

"My dad and mom never did *that* to have me!" he said one hot afternoon, his eyes blinking in horror. "Not my mom!"

"Well," Leah said crankily. "How'd you think you got here?"

"Ho! I know I came out from under her heart. She told me that."

"And how'd you get there?" And how at six did Leah know so much? Spying, eavesdropping, nosing around. The sauna, before she'd been banished from bathing with her parents; she remembered seeing her father's cock and testicles dangling, swinging, and knowing that that was where it all began. And her father, catching that bright, that interested, that beady eye of hers, bellowed for her mother to come and take her away. Now she said to Joel: "Well, if you'd look at yourself, you'd see you have a little weenie. And those little bitties in there are where babies are."

He made a horrible face at her while he thought about it. "Let's go sauna right now and see."

They did. They crept into the warm sauna and looked at him. He had a tiny baby-cock, more like a naked mouse than anything else Leah had ever seen. Joel raised one eyebrow at Leah. "And *this* is gonna make babies?" He held it between his forefinger and thumb, turning it, stretching it. "Nah."

"We-ell. Maybe when you grow up it'll get big. You're only a pipsqueak now." But as they played with his mousie it grew by half a thumb in length and looked like a new toadstool, only pink.

"I can make babies right now. So there!" He pranced around the sauna dressing room waggling his butt. He held the mousie in his hand and pretended to shoot Leah with it. And quite suddenly his face turned beet red. He turned white in patches and shivered. Then he fell on his back and laughed or cried.

Leah goggled at him. "What's wrong with you?"

"Oh! Oh! Woof!" He rolled over onto his stomach and wriggled on the braided rug for a moment and then sighed.

Leah squatted beside him, curious, maybe a little frightened. "Did you die, or what?" she asked. His eyelids were heavy. Then as she watched, he slowly opened his eyes.

"Do you know how to do that?" he asked. He watched her, but he had knowledge now that she didn't have. He was dividing them. She could feel him moving away to the land of maleness even as she studied his face.

She grimaced at him. "No. But who cares? Who wants your mousie anyway?" she sassed, and walked away from him. And missed him terribly. She felt tears coming into her eyes and frowned to hold them back.

"Aw, Leah, it ain't so important. You're only a girl anyway." She heard him get up and tuck himself into his pants and button the two buttons on the front.

She didn't want to talk to him. She didn't like him. She pouted and went outside. When he followed and tried to put his arm around her waist, she pushed him away, sticking her tongue out and glaring at him. Then she went to sit under the willlow tree until her face got tired of frowning.

He swaggered into supper for the next few nights. Full of himself, he sidled up to Leah's father and drank coffee in front of everyone, bold as a jaybird. He clumped around the house, his Buster Browns suddenly man-heavy and important. He chewed on a stalk of hay, hitched one thumb through the belt loop of his pants, cocked his straw hat over one eye, and tucked out his lower lip. Her father laughed and took him up on the tractor seat with him and let him fill his pipe with tobacco, even let him strike a match on the seat of his jeans.

Leah genuinely hated both of them and hid in the barn.

"Don't you come weaseling in here at night," she snarled at Joel when the lights went out and they were put to bed. "You stick to your side of the bed." And she knotted herself up, knees under her chin, elbows out, bristling with rage.

But she couldn't hold on to the rage. It slipped away from her and she fell asleep, Joel's scabby knees tucked up behind hers, his baby breath moving the air over her ear.

Joel came and went from the farm: he exploded upon the family, firecracker bright, and stayed to sizzle and pop through the school year, then left for a summer and returned with the new year, face stitched up in black from a recent temper tantrum through a plate glass door; he did not change ever, but remained more and more the same: frowning in awful rages, running head first at walls to butt with all his might when crossed, melting at the eyes when an arm was thrown around him, his shorn head nuzzling in Leah's back when an orange was peeled for him, when a bed of sacks was made for him in the cozy place under the weeping willow. At seven and eight he was the same. Blue eyes blackened, blond hair shorn, gap-toothed, scabby-kneed, a nose that bled at a glance, scars, bruises, Band-Aids, smelly, grumpy, pouting, infinitely in need of a laugh and a cuddle, he loved with a devotion that was total and daunting.

They shared Christmas stockings and scoldings, chased the chickens eggless, roped and tied the hogs in spring, tore the woodshed apart after a rabbit and left the firewood out to get soaked by a night rain, bawled when whipped by Leah's father, swore to run away, stayed because Easter was coming, swore to run away for good when disappointed by the Easter bunny, but forgot about it when the circus came to town and the elephants and camels *were* huge and did stink and they ate themselves sick on circus peanuts and cotton candy and warm pop.

They ran and sang and yodeled and swung from the ropes in the hay loft, licked the cows' salt block, drank from the trough, came down with stomach gripes that kept them glued to the outhouse in shared misery with Monkey Ward pages. Slept in the same bed, dreamed together of riding the circus horses and taming the molting tigers who coughed and drooled in roars, pawing the air with paddy feet.

Dragged to church on Sunday nights, they discussed God, dismissed Him in favor of hellfire and brimstone and a harmonica played by the minister's wife (no hands!); loathed the altar boys: hair slicked down, nicey-nicey faces yearning for a slap and a pinch; Joel and Leah made faces at them, threatened them behind Leah's father's back, tripped them in the processional, meowed at them during the recessional, sang themselves red-faced and mute, grinned at each other, licked their paws in malice when the minister turned an accusing eye upon one of the altar boys after Joel had got him a good one with a spitball.

Then one winter, when the earth turned and heaved under the snowfields and foamed stones up out of the deeps, Joel was sent back to the city and Leah stumbled into her twelfth year and puberty. It seemed to her that she turned with the earth, heavy as clay, lumpen, sore in the joints; she felt the peculiar and unwanted shiftings within her own bones and spaces, with seepages that began and seemed never to end. In her twelfth year she shot up to five feet ten inches tall; she thought she could see her arms shooting away from her, her wrists great knobs that dangled and banged tables, doors, the hot edges of the kitchen range. Her feet became remote; she required conscious thought to maneuver them; they spurted out of her shoes and socks; long stocking and suspenders no longer met but snapped apart with the finality of doom—snapped in class when she stood at the blackboard, one moment silently scraping away with the chalk, the next frantic to keep her skirt down, her stockings up, as the electric eel of suspender darted free, writhing up from under her skirt to pop up under her chin. Her body grew in all directions: rising like bread dough to expand through the flat-chested blouses, her bony chest became breasts that lunged and heaved even when bound in a brassiere that had straps, straps that snapped and broke whenever she moved at more than a tentative pace. "She's a big girl," she heard. Someone said, "She's developing." Someone said, "She's well developed." She hated her body. She hated being a big girl when everyone around her was tiny, petite. Her mother, aunts, playmates, teachers—all, *all* were petite, dainty at five feet two with tiny bones; and breasts that were teacup-sized, not the baby-bonnet burden that Leah carried, slouching, hunched over, blushed about, hated. And she thought she was not pretty. "She has a sweet face," someone said. "She has character," someone said. "She has a way of looking at you," someone said. And someone said: "She's moon-faced, isn't she?" She knew. Too tall with a great moon face, eyebrows that almost met in a black frown, a short broad nose, a forehead that was inches too high, gray-green eyes that were too far apart, a mop of hair that roared and fought the hairpins and curlers her mother forced upon her—hair that was ash colored in winter, brindle in the summer, too thick for a comb, in need always of a curry and a brush, tied with store string or rubber bands into a club or a tail that switched, that tangled, that got stuck with ink or gum or whatever ratty boys devised to tease her. And to add to it all, she began to sweat under the arms, to grow hairs in private places, to *itch* in private places, to seep and ooze from private places. A slow red trickle that astonished and enraged her that first morning. "Goddammit!" she snarled. "I hate it! Ain't enough with the bras and the straps—now this!" "This" was the sanitary napkin and belt her mother thrust at her. "'I won't wear all these contraptions!"

"Then you'll flop all over. And you'll leave a mess every time you sit down. And everybody will know you've started menstruating."

"Ow!" Leah clapped her hands over her ears.

But there was no help for it: she had been pitched out of childhood, she knew it.

And to make things worse, Joel had been left behind. When he came to the farm that following year, he was still five feet tall, if that, standing straight and looking at her from behind a fist-closed eye, peering at her as he would at a stranger, treating her as if she were a strange grown-up and not Leah. She was still herself, she wanted to tell him. But she felt what his look told her: that Leah was buried under the grown-up and could not be found.

The Cups turned up and Leah saw the string ends of childhood, the chaos and hurly-burly of her kidhood, when she was tough as eggshells. And her family lived down the ore-red road that ran beside a lake; between the lake and the pine forests, a saltbox house with a weeping willow—her wishing tree—where dolls appeared, where she took the sacks and pillows of childhood rages, to sleep under the green sighing branches. The farm was a margin of land between the forest and the swamp; the cows grazed with moose and deer, the deer fed on the vegetable patch, the hens pecked cheek to wattle with partridges and a wild goose or two. And at midnight in summer the skunks came to raid the henhouse and Leah's father made strange moonlight dances in his underwear, threatening the skunks but always standing in foaming impotent rage when they came parading out of the henhouse with stuffed cheeks and the flirting tail that could blitz and blind. The saltbox house seemed to drift atop a wave of stones and shifting earth. It moved the house, the earth did, every spring and midwinter, shifting it like an insect on the skin; or the earth lifted the house in gigantic waves like the great tides of the sea, only slowly, so slowly and so unyieldingly that the timbers of the house creaked and the curtains swayed when there was no wind, but only the giant turning of the earth. And they sat mute, Leah and her parents in their separate rooms, watching the walls change their angles, seeing the china slide down the shelves, hearing the pipes under the house groan in the grasp of the earth's jaw. And as the house moved up and down, so did the fences; they'd lean first this way and then the other, like bobbing fishnets on water, the barbed wire twanging as it split from the wooden posts and became hooks and whips. And it seemed to Leah that there was nothing that was snug and safe now that childhood had been left behind, bobbing and slipping away from her just as the house moved on the earth's waves.

Her parents, too, seemed to slip away from her, moving on a slow wave of time, the distance increasing silently, almost unnoticed, until Leah tried to reach them, to touch them. But her father, struggling to keep the farm, took jobs away from home with construction companies, road-building companies, and went to Alaska, Montana, Canada, wherever the huge earth-moving equipment was needed. And her mother crossed at night into the north bedroom and closed the door, talking to her twin sons, folding their clothes over and over, dusting their twin silver picture frames.

Her mother and father did not shut her out so much as put her gently away from themselves; the spontaneous hug she needed was not given. Her mother's warm blue eyes could cool and turn Leah aside; the footsteps in the hall at night always passed Leah's door and went on to the north bedroom.

So Leah, too, became a night watcher, watching distances, watching stars and the shifting earth. Now she was isolated, with Joel gone back to the city and her parents at their own distance; she was solitary and learned how to tell time by the turning stars, the careening sun. She walked, ran, danced alone over the snows, paraded over the frosty grasses, slid in and out of the black shadows of the forest; she found snow there deep in the moss, deep in July, and blitzed the dogs with snowballs, chasing them home, yodeling them back to leap around her as she wandered far away from the saltbox house and the isolation it contained. She swam with her horse, Valko, swam holding his mane and tail, swam alone naked, learned how to swim alone and had to relearn how to swim in gym class that following fall. She fell in love with water, decided she was a sea creature, a whale. Not a mermaid, because they weren't real, they were sad, they fell in love with the wrong prince: he asked them to come dance with him, and they danced on broken glass in their innocence, in their wish to please him, and then left teardrops of blood tracking back to the sea. But the whale, she believed, she *knew*, would be wise and gentle and watchful, and was real; it could sink to the bottom of the water and comb its beard, and it had a soft white hide and a gently deep eye that could see past the seaweed and the weed of the real world. She swam in lakes, swam in the pool in gym class, rolling over and over, floating at the bottom of the pool, at the bottom of the lake, letting legs glide past her, letting minnows drift next to her and stare at her; she knew she was a sea creature and she didn't mind the quiet, the solitude at the bottom of her deep private world. And she ran with her tall body through the forest; in summer she picked blueberries in the mossy shadows, picked strawberries, blackberries, pin cherries, chokecherries, bringing the buckets full of berries home, her own face berry-stained and sunburned, her clothing and hair burr-tangled, her heart light as summer smiles, and as innocent.

She liked school, but felt it had little to do with her; she liked her classmates but felt displaced; the girls liked boys, played with them some kind of game that had rules and triumphs that led to giggling and dire happenings like pregnancies and engagements and showers and a kind of lewd scummy talk in the back of the school bus that she didn't understand totally, but understood enough to feel herself become boneless, become ectoplasm, become invisible, she hoped. She watched with lively interest, almost avidity, yet with a readiness to disappear, as the girls played the game. The Game. She thought of it that way, the erotic ticklings and teasings, the brushing of breasts against a boy's arm, the flicker of a thigh at a football game, the somehow sexual slant of a book against a girl's sweater. The Game, the constant whisper in the walls; secrets tucked into books, folded into papers; whispers in the glee club, in the choir, in the girls' gym; the shout at the baseball game or football game: to catch a boy, hold him, make the trade with him without being "caught," without becoming pregnant, but to kiss and fondle in the back of the school bus on the way home from a basketball game, or in the back seat of a car after a movie, the white cotton socks flashing in the dark, the heavy and sensual sounds of zippers, and the exclamations of "Don't!" and the whispers: "Don't worry, I'll take care of you." And everyone did, and no one took care of anyone, and the girls counted on calendars and fingers and the boys became resentful and guilty as the counting went on past twenty-eight and thirty-two and the school sweaters and class rings changed to engagement rings. And then the relief when a girl got her period and everyone could catch their breath; or almost everyone, because Leah's cousin, at fifteen—it was Vivian, who was a cheerleader and wore a blue angora sweater, *she* who was sophisticated and had Vaseline in her school locker—she "missed" and was caught and dropped out of school in her sophomore year. And Leah, who had been daydreaming through it all, was a bridesmaid, tall and gawky in a blue net formal, and she and the bride shared acne-cure secrets. Leah slunk through the wedding, watched her cousin and the groom dance like mechanical dolls to the tune of the small accordion band, to the tune of parents (four), to the tune of malicious tongues that sang an alleluia chorus of "Thank God it wasn't *my* daughter (son)!" and "That's what comes of letting them date so early." Leah survived the wedding but almost succumbed to her own mother's suspicious blue eye: "Mom, I'm not even dating!" Suspicion was heavy in the air that year until Leah's grades came home, all honors, and her mother went back to the north bedroom with only a backward glance glinting ice blue.

Leah, at fifteen, liked school, read all her textbooks the first weeks of September and then needed only to glance at them for the rest of the year. She dreamed through most of her classes, nodding according to some internal rhythm, coming up for air to answer questions, to pass the examinations effortlessly; and then she submerged, reading everything that she could get her hands on, dreaming, discovering classical music and bringing home recordings to play on her phonograph, listening to

Texaco and the opera on Saturday afternoons while scrubbing the kitchen floor and washing and waxing the rest of the house.

Then suddenly her mother looked at her and spoke to her father: "She should be looked after." Meaning: married.

Leah, when she became aware of the plan, balked. But she didn't know what to do about any of it: the young men, army veterans, construction workers, farmers, whom her father invited to dinner, to supper, for a beer on Saturday, come to the dance at the co-op hall and meet my daughter. She stood still for most of it, in her white blouse and navy skirt, the nylon stockings tugging at the suspenders under her cotton slip, her toes curling up inside her shoes, her hands taken in a grasp, her mouth dry, the hairs on the back of her neck shifting as anxiety and then rage swept over her.

One young man, all blond and dark, came several times to the farmhouse, his boiled blue eyes seeking Leah out, prying her out of her shell, fishing her out of her solitude; on Saturday night he hauled her to two or three country dances, bought her a hamburger and a Coke, thought, she knew, that he had acquired some property rights, some hunting license, some tenantship. And when he laid his hand on her thigh, placed his weight on her shoulder, she felt that he would dim her somehow, if not extinguish her. And when he kissed her, placed his heavy arm over her, she became boneless and slid out from under.

"Why not, Leah?" he asked, sliding his body after hers on the car seat.

"I don't feel that way about you."

"Ho, I'll show you how to feel. . . ." He reached for her, his blue eyes hard under the blond lashes.

She opened the car door and got out.

"No, you'd never walk home. Nobody's ever walked home on me."

She looked at him and shook her head. She set off down the gravel road, walking easily, thinking about something else, concentrating on walking the eight miles home. She heard the car motor start up and heard it follow her. She shook her head and continued to walk.

"Aw, come on. You don't have to walk home. I'll bring you home. No fooling."

She got back into the car, but stayed close to the door.

"You ain't gonna have many dates if you act that way," he said. "How'll you find anybody to marry?" He grinned in the dark. "You'll get a reputation. Prick tease."

"That's all right."

"Oh, is it? Lot you know about how men talk."

"I know how you talk. If you got me to give in, you'd spread the word about me. That I was easy."

"No!"

"Yes. I know. I hear it at school about different girls." She paused to let him say something. He didn't, so she went on: "I heard. Even girls that are really nice, if they give in, if they aren't careful, you all talk about them. You don't care if you hurt them."

"You ain't so pretty you can get a lot of dates, you know."

"I know." She felt his words slide in under her skin, the thin knife of them slicing beneath the toughness to where she was quivering and unable to protect herself. She didn't say anything, but watched the road ahead.

"You gotta understand, Leah. Men have needs. You know. And you gotta be realistic."

She could see the white fence post that marked the beginning of her father's farmland. She could also see that he was slowing the car, easing it to a stop under a stand of trees.

He reached for her again as if they had resolved their argument, as if she had been convinced, as if *he* had convinced her and now would take his reward. His eyes gleamed in the dark; she could feel his breath on her cheek, see his mouth seeking hers.

ᓌ The Black Magician ᓍ

I light a cigarette. Let him hang there for an eternity, mouth seeking, hands rude, cock erect and prodding at the fabric of his pants. Who else would I leave thus, suspended with an erection, suspended in that state of delicious anticipation, so delicious, so lubricious, so cockalacious! I think, fondly, lovingly of you, Ben, and wish it for you. A hell of delight for you, to linger forever with that erection and that confident look, that arrogance, that certainty that you will not be refused.

The next Tarot card turns face up: the Black Magician. And I make the first of my wishes: that you, Ben, Lover, with that long elegant cock of yours, that selective, particular cock, will have an eternity of suspended delight. I look at the Black Magician, his bat wings, his potbelly, his goat thighs, he is indeed the Goat of Mendes, well named, I think, and the card I choose for you, Lover, the goat, the cockeyed goat of lechery, slavishly jumping and humping and pumping any available orifice. And the two imps, male and female, carnal desires, rolling their eyes, forever chained to the Magician, always and forever at the command of impulse, of appetite.

And I remember what you said to me one night, one of the last nights I shared with you in the big bed; I remember, lying there in the dark, a cigarette glowing between my lips where you had just moments ago been glowing; that cock of yours seemed to glow, for me, in the dark. Now I sit in my study and remember your words, your voice. "Men do go around always slightly excited. We have a kind of antenna, a sensitivity, an awareness. I can always tell when I've turned someone on. It happens often."

I remember saying: "How can you tell? Something they say? A gesture?"

"No, it's a vibration on the eyebrow, like I have an antenna."

"A cock awareness? Cockeyed?" I smiled fondly in the dark, but was incredulous too.

And you said, "Yes. And I'm rarely, if ever, wrong. About someone being sexually attracted to me. I am sexually exciting, powerful. I have that power."

"Hmm." I lay there, still warm from the pleasure of you, Ben. And you absentmindedly continued to stroke my body, to run your hand between my legs where you had lain and into the cleft where you had thrust, where your semen came seeping down to wet your fingers.

"Yes, it's true. Anywhere. Theater lobbies, in the line at the airport, just walking down the street, I'll see someone's eye on me and know, my antenna will vibrate and I know they're sexually excited. And I get excited, too, just by looking at them and knowing they want me." I could hear it in your voice, Lover, you were becoming warm, sodden, heavy with lust and excitement.

So, Lover, I wish for you the hard desire, eternal sexual excitation, nightstalking with your cock erect and tingling with anticipation . . . and nowhere to put it! That is the hard part of the desire, my love, that you with your hot cock may follow the next pair of eyes, the next cleft, the next pair of lips and find them always just out of reach: I think you deserve that, to reach and reach with dripping one-eyed cock for the unattainable.

ᓃᓄ The Horseman of Cups ᓄᓃ

I put the cigarette out, dabbing it in the ashtray. And set aside the Black Magician, his imps grinning at me. He sticks his tongue out. Yes. Carnal desires, appetites, we feed upon them even in fantasy; even in revenge.

The Horseman of Cups, smiling, capped with roses, riding a white pony: the lover in a fairy tale, the darling prince, he carries a chalice of love in his dimpled hand.

He tasted of salt. Mike, his name; blue of eye, silvery wheat-colored hair, his fair skin burned and peeling that late May afternoon on the Mississippi River bank, holding my hand as we dallied along, talking. Never had there been so much to talk about with anyone before, I'd thought.

We had met in English class by laughing at the same pun and, magically, had become friends in that same instant. "I'll give you a ride home," he said after class.

"I live on campus, Comstock Hall," I said.

"I'll give you a ride anyway. Come on." And we rode the long way around the Minnesota campus to my dormitory.

Meetings are important, even now as I sit at the Tarot; important in an arcane way: so I read the Tarot, throw the joss, scrabble in the entrails. Remember . . . Mike's fair skin, fairer than mine, milky white and blue-veined just over the pubic hairs and along the insides of his thighs until he sunburned there that May afternoon when we lay sprawled and secret along the Mississippi. The crisp peeling skin of his neck and shoulders tasted of sun and salt; popcorn has that coarse skin taste.

They did not become lovers that first evening, or even that first week. But he liked her, he let her know that so easily, with the laughing blue of his eye, the nod of ap-

33

proval that was not dangerous or boding, and so she liked him in return. She liked him, trusted him; did not feel that lustful lunacy about him, that smoldering desirous tickle at the pit of the stomach. No, not then, not yet. They could walk to the library holding hands and grinning at each other, even kissing and nuzzling in the shadows. She remained cousin to him, she felt. She could watch him walk away from her and go back to her dormitory cell to study and sleep untroubled; she did not gnaw on her pillow nor jounce around on her bed nor grapple her blankets with her thighs. No. Somehow he did not stir her that way; her fantasies were elsewhere, still forming. She was a past master/mistress of masturbation; oh yes, she had her Gothic lover, her Heathcliff, her dangerous lover who came to her in the middle of the night and put one hand on her breast and grasped her knowledgeably with the other, a thumb hard on that tender and mysterious place tucked away between the lips of her body; she rode out the nights alone with her fantasies, rocking herself to a satisfied sleep.

So then, with a head populated by fantasies, how could she fall in love, or fall in like, with Mike Golden? His liking created it: that answering affection that she felt. He filled a space that she hadn't realized was vacant. No, it was more than that. And it was less than that. What it was, to be honest, was curiosity and the faint shimmers of heat lightning along the horizons of her fantasy world.

"What are you doing this summer?" he'd asked.

"I'm going home first, and then I have a job at a summer resort on Lake Vermillion."

"Why don't you stay in town? Find a job here." He'd put an arm around her shoulders and, bumping hips, they walked under the trees on the mall.

"It's too late to find a good summer job here. I'd have to pay room and board, too, if I stayed. At the resort I'd get that and a paycheck. You could come up weekends and see me, we could go swimming."

"You should stay in town. We could see each other every day, not just weekends. I'll help you find a job."

"Mmm. Mmm. We'll see." But that night he kissed her with something like urgency. Startled, she backed away from him.

"I just think you should stay in town," he said. But he

touched her breasts and held her close to him, and something in his voice touched her, moved her so that she wanted to please him, wanted to be with him.

She lined up a full-time job in the university hospital kitchen and began filling in part time on the dorm switchboard. "So I can eat free and live free," she told Mike. "And if my scholarship gets picked up, I'll be in fine shape by the time school starts again." She found herself looking at him and feeling unsettled. She blushed. She could not look at Mike, not look him in the eye, not look at him without undressing him; she looked down at her feet, then looked at the front of his trousers, looked back at her feet. A warming had begun.

Without speaking of what they were thinking, they drove out along the river road to where the river left the city and became itself again, deep and purposeful. "Let's get out and walk awhile," Mike said. And he looked at her with concern, affection, almost a worried look, so that Leah took his hand and kissed it.

Then: Was it better? Worse? He lay heavy on her breasts, watching her; that concerned looked remained.

"You look like someone I didn't know for a while," she said. "You looked like a stranger looking at me."

"Are you okay? Was it good for you?" he asked.

"I don't know. It didn't hurt. It doesn't hurt now. Is this all there is to it? Just this?"

Mike hid his face, himself, by pressing into her neck. He said something.

"What? Did you . . . come? Have an orgasm?" Her legs were beginning to cramp in the joints. "Maybe it's something you have to cultivate a taste for. I think I could have . . . uh, had a climax before . . . uh, without going all the way."

"Jesus. Will you be quiet for a minute?"

Mortified, she closed her mouth. She violently wanted him to disappear. She wanted *herself* to disappear.

"Now, wait, Leah." Mike lay beside her. "It's the first time, isn't it?"

"I told you."

"Okay. Trust me. I'll take care of you. And it does get better. I think I rushed you and I'm sorry. Okay?" He had that look of concern again, a vertical line between his eyes.

"Okay."

"And don't cry." He kissed her eyebrow.

"I won't."

"What were you thinking?"

"When we did it?" She was of two minds now: tell him, don't tell him. She didn't want to tell him, she realized. Her thoughts were stilll too much a part of her. She had separated from her body, from that part of her body that he had entered, and now she did not want him entering the rest of her. Or she wanted to *share* herself, her thoughts, but she did not want to be dimmed, taken over by him. Thoughts, feelings, impressions flooded over her, overwhelming her. "Stop. Wait a minute," she murmured. And the whale, gentle, feminine, surfaced for a moment and gazed at him. She smoothed his face gently and held his head on her breast. She wanted a minute, a quiet space, to stretch out, to accommodate, to . . . she didn't know the word for it, but it meant to grow enough to understand what she was feeling, what she was perceiving. She said, "I want to osmose this. . . ." Then she shook her head: the whale retreated to the secret places of her thoughts and she felt the sand grate under her back.

Mike got up and helped her to stand, brushing sand from the back of her skirt and blouse. He glanced at her. "Are you okay? You look kind of shaky."

"I'm okay. It wasn't like what I'd expected. I don't know . . ." She was interested in her body's feelings. She wanted, fiercely, to look at herself, to see if there was anything different. But she couldn't, not with him standing there. She didn't feel, then, that they were intimates. She felt their separateness more now than when they had been holding hands, walking across the campus.

"Leah, you aren't feeling bad about what happened, are you? Please don't. And don't worry if it didn't happen for you this time. It will next time. Or the time after that. I'll take the time, I promise, not to rush you. It's okay. Women don't have the same sexual intensity as men; they don't have the same capacity for orgasm." He had folded the blanket and now took her hand. "Come on, I'm hungry. Let's go get a hamburger."

"I can't. I've got to work switchboard tonight."

They drove back to the campus in silence. She was muted, silenced by the explosion of her feelings. She was learning more than she could handle, more even than she wanted to handle. Mike looked at her with such concern that, again, she took his hand and kissed it.

"I'm okay," she promised him.

"I'll see you tomorrow? You don't have finals this week, do you?"

"No. My first one is next Wednesday. And then I have two on Thursday." She tried to see him the way she had seen him before. But he was somewhere between the laughing Mike that she knew and the Mike with the stranger's eyes. "Tomorrow will be fine." She kissed his nose and got out of the car. And ran into the dormitory without looking back.

"You were almost late," Rita, the day switchboard operator said. "I can't sit around here waiting to train you while you gab with your boyfriend."

"Sorry. I think I can do it myself by now."

"Ready or not, you will. I have a date of my own waiting." She handed Leah the headphone, grabbed her book bag, and left.

The board lighted up. Leah stuck the head phone on. "Comstock Hall," she said. ". . . She's in three forty-two. I'll ring for you. Thank you." And stuck the first call in.

"So! When is a lemming not a lemming?" Zulu grinned at Leah over the top of the switchboard. "I saw you and dream boy necking in his car."

"You did not. We don't neck." Leah could feel the blush moving across her face.

"Well, dontcha know, I don't care about that. Only it seems pretty funny to see *you* out with a guy. After all that hoohaing about how girls are lemmings rushing mindlessly into the sea of matrimony. Hah!" Zulu—Zoe Lu Joann Howell—had bounded into Leah's freshman year in a Peter Pan costume. Zulu, green legs flashing, red braid snaking down her back, had come careering across the knee-deep snow and run headlong into Leah, spilling books, cartons of coffee, sacks of doughnuts and a string of expletives that made catherine wheels in the air. She had helped Leah to pick up the books and to sort everything out, saying, "I'm an actress, dontcha know, and I don't have time for the rituals. I'm Zulu and you come see me in *Peter Pan*, hah? I'll give you a free ticket —here. And be sure to vote for me in the Winter Festival. My ass is hanging out in the poster of the girls in the opera hose and black leotards." She had looked Leah hard in the eye, grabbed her belongings, and galloped off again. After that, Leah realized that Zulu lived in the same dormitory, that she'd seen the bristle of Zulu's hair over the shower stall wall, heard the muffled expletives in the middle of the night when Zulu trundled home with a costume or prop from some play.

"I'm not rushing into matrimony," Leah said. She waved a hand at Zulu and turned back to the switchboard.

"You hungry? I haven't eaten yet. I'll get sandwiches and coffee and bring 'em up here. I don't want to sit in the cafeteria with the Friday night leftovers. Gawd, they are dreary. I wish I could live in the theater building. Let's get an apartment and room together, for our senior year."

"I can't. If I get another scholarship I have to live in the dorm. I'd never get enough money to support an apartment."

"Oh, yeah. Well. Say, are you staying in dorm this summer or what?"

"I'm staying. What about you? Did you hear anything about the auditions?"

"Jaysus! You'd think they'd grab me in a minute. No, nothing yet. And I've been in every damned play, every lab production, even every damned skit on campus so it's not that I don't have talent. Well, I can always go home and watch my brothers repair their cars. And do my swimming for the Aqua Follies. What we oughta do, you and me, is get our boyfriends together for a double date. You wanna?"

"I'll ask Mike."

"Okay. I'll go get the sandwiches. Listen, can I study for Lit Three forty-one with you? I just need to bone up a little, ya know?"

"Okay." The switchboard lit up in three places. When Leah looked up, Zulu had gotten the sandwiches and coffee. "Did you bring your notes up here?" she asked, handing Leah a sandwich. "I could look at 'em now and save time. Ya know, I could memorize 'em."

"My notebooks are under the counter. The blue one is Lit."

When her shift was over, Leah turned the switchboard

over to the night girl and went to her room. Zulu had copied her notes and gone off for a late date. "See ya!" She'd capered out of the dormitory, her long red braid whipping down her back.

That week Leah studied with Zulu, worked the switchboard, learned how to fill the diet trays in the hospital kitchen, and tried to understand what was happening to her. She and Mike went to supper and then to a movie on the evenings she didn't work the switchboard. And she cultivated a taste for lovemaking. Mike would let her touch him everywhere, lying on his back, his hands clasped behind his head, a half-smile playing at the corners of his mouth as she tongued his nipples or touched the crisp, almost brittle pubic hairs. His buttocks charmed her; there was a dimple at the base of his spine that, when touched, made ripples of goose bumps along his baby skin.

"It's like having a toy," she told him. "They should make a boy doll with the parts for little girls to play with."

"Didn't you ever play doctor when you were little?"

She thought about her cousin Joel. "Not doctor."

"I loved playing doctor when I was a kid. That's why I'm going to be a doctor now. So I can play it all the time. You want to play doctor with me? Come on, give me practice."

"I get a sheet, don't I?"

"Okay." He draped the sheet over her. "Now, just relax and I'll be the doctor." He grinned at her over her sheeted knees. "Just relax. I won't hurt you. See, I'm being gentle."

His hands were gentle, cupping the tender places between her thighs; the probing finger moved in a back-and-forth rhythm, entering and leaving her body, giving her rushes of warm excitement. "See, I'm not hurting you," he said. Now his shoulders were under her knees, she felt his head brush between her thighs, his mouth, his lips sucking at the tender place, his tongue a sweet serpent licking and moving between the lips of her body, licking a flame of wetness from front to back, until the cleft of her body was hot and moist and she was losing her breath, had lost her breath and wanted him not to do that, or to kill her; he was killing her with this breathless delicious shiver that made her body buck under his, that made her want not his mouth down there, not just his tongue down there, but his cock, which she had grasped and stroked; and now, watching his grin between her knees, she half sobbed as she struggled to bring his cock inside her; she clutched him and held him and begged him until he slowly allowed the warm bobbing head of his cock to move into her; and then they moved together, struggled together to reach that place inside of her that made them both cry out, gasp and shiver ferociously; and suddenly Leah was afraid of that place, afraid of reaching so far within, away; and she tried to hold back from it, but Mike carried her along with him, forced her almost against her will to thrust with him and enclose him with the great muscles of her thighs and belly so that he moved deep within her, filled her with himself: his cock and then the rapid tattooing of his seed.

"Ah!" he groaned, and shuddered, his whole body convulsing into a deathlike rictus and then subsiding to lie softly upon her breasts, a dazed look in his eyes, his hands clasping her breasts, cuddling close, a child.

Somehow that cuddling close was as delicious and as filling as the struggle, perhaps more so, for it lasted longer, was peaceful, and they were *seeing* each other again. Leah could lie there, resting, reflecting, osmosing; she could at this distance see her own body, its blushes, the ripples of goose bumps, the hardening of her nipples and the tiny, tentative climaxes that rocketed to convulsions that threatened to kill her with deliciousness. It was during that cuddling time that Leah fell in love with him, melted away from like and curiosity into the slow dissolve of her bones, the dissolve of selfhood; she felt, she thought, like the mermaid, coaxed out of the water and into a delicious slow dance.

"Ya know what you're doing dontcha?" Zulu asked. She was packing her winter clothes for the trip home to Duluth. She'd been hired for the summer season at Tanglewood as an apprentice actress. "Spear carrier," she'd said. But she'd also bellowed an Isolde-like howl of triumph when the letter of acceptance had come. "You're playing house and he's playing doctor. Are you and he serious or what?"

"You mean serious like getting married?"

"No. Serious like . . . serious like taking precautions."

"Oh."

"Oh. That's the answer I expected. You'd better do more than 'oh.' Dontcha know he's going away to med school in the fall? And what you said about your folks, they weren't so red hot about you coming to university. I don't think they'd be hot about your playing house either. Especially if you brought home a little bastard, excuse me for saying so."

"I know."

Zulu slapped a corduroy skirt into a cardboard carton and shook her head. "Precautions. You know about precautions? I am not rooming with an idiot who thinks babies are found in cabbage patches, am I? I mean, this fall it would be nice if my roomie knew what the score was and didn't fish my diaphragm out of its box and think it was a bottle cap. Or are you doing the gel thing? Excuse me for being nosy, but I get anxious about my best friend when she shows no interest in the facts of life. You did go to the doctor? Hello?"

Leah had let her hair fall down in front of her face and was combing her fingers through it, making a curtain. She sighed. "I went, but it . . ." She shivered. "He wasn't at all what I thought. I thought it would be easier. You said it wasn't so bad, going in and asking for a . . . contraceptive device. But . . . first he was nice, you know? And then when he knew what I was asking for and that I wasn't married or even engaged, he got so ugly to me. As if I were doing something terribly dirty to myself. And . . . he said he'd examine me but then I couldn't face it, couldn't let him touch me, not when he had that sneering, cold look on his face like he was going to be touching something dirty."

"Jaysus! I'm sorry. You got the old man. I should have gone with you. The younger guy is nicer. Well, not nicer but he doesn't act like such a shit. What are you gonna do?"

"I don't know. We haven't talked about it. Mike's been studying for his makeup exam in organic chemistry, so I haven't wanted to bother him."

They looked at each other. Zulu went on with her packing. Leah sat on the bed. There was nothing more to be said.

* * *

Leah put the phone receiver back on its cradle and sat absolutely still. She'd have to go home. "Dad had a heart attack last night," her mother had said. "Come home," her mother had said. Leah, numb, could not make her mind work. Her thoughts clotted around two sentences: "I'm pregnant. I *can't* tell Dad." Then, sadly: "I can't tell Mom either." And then the thoughts came, the unwanted thoughts and memories: Mom pacing the floor in the middle of the night, always sitting down in the north bedroom with the cedar chest of the boys' baby clothes and their one picture. I've done it now, Leah accused herself. Mom will nod her head in that final I-knew-it-all-the-time look. And I can't tell Dad. Leah stood slowly and dug through her shoulder bag. Twenty-nine dollars. "I can get home on the bus with that," she said aloud. "I'll see Dad, how he is. Then I'll think about the other."

She went home, to northern Minnesota, to the lake country, the bus trundling through the black-green forests, and caught a ride home with the mailman, Mr. Johnson. "Sorry about your pa, Leah," he'd said. "But the doctors can do a lot nowadays. Your pa's still a young man, not even sixty. If you need a ride or something, you call." And he'd shaken her hand. Adult. She thought: He treats me now as if I were adult. And last Christmas I was still a little girl. She walked up the road from the mailbox, feeling the world teeter dizzily under her feet. Adult.

Her father's car stood in the driveway. She almost expected him to be home. But when she opened the front door there was no pipe smoke. That told her.

"Mom?" She heard her mother come out of the north bedroom, saw her now diminished. Then her mother was her mother again, the commanding blue eyes arrowing questions even now.

"I'm okay, Mom," Leah said. She put her arms around her mother, rested her cheek against her mother's forehead.

"You look puny." Leah's mother stepped away, eluding the embrace, yet holding on to Leah's arm. "We'll have supper after you've seen Dad. Can you drive me to the hospital now?"

"Yes. How is he?"

"He says he feels good. I've got my purse. Here are the

car keys. I'm bringing him some shaving things. You better bring him some candy or something. Did you?"

"I've got magazines. The sports one and a hunting one."

"*Reader's Digest*. He likes *Reader's Digest*."

"I brought it." Leah had set her overnight case down near the door. Now she waited for her mother to tell her to put it into her old bedroom.

"You did well in school?" Her mother walked through the kitchen, checking the gas range and heater. She brushed invisible crumbs from the gleaming counter and refolded the dish towel, her purse hanging from her arm. She paused in front of the buffet to inch the cut-glass bowl to the left.

"Yes. I sent you my grade report in June, remember? I'll be on scholarship again this year."

"Um. You still working part time."

"Yes."

"Well, let's go. I'm ready." Leah's mother urged her out of the house, locking the door behind them. "Now don't talk to Dad about anything that might upset him. Talk nice about the farm and the weather. Oh, and your good grades, too."

"How did it happen? You didn't say on the telephone."

"He started the haying. I said it was too much, haying on top of working graveyard shift at the mine."

"Oh. I thought he'd gotten sick at the mine."

"No. He came home at eight. I made him a nice breakfast and he went out with the tractor to get the cut hay raked. I went out to the field at ten with his coffee jar and some biscuits. And he just slid off the tractor seat. I just remembered; I left the coffee jar right there in the field. Well, he didn't say anything but took hold of his chest and arm so hard I knew he was sick. I got him back up on the tractor and drove him home by myself. And I called your uncle Lee to come. We didn't even change clothes. We just brought your dad to the hospital and Doctor Bray put him right to bed. I'll have to remember to get that coffee jar out of the field."

Leah listened, nodding her head, driving the old Buick harshly, stripping the gears until she remembered how to shift.

"You can park over there in the lot behind that brick

building. They got a parking lot for visitors now. Now, comb your hair and wipe your face." She dabbed at Leah's face with a spit-damp handkerchief. Leah bore it.

The hospital floors were linoleum, highly waxed and polished. The nurse's heels clicked in patterns of sound as Leah followed her mother through the reception hall and down the long corridor to her father's room.

"Hi, Dad!" Leah held her father's hands and kissed him. She stood on one side of the bed while her mother stood on the other. "I came home right away after Mom called. How are you?"

"Oh. I'll be fine." He smiled at her, that bittersweet grin, one corner of his mouth higher than the other, his eyes narrowed even now against the perpetual smoke from his pipe.

Leah caught her breath, forced herself to smile into his eyes. He's lost all of his suntan, she thought. She looked down at the hand she was holding—the energy had gone out of it. She gripped his hand fiercely. "I brought you something to read. And a sack of peppermints." He'd always brought her a sack of peppermints when she had measles, mumps, whatever.

"I'll have one now," he said. He took the paper sack from her and held it on his chest. For a moment he closed his eyes, frightening Leah and her mother. But he opened them again. "I just get tired so fast anymore."

"We won't stay long." Leah's mother looked across the bed at her. "You go on out, Leah. It's too hard for you. I'll sit with Dad for a few minutes."

"I . . . It's not hard on me, Mom. I'd like to stay, too." Leah hung on to her father's hand, but the command in her mother's eye was too strong. "I'll come back tonight after supper, okay?" She kissed her father's cheek. He held her hand and nodded. "You come back, flicka. How's school?"

"She's fine," Leah's mother said, taking both his hands. "You lay back and rest. I'll sit with you." She inclined her head at Leah.

"I'll be right outside in the hall," Leah said. She kissed her father's cheek again and walked out into the hall.

On the drive home Leah asked: "How *is* he? Will he be all right?"

"Doctor Bray says he should be all right, but he needs

rest. And I think he better give up the mines. They take too much out of him. You got to remember he worked hard all of his life. He don't need worries now."

Leah glanced at her mother, blushing. The back of her throat hurt. "Is the farm okay? You don't have money worries?"

"*I* don't have money worries. The insurance from the union will pay his hospital and doctor. And I got something put away." She sat back and sighed.

They drove home in silence. Leah changed into old jeans and a cotton shirt and helped with the milking. "Rosie still doesn't want to come in for milking, does she?" Leah asked, panting from having chased the red cow back and forth in the barnyard.

"No. That old meatbag. I'm going to sell her off now your Dad's sick. She's too much trouble anymore." Leah's mother handed her the milkpail. "You take Cranberry and Pearl. I'll do Tiny and the others. Let Rosie stew until last."

The milking done, the pails washed, the cows let out for the night, Leah and her mother sat at the kitchen table eating sandwiches. "Now, we'll just run up and see Dad for a minute," Leah's mother said. "I'm going to call Nestor to come by tomorrow. He can take Rosie off my hands. She's a fall freshener and she'll bring some money. Dad doesn't need to know. I'll tell him about Rosie when he's better." She poured herself a cup of coffee. "You plan to stay in school, do you?"

"Yes, Mom."

"Well, we won't talk about that to Dad. You don't have a serious boyfriend? Dad was worried about that Mike you talked about. That hasn't worked out to any kind of seriousness, has it?"

"No."

"No. Well, all that schooling will be a help when you're settled once and for all. I suppose another year won't harm you. And all the boys from here are married by now. Except for Toivo . . ."

"No. I'm fine, Mom." Leah met her mother's eyes with the lie. "I am fine."

"Well. You heard that Celestine got a nice job with Honeywell? She did fine with that secretarial course. And now she's engaged, so she's going to be settling down nicely." Pause. "And your other friend, she's got a nice little family started even if they did marry fast, before she even graduated high school. Well, Iggy's done right by her. He drives a truck in the iron mines."

"I haven't heard from either of them for a while."

"Well. They're settled nicely. It's nice for their folks, knowing their daughters are taken care of and not running around. Folks worry about daughters until they're safely married."

"I know."

"Tomorrow you can drive me to the bank. I have some business to do and some insurance forms to fill out. Then you can go back to school."

"I thought I'd stay a few more days. Don't you need me? I could stay."

"No. Just so long's you're in school and working. Dad won't need you. And I can get the Lahti boy over to give me a hand. I'll hire the haymaking out." She drank her coffee, then took the dishes to the sink. "If you want to see Dad tonight, we'd better get a go on."

"He's sleeping now, but you can sit by his bed," the nurse told them when they arrived at the hospital. "Doctor says he's coming along just fine now."

"We'll just sit for a minute then." Leah's mother sat by the bed, one hand patting at the white sheet.

The paper sack of peppermints was on the bedside stand. Leah looked at it. She felt awkward, extra.

"Mmm . . . Hi. I had a good sleep." He smiled at them. "Were you here long?"

"No, no, we just came a minute ago. Did you have any visitors? Anni said she'd come when Rikku could drive her over."

"Only Pastori Napa. But he only comes to help with the hay on a rainy day ever. He came in and prayed. I fell asleep, so he must've gone again." Leah's father laughed.

Leah's mother said, "Well, we won't stay but a minute. You look better. Leah's going back to school tomorrow."

"So soon? I guess you have to go back this quick?"

"I told Mom I could stay longer. If you need me, I could stay. Even a few days might help." Leah looked from her father to her mother.

"I said we wouldn't need her, Arvo. I can get one of the Lahti boys to help with the work. And I'll hire out the haymaking. What can she do?" She took his hand and stroked it. "We'll do fine. The two of us, Arvo."

Leah's father seemed to let go. He sighed, let his head sink deeper into the pillow. "Yeah. I guess you'd know best. But you'll come home for a little rest before the fall term starts, won't you?"

"I will." Leah meant to say more, but her mother's blue eyes glinted her into silence. She kissed her father on the forehead. She spent the rest of that visit sitting stiffly in the chair, watching her mother pat her father's hand. After a few moments her mother relaxed, chuckled at them both.

Late that night Leah awakened to the familiar padding steps in the hall. She watched the halo of light that ran before her mother's shadow, and heard her mother go into the north bedroom. The cedar chest and the boys' picture, she thought. Then she dozed until morning sounds awakened her; she went to the kitchen and found her mother sitting at the kitchen table, the cards spread out on the oilcloth, a cup of cold coffee beside her. "Didn't you sleep at all, Mom?"

"No. I never sleep anymore. I've been reading your fortune. There's spades ahead, losses and tears."

"Oh. What about Dad?"

"He cheated the Devil this time. See, there's a journey ahead for him. So he'll be fine."

Leah nodded. She thought: Whatever I do now, I'll have to do it alone.

She saw her father once more before she left for the Twin Cities, kissing him on the cheek, gently hugging him. Her mother, accompanied by a Lahti boy (the same one who would do the farm chores) came to the bus depot. "Write to me," her mother said. "I miss you so much." She held on to Leah's arm. "You know I love you, Leah."

Leah got a window seat and waved to her mother, promising to write, promising to call. "Call me if you need me home, Mom," she said.

She dozed in the bus, dreaming those fractured dreams: the cedar chest, her mother playing cards with the twins' pictures, Rosie glaring wall-eyed from the barn.

That night of her return, she opened her dormitory room door with one hand, juggling overnight case, laundry bag, letters, the fall schedule of classes, and a package.

Absently, inside her room, she shuffled the mail: a postcard from Zulu at Tanglewood, ads for magazines, junk mail, and a letter from Mike. She hadn't seen him for a week.

> Dear Leah,
> I'm sorry about your Dad. I know he'll pull through.
> Wish we could have spent our last day together but I understand you had to go home, and I had to leave early. I'll be in Georgetown by the end of the week. Maybe you could come up for a weekend?
> My classes will be tough but we could spend a weekend together. I'll write soon.
> Love,
> Mike

She turned the envelope over. He'd misspelled her last name. She folded the letter and replaced it in the envelope. Then she went to bed.

She worked the afternoon shift at the student union in the kitchen, making salads. She wore a pale yellow uniform, a white apron, a hair net, her saddle shoes and socks. She washed baskets of lettuce, chopped green onions, cabbage, and carrots, sliced tomatoes, peeled eggs, and stirred mayonnaise with chili sauce for dressings. She earned ninety-five cents an hour. "Boys make a dollar an hour," the supervisor told her. "They need the money more than girls do. And they're going to be the men in the world anyway." She washed up the stainless-steel bowls, scrubbed out the walk-in refrigerator, carried laden trays back and forth from the kitchen to the serving counters.

She needed more money. She asked around. She read the bulletin board. She took the graveyard shift in the university hospital dishwashing room. She scoured pots big enough to bathe in, she scrubbed down the steam carts and ran the autoclaves at midnight; she set the coffee urns up for the morning shift. She washed the tray carts and hosed down the dishwashing room floor.

She needed more money. She needed three hundred dollars. Red-haired Helen, the dishwashing super who had known where to go: "Out toward the airport. A trailer court. You'll find it. It's the Easy Rest Trailer Court, one-oh-one-one-seven Chamberlain. Your little friend, the one who's preggie, she'll need three hundred in cash. Too bad college girls don't know everything." Pause. "You gonna go with her? Take cab money along. There's no place to stay after. Here's the telephone number. She should call and make an appointment. They don't take just anybody."

August. Leah worked the switchboard in the dormitory from seven until noon. Then she made salads in the afternoon and evening, walking across the street to the hospital kitchen under the full moon, watching the river glint and dimple. She added her hours, figured the tax, the social security. Not enough. She sold books, even her favorites: Thomas Mann's *The Magic Mountain* and *Buddenbrooks*, her hardcover Shakespeare, illustrated by Rockwell Kent, Joyce's *Ulysses*, all her Dostoevsky. Then she sold her suitcases, taking them downtown to a pawnshop, nodding, biting her lip because: "These initials, see they make it harder to sell 'em." "I'll be back for them before Christmas. My grandmother gave them to me. With her ivory brush and dresser set." Pause. "No. I can't sell them."

And, finally she had enough money. Three hundred and ten dollars. "Be here around five tomorrow afternoon," she was told. "Don't eat anything, starting tonight. Bring cash and a box of Kotex supers. We're in cottage four toward the side."

Leah called her supervisor in the cafeteria kitchen. "I have some kind of stomach flu, Minnie. I'm sorry. Could I miss tonight and tomorrow if I don't feel better?"

She called Helen and said the same thing. "Yeah," Helen said. "I guess you won't be in for a couple of days, huh? Well, be careful, kiddo."

Leah took the streetcar downtown and changed to the airport bus. She carried the Kotex in a grocery sack.

Number four. Leah tapped at the door. The light bulbs around the trailer court were on, even though the sun had not begun to set. She tapped a second time.

"Miss Knutinen? You the one who called?" A woman held the door partially open.

Leah nodded. Her mouth was dry, her breath had gone sour.

"Come in. You alone? You should bring a friend . . . your boyfriend."

"He . . . couldn't come." Leah stepped inside. The linoleum rippled under her feet. A brown couch with striped pillows sat at one end of the narrow room. A brown fabric curtain separated the kitchen from the rest of the trailer. Plastic sweetpeas and ferns in a copper vase stood on a tan coffee table.

"You didn't eat anything?"

"No." Leah had trouble with her breathing.

"You just come in now. Doctor will be right with you." The woman held her hand out and waited.

After a moment Leah understood. She handed the three hundred dollars to the woman.

Counting the money, the woman said, "Seeing you didn't bring anybody, I'll run you over to the motel down the road. You shouldn't do anything tonight, you know. Just rest up. Course, it depends on how far along you are."

A man pushed the curtain to one side and looked at Leah. "I'm about ready. You tell her what to do?"

"I am just now. You just slide off your panties and we'll put 'em in your purse. You brought the Kotex? That's fine. Well, you come along in here and get up on the table. Doctor will examine you and we'll get you started."

Leah faltered for a moment, then allowed herself to be handed up onto the porcelain-topped kitchen table. Her skirt hiked up around her hips.

"Just kick off those shoes and socks, will you? Fine. Put your heels in the stirrups here, that's right. Kind of cold isn't it? Well, just you relax and Doctor will give you a quickie examination. Relax, how's he gonna get inside you if you keep your knees together?"

The man washed his hands at the sink, dried them on a towel, and brought an instrument to the table. He turned on a light bulb and angled it over Leah's lower abdomen. "Let's see. How far along are you? If it's too far gone I can't help you out. No more'n three months?"

Leah shook her head. She was trembling.

He took her knees and forced them apart. "Now, I can't do you any good if you don't relax. Just lay back there and let me see what I got to work with."

The woman forced Leah's shoulders down, nodding

to her: "He'll be quick. You just lay there and let him look. This part don't hurt at all."

"I don't ... Please ..."

"Listen here, young lady. You made this appointment. Now, whether you let me operate or not, I keep the money. So make up your mind." He'd slipped the instrument past her labia, and she could hear it being expanded, she could feel the heat from the light bulb as he swung it down and around between her legs. "You're pregnant, all right. Well ..."

Leah said, "Please, I don't ..." She trembled again. "Oh, please won't you help me?"

"That's what I'm doing."

She heard the woman moving behind her head, and then the rubber cone was over her mouth and nose, choking her, nauseating her, looping her backward into a void.

Which was not without pain. Something was being done to her that tore with small teeth at the tender insides of her body; she could hear it, a sound of scraping, like the sound of scraping squash; she thought she dreamed it, she dreamed she thought it, and she heard a bloody thread being pulled from within her, a bloody thread that brought with it a sac with one eye looking at her, and that thread caught around her and around her....

She awakened, tasting of blood and sourness in her mouth; she'd bitten the inside of her cheek, she thought. She was cold; her hair had come undone and now stuck to her hips and back. She sat up on the bare mattress, and then she remembered. She was curled up, knees to chin, her hands between her legs, and when she brought her hands up they were bloody. Her thighs were bloody and her hair was stuck to her body with the blood. She was cold, but to move meant to be colder, so she huddled back into her fetal knot, clasping her arms and legs to her, trying to sleep.

Something warm and wet slid between her thighs, waking her again. She smelled salt and something more. More tired now than if she hadn't slept at all, she looked around. Her purse was on a Formica nightstand beside the bed. She reached for it. The ten dollars she had kept for cab fare was gone.

ಒ‌ The Angel of Time ಎ

UNIVERSITY Hospital sent Leah home after three days: but why worry over minutes and seconds? She thought she was balanced between the physical and spiritual world. And then she resolved into the physical. She didn't go home to the farm, but home to the dormitory. Where she lived. The dorm was quiet. The rooms were still, the doors left open, the mattresses and furniture smelling of stale air and disinfectant. The maids and janitors moved in squads to clean, repair, paint, scrub, and wax one long echoing corridor after the other. Leah, huddling in her room, felt a kinship with the spiders and cobwebs being brushed out, banished. She slept badly, dreaming frequently of the whale, the wounded, scoured-out, scraped-out whale sinking to the blue deeps of the sea, a thin red thread reeling from her belly, that red thread, a blood thread, looping higher to the breaking waves, there to fray in the foam, to wash away, to disappear.

Leah was numb. She worked the switchboard part-time the last week before the students would return. And she read the Russians, the long, detailed accounts of Russian wars, of Russian life, of their French mannerisms, of lace and coarse fabrics, of wronged women, of faithless wives, of revolution, of wars, of retreats; she read the English novelists, the stylists, the Gothics, the satirists; she read Americans, she read Finnish, she began Icelandic and German; she dug into books and languages, finding that she could dull the edges of pain with words, could lose the first bitterness of pain with words.

Her father died during the first week of full-term classes. Numbness added to numbness; Leah went home to the farm.

"I'm glad you could come," Pastori Napa said at the bus station. "Your ma is taking it some hard. She's got her sisters to help some, but you're the best help." He held her hand in his moist little hands, his round eyes shining up at her. "We already got the casket ordered. We knew your pa was bad when they took him in this time. He just never got back to himself."

"Where is he now? Can I see him? Is my mother all right?"

"She's to home now. I'll take you straight home."

"No. Could I see my dad first?" Leah knew she would be all right if she could have a moment with her father first, before anything, before anyone else.

"Sure thing! You pile in here and I'll just drive us over. He's in the mortuary chapel now. But tomorrow we'll have him out to the church. We got a nice funeral planned. You'll see." The minister drove his black Chrysler carefully, fussily, over the gravel road, almost stopping for every turn. "Ya-as, Missis Napa and myself, we planned a nice turnout for your pa. We got the songs picked out and got Paul Lopp to play the organ—I'll sing 'Rock of Ages' and Missis Napa will play the guitar. And I wrote a nice eulogy for your pa. And flowers have started to come already. Some even from Virginia and the flower shop there. I say that's nice, ain't it? And a big floral tribute from Eveleth. Your ma ordered a little boo-kay of five roses with one white one. She said that was personal, so we put it right on your pa's chest, or where it is when the lid is opened."

Leah opened the car window. Nausea slid oil around the base of her throat.

"So it's all set up for you, nice and smooth. And we'll have the funeral supper right in the basement of the church so's there won't be any upset at home for you. I got the grave digger out this morning and we took your ma out to look for a site. Well, we got a nice place on the side of a hill there, with space for your ma right beside. She wants to be cremated, she says, and put in the same resting place. But we figured you'd be taking care of that, so we just went along with what she said, upset as she is right now."

Leah nodded.

"I went ahead and made up the little souvenir cards. The bill will be right in with the rest of the expenses. I don't know, do you want to take care of it all now, or would you want to wait and talk with your ma?"

"I think I'll talk to Mom about it."

"Well, if you say so. She was handling things pretty good. Although, if I was asked I'd have wanted a little more impressive casket. But she's got her mind set on wood with brass handles. Well, she's got a lot on her mind." He eased the Buick into the parking lot behind the mortuary. "Ya-as, we'll see your pa and then take you on home." He scurried around the car to hand Leah out, but she forestalled him by moving quickly out of the car and walking across the pavement to the carved doors of the mortuary. He followed her inside and directed her to a closed door. "He's in there. Will you want me with you?"

"No. Thanks." Leah hesitated, then opened the door and walked into the small room where her father's casket lay. The lighting was peculiar, she noticed. So were the walls. Pink. Or skin color! She could not get air into her lungs, wanted to open a window, but there was none. Her eardrums clanged so that she had to close her eyes for a moment. She walked resolutely across the rose-beige carpet to the casket.

Her father lay against the ivory satin pillow, his unruly black hair finally subdued, parted neatly to one side, the sideburns still bristling, still pitch black. His weather-stung skin was still tan over the pallor. His mouth, dented where he'd held his pipe for most of his life, curved in the familiar bittersweet smile.

Leah touched his hand. Cold. She drew back in horror. Cold. Not with death but with refrigeration and preservatives, she thought. Not even dying could cool him this way, or stifle the curl in his hair, or glaze the ironic humor of his smile.

She had withdrawn her hand, recoiled. Now she touched her father's hand again, leaned down to place her cheek upon his. Her face felt almost bruised by the hardness, the opacity, the absence of her father—no, not her father, she thought, but a dime-store dummy. She straightened and stepped back a pace to look at him. "They should've left you with your pipe in your hand. Not that white plastic-covered Bible." She hadn't realized she'd spoken aloud until Pastori Napa touched her on the arm. She spun on her heel, almost losing her balance, clutching at the casket for a moment. Then she said: "Where's his pipe? That would be more like him, more like what he really was."

"It wouldn't look right."

"Well, then his little birch-bark tobacco holder. It's carved. He made it himself and carved it."

"No, leave the Bible be. It's the New Testament." Pastori Napa smiled and patted her hand. "Your ma said to put that there. We always do anyway, but she said to."

Leah wanted to argue. But she shrugged and turned away from the casket. "Well, if that's what she wants." Not looking back, she went to the door and walked out of the mortuary.

"Will you be wanting to order flowers while we're still in town?" Napa had followed her outside.

"I guess so. I don't know what would seem right to him." She wanted, badly, to sit quietly and think, to sit in silent aloneness to gather her belief that her father was dead. "Osmose," she said aloud.

"Roses *would* be nice," Napa said. "Or carnations."

"No. I . . ." She concentrated. "Nothing seems right. Not hothouse flowers or cut flowers. Sprigs of leaves, pine branches?"

"I think your ma'd want flowers."

"Oh." Leah got into the Chrysler. "I'll ask her what she wants."

The yard in front of the farmhouse was crowded with cars. "Your pa's sisters and their families are here. I expect they'll be here tomorrow too, after the funeral, and you'll have time for a nice visit with 'em." Napa parked the Chrysler and took Leah's elbow in time to walk her up the steps.

The door flew open and Leah's Aunt Anna rushed out to seize her in an immense and powerful hug. "Oh, flicka! I told Vilma you'd come as quick as you could. And here you are. Did you eat yet? No, come in, come in. Vilma is in the living room, you come see her and I'll put on more coffee and some supper for you." She hauled Leah around as if she weighed no more than twenty pounds. Leah, in spite of herself, held on to her aunt, returning the hug, almost clinging to the short slab-sided mountain of a woman.

Leah's mother sat on the couch between two younger aunts. She looked up at Leah and held out her arms. Leah hugged her mother, kissed her, looked at her, felt her own chest tighten with pity and grief.

"Sit down, Leah," one of the aunts said. "We'll move over so you can sit with your ma."

"No. No, that's all right." Leah's mother wiped her eyes and smoothed the collar of her dress. "We'll be all right."

Leah sat down on a kitchen chair, and didn't know what to say that might be helpful. She looked across the distance of braided rugs, handwoven rag rugs that drifted over the highly polished wood floor; she listened to the silence collect in the room. The clocks ticked relentlessly, dust seemed to settle gently everywhere, the walls ticked, something in the walls ticked. The ticking made Leah's eyes brim with tears, and when she swallowed them they tickled down inside her.

Aunt Anna stuck her head through the living room doorway: "I got you some supper fixed, Leah. You just come in here. Richard is out doing the cows so's you won't have that to worry about. And Walter'll stay the night if you want." She had bacon, scrambled eggs, and toasted homemade cardamom biscuit on the table for Leah. "I don't know, do you want coffee or milk? You look some punier than when I saw you last. You been studying too hard? Lookit, I can see the veins up here on your neck, and you do look peaked." She poked Leah's ribs and waist, patted Leah's hips and belly. "Nah, you eat up. You're meant to be a big healthy girl, not a stick. What do you weigh? I bet not a hundred and fifty. Tch. Eat up. Here, put some of this whipping cream on that there biscuit, that'll put the health back on you." She dolloped cream into Leah's coffee and then spread more on the toast. "I think you should stay home a bit. Fatten you up. Anyways, you're of marrying age and there's plenty of boys around here looking for a nice girl like you. Girls don't need that college business. Now, your ma should've kept you home. I know, she put such pains into those twins and they died, but she coulda put more pain into you. I shouldn't say it but I do, where'd all that pining get her? Especially now, she's going to need you and not those dead babies of hers. Well, you eat up and I'll make a nice tart for you quicker'n you can imagine. I found this easy crust they make out of graham crackers and butter and add a dab of sugar and put in the cherries or apples like I got here already peeled and you know it'll taste good with cinnamon and brown sugar and cream on the top. See, I'll just pop it right in and you finish eating and we'll have a sip of coffee together and you'll have dessert before you know it." Anna could not sit still. Leah had grown up knowing an Anna in perpetual motion; even visiting, comforting the ill or burying the dead, Anna cooked, cleaned, messed, piddled, made things, crocheted, sewed, washed woodwork, cleaned ovens, pinched pie crusts, carried wood for the cookstove, changed babies' diapers, scolded, hugged, kept secrets, blabbed secrets, scandalized, gave advice, took none, kept her eye on every living thing within sight, and, as far as Leah could tell, was next to God.

The ticking stopped. Leah bit into the biscuit and was suddenly at home. "I don't know what kind of flowers I should get for Dad."

"Was that Napa at you? I'll take a spoon to him one of these days. Get no flowers, I say. Your pa would smile at that. Evergreen. I'll come with your myself, put on my barn boots and a towel over my head and we'll take Richard's hatchet, he's got one in the backbox of the truck, and you and me, we'll get evergreen boughs. Flowers. His half of the florist shop! Well, Jesus Christ, that Napa can squeeze money out of the grieving family and not even blink." She looked through the kitchen window. "Is his car still here? I think I'll just go out and help him leave, that pisshead." She shook the curtain back into place. "No. Gone. Well, he'll be here tomorrow after the funeral with his hand out again. Your pa had no use for him, you know that. And now I'm here I'll see to it he don't take advantage. He knows better'n to mess with me." She went to the oven, opened it, peeped in, then sighed and closed it. "Be another few minutes. Now, I'll have a sitdown with you."

Anna poured herself a mug of coffee, looked at Leah's cup, added coffee to it and went to the living room door. She gestured with the coffeepot. "Anybody ready for more. I got plenty here." She nodded and brought the pot back to the stove. "Ech. They're in there with your ma.

She took it some hard, but she'll do fine now. Did you see him? Don't he look nice? Course, they couldn't get the stains out of his skin from of all those years of work. Well, who'd expect he'd go with lily-white hands? I remember when he left home the first time. He runned off to join a lumber company and got a job as coffee boy, he was so little and young. But he come home with his purse full of money, and was he proud! There wasn't no mines then, no, we had the farms and lumber and, of course, hunting which got us through when we were kids. Then he run off again when he was nineteen, but he got a regular full-time job with the lumber company and they took him all the way out to Montana, he come back with a cowboy hat and fur pants. We did laugh, he looked like a bear in those pants." She laughed now, her black eyes bright as berries, her black hair doddering in its heap at the top of her head. "Oh, and he had his hair pomaded when he got dressed up in his fancy shirt. He was good-looking. Well, our side of the family has the looks." She smoothed the dress. "You got your share, too, don't think not." Winking, she took a bit of Leah's biscuit and popped it into her mouth. "You didn't see that, did you? No, I got quick hands. Well, but your pa looks nice. I don't expect him to sit up and wave the way Mattie says, he's dead, she knows that. So why she says he looks lifelike . . . well, you know Mattie, she's sweet but tries too hard to please. She's godmother to you, so that's all right, not as if she was blood kin and we'd wonder if she was a sign of things to come."

She took another bit of Leah's biscuit. "I don't have any appetite myself, a nibble here, a bite there, that does for me, I don't eat more'n a birdie. Your Auntie Virginia ain't here yet. I expect she'll be at the funeral. Nice. Nice. She moved to town and she got *nice*. We're not good enough for her, as if I didn't wipe her ass off when she was in didies. Well, she married Savolainen and got nice. It's hard, though. We had twelve born, some in Finland, some right here not five miles away, and what's come of it? Eckstroms, Makis, Lahtis, Jarvis, Waisanens, Lappis. More even. And we dwindle down so there's more of us in the ground than upright. Well. And the men always going off somewhere, running off to lumber camps, running up to Canada or Alaska to work highways even before the big wars, and the women left to milk the cows and turn sour. Well, I don't have to start feeling bad, I got my own boys at home yet. And you went and run off, too, like a boy. Your pa, he went off to Alaska. But you were born then. So your ma had company. I remember how little and yellow-haired she was when they got married. She made me look downright black, she was so light-skinned. Not sickly, no. But white so you could see the blue veins on the tops of her breasts. I never saw such white breasts as she had. She was a little dickens then. Oh, she'd get to giggling and fooling in the sauna and even your Aunt Virginia would have to laugh. Oh, she was a dickens. She'd make your pa jealous by playing sniff with Pastori Napa at the church suppers. Or pass-the-hanky. So we saw she'd get your pa to stay home at least one winter. And he did. Two winters. The first one they were married and they had to live in our downstairs rooms. Houses for just young folk were hard to come by and they tried it, living downstairs of us. But I could hear everything they did. "'Don't bite!' she'd say in the middle of the night.'' Anna laughed softly to herself, took the rest of Leah's biscuit and ate it. "Well, then they had to live alone. Your ma had her own ways and so did I, and we tried but the looks got going and I'd be a little sharp with her, it was my house! And she got too nice to live with us. So they moved out and lived in your gramma's sauna and fixed it up nice. But it seemed like it didn't work right for them because the twins died right off and your pa went off for the next winter. Well, I'll be quiet now. I get talking about things. Och, the tart!" She jumped up and opened the oven door. "It's just coming now. Well, that's a relief."

Leah could hear cars arriving, doors slamming. "Should I go and be with Mom?"

Anna shook her head. "No. When she wants you she'll let you know. She has her ways, you know." She closed the oven door, peeked out the kitchen window. "Oh, I thought I recognized the voice. Your cousins from Sparta. You want to talk to them? They'll come out to the kitchen in a minute. I better get the other big coffeepot out." She pulled a large white enamel coffeepot out of the cupboard, rinsed it, filled it with water, and set it on the stove. "I'll get the egg and the coffee in it soon's the water boils nice." She stopped to look at Leah. "Well, you're like my own little girl. You got left with us so much. Us or your gramma. I don't see as it did you any harm and we were glad to have you. It was nice to have a little girl in with our boys. Do you remember playing so late Fridays and Saturdays when you were with us? Well, the boys do even now and they're working and grown up. Ray's got engaged already and got a good job and he's building a house back of ours. I still have that chip off the bureau that you and Joel knocked off when he came to stay with us."

"Leah." One of the younger aunts was at the kitchen doorway. "Your ma wants you now."

Leah nodded and went into the living room. It was crowded now with relatives, blue-eyed and serious.

"Here's space on the sofa," an aunt said, beginning to rise from where she was sitting next to Leah's mother.

"She'll be fine on the kitchen chair," Leah's mother said. "Move it closer, that's all." She dabbed at her eyes and sighed. "It just came so fast."

Murmurs of condolence rose on dove wings, feathering the empty space in the room.

"You don't know how hard it is, Leah, to be all alone." Leah's mother sighed again, her voice coming in plump little bursts, plump as the tears that escaped her fingers and ran down her face.

"I'll stay home now if you want me to," Leah said, hitching the chair closer to the sofa, reaching for her mother's hands.

A blue eye glinted at her for a split second, then closed. "No, no. You have your school. I'll do all right here alone. I always have." She trembled and wept into the handkerchief.

Guiltily, Leah said: "No, I will stay home."

The mother shook her head, dismissively waved her handkerchief. "No."

The cousins and aunts looked at Leah, silently willing her to be kind, to be patient, to understand, to change the subject.

Leah said, "I didn't get flowers yet, Mom. I couldn't think of what would be right. Anna and I'll go and get pine boughs for the grave tonight."

"Don't be stupid," her mother said. "Whoever heard of pine boughs for a grave? It isn't a sauna."

"I just thought . . . What would you like me to get?"

"Gladiolas are nice," one of the aunts said. "We'll take you into town tomorrow morning if that helps."

Anna came into the living room with the big coffeepot. "Who needs coffee? Leah, you come help me in the kitchen, that's my good girl."

"Leah should stay here with her mother," one of the aunts said.

"Bossy!" another aunt hissed.

"Oh. Bossy, is it? Well, he's my brother. I guess I know when I'm not wanted when I hear it, though!" Anna slammed back into the kitchen.

Leah looked to her mother for instruction, got none. She sat still in the chair for a moment, then got up and went into the kitchen. "Oh, Aunt Anna, don't listen to them. Let's just sit out here and have coffee and talk. It's a mess in there."

"Well. I put the pot back on the stove. And the cups is set out. And I sliced the biscuits and the roast is there under that towel. And if they want to eat, they can. And if they want to shove it up their *ears* they can. I have feelings too, even if I don't set la-di-da on the couch and sniff." She spoke ferociously; a tear shot out of her eye and splattered against her glasses. "I won't be stepping foot in this house after tomorrow, kiss my ass if you like!"

"Oh, Anna. Mom didn't say anything. She's fond of you. It's just today is hard on her. You said so yourself."

"Well, it's hard on everybody." She rounded on Leah and hauled her into her arms for a gargantuan hug. "Let's have that little tart I made. The la-di-das will be getting their coffee and going home. You and me, we'll wash up and then it'll be bedtime. You want to come home with me? No, I guess you better stay here with your ma. She expects it. Anyway, she's got her own ways so we'll say no more." Anna twinkled at Leah. "But *that's* hard on me."

Eventually the aunts and cousins did go home. Anna pulled a sweater on, dangled her bag from her arm, kissed Leah, pressed her cheek to Leah's mother's, and enthroned herself in the front passenger seat of the battered ford. Her husband, Richard, came from the barn, having checked the cows and the lamps. He smiled shyly at Leah. "We ain't seen you for a while, flicka. You better come to visit before you forget all about us."

"I will. I'll see you tomorrow, won't I?"

"Yas. I'm pallbearer. I'm awful sorry, Leah. We'll miss your pa." He took her hand gently and patted it. "Well, you take care of yourself now." He got into the car and started it, waving to Leah as he backed around the weeping willow tree.

Leah's mother had moved from the living room to the kitchen. She was wiping the counter with a dish towel when Leah came back into the house.

"Can I do anything to help?" Leah asked. "Do you think a cup of tea would help you to rest?"

"No. You go on to bed. I'll sit up a little."

The ticking began again. It moved from the clock on the kitchen wall to the stove, where the embers vibrated with it and fell apart, then it moved to the cupboard door, then to the curtain at the window, tapping against the glass. Leah's mother tapped her fingers on the counter briefly, then walked out of the kitchen into the hallway.

"Mom?" Leah followed her. They stood in the hall for a moment with nothing to say. Leah hugged her mother, then allowed herself to be pushed gently away. "Try to sleep," Leah said. She went to her bedroom and sat in the dark, listening to her mother's footsteps move along the hallway.

The house shifted and creaked, the earth making the slow turn toward the deep Minnesota winter, the moraine heaving invisibly, inevitably against itself. Leah listened in the dark, could almost hear the earth speaking to itself, could hear the house creak as it rode the earth.

Without putting on the light Leah undressed, pulled on an old flannel pajama top, and crept under the cold sheet. She tried to find a familiar place on the pillow, but it had lost the old cuddle spot, had become a resisting lump. She felt like the house, riding on top of a cold earth that had closed against her; she dozed, wakened, dozed again, and finally wakened to see the light creep along the hallway floor as her mother made the journey to the north bedroom and the twins' belongings. The light grew, subsided, blinked out as her mother opened and closed the north room door. Leah turned over on her side, folded her knees to her chest, and tried to sleep.

The floor creaked again, this time with the weight of her mother's steps as they approached Leah's bedroom.

Leah sat up in bed, shoving her feet out of the warm space she had made.

"I'm sorting through your dad's things," the mother said. "I thought you'd like to have something of his to remember him by." She stood in the doorway holding the night-light in one hand. She set the light on the chest of drawers and stood thoughtfully for a moment, then laid two dark objects on the chest.

"Turn on the light, Mom. Don't you want to sit down?"

"No. It's light enough. His pipe and tobacco pouch, is that all right? I kept his watch back with the boys' things. I'll give his clothes to the cousins and whoever needs them."

"Whatever you want. I'll take care of the pipe. Thank you. Won't you want me to stay home with you?"

"No. I thought it all out today before you got here. I'll take care of everything." She picked up the night-light. "Well, you sleep now. I'll sit up a bit. Walter's coming to do the cows for me tomorrow. Did you bring a dress suitable?"

"Yes. That dark blue dress with the white collar. I can wear a scarf. Isn't there anything I can help with? I can stay for as long as you need me."

"No. No. I settled it all in my mind already. Get some sleep. Coffee will be ready at six." She left, taking the small light with her. Leah could hear her take the cards out of the drawer in the kitchen cupboard.

Leah could not look at her father again. She went through the motions at her mother's side, but when they came abreast of the open casket, she closed her eyes and allowed herself to be led past it. She tried to take her mother's hand, but found it motionless, resisting. Her mother kept the handkerchief to her eyes, nodding when spoken to, offering a blind face to the aunts and cousins who came to kiss her.

Pastori Napa, freshly barbered and gleaming with pomade, pattered through the funeral ceremony, smiling with condolences at every turn, every blink. He and his wife stood together beside the casket and, casting limpid glances at Leah's father, sang in the falsetto and dulcet tones of the old Finnish tradition, the guitar and organ accompaniment almost managing, in Leah's opinion, to make things bearable.

The church bell tolled, the casket was closed, and the pallbearers stepped the length of the church, treading somberly in time to the organ. Leah was numb. She remained numb through the rest of the ceremony, following the hearse to the cemetery and standing on the wind-battered hill, watching the leaves fall into the open grave, watching the artificial grass flap, watching the casket descend into the dark red earth.

ঌ Seven of Wands ॐ

The Seven of Wands turns up. Teaching. Writing. Publishing. A card with seven wands, scepters, magic wands almost. I go backward and forward, hunting the scraps, the fingernail clippings, the dropped hair, the lint from a jacket, a tobacco crumb, everything, anything of the detritus that has collected, amassed, the detritus that marks the way deeper and deeper into the maze. I know I follow the spoor now, although I hear the coughings of two different throats, the shuffling of many feet here in the half-light of introspection. Disbelief: I feel that. I know that even while my tears are drying on my face, my eyes are stretched wide open with disbelief: This is not happening to me!

"You let it happen."

Who said that? I stare around, touch again the Seven of Wands. . . .

Zulu came bounding into Leah's room. "I'm tired of being a sex object!" She threw herself down on Leah's bed and kicked her heels against the spread. She lay there for a moment, then rolled over onto her stomach to look at Leah, who had gone on typing a paper. "Yah. You're cool, you are. The Equivocator. The Observer. I s'pose you'd say we're *all* lemmings *now*."

Leah nodded and continued to type to the end of the paragraph. Then she stopped and sat back to grin at Zulu. "Aren't you? I'm not belittling you, but you all seem to be rushing off to sex just as crazily as you all did to marriage. Just the pill makes the difference."

"I'll say! And you shouldn't belittle us. You sit here working away, but I know you'll fall for somebody and it's all over for you. You ought to let me introduce you to a few of the guys. You graduate and go on to grad school and be a librarian and all your sex life will dry up. You already have that kind of pinchy look around your lips. And I bet all your body fluids are drying up."

"I'll find someone my own way. You don't really mean that you're in love with every boy you go to bed with? No one is in love that often."

"We-ell, sometimes it is just curiosity. Or like last winter it was just too much bother to get dressed and come back home—you know. And what's the sense of being free if I don't take advantage of it?"

Leah nodded thoughtfully and turned the page of the handwritten copy she was working from.

"You aren't still mad at me, are you?" Zulu sat up on the bed and lit a cigarette, offering the package to Leah.

"About Carl, you mean? No, I guess not. It would be different if I'd really thought he liked me. Or if I'd really started to like him. But it doesn't say a hell of a lot about your loyalty or your friendship, not the way you—what is it anyway with you? You blab about loyalty, but when you see a man, and somebody likes that man, *you* have to move in. You really did, you know. You send off those sex vibrations or waves or musk or whatever and take over."

"You are mad."

Leah took one of her own cigarettes and lit it. "Yes. Angry, disappointed, even hurt."

"Well, it couldn't have been much of a relationship if he got distracted so easily." Zulu shifted her weight on the bed, not quite looking at Leah.

"No, it couldn't have been. And the relationship you and I have—had—couldn't have been much either. It was distracted, too."

"Jaysus! All this about some guy." Zulu got up and went to the tiny kitchen unit in the closet and opened the refrigerator door. She took out a can of beer, popped it open, and drank some, watching Leah from the corner of her eye. "I have the feeling you are really upset about this." When Leah said nothing, Zulu continued: "You know I've always really liked you. And respected you. Almost like a crush on you, you know, because you're so mature and bright and kind of always thinking so hard. Like you're my older sister. Not that we're at all far apart in age, but you seem older this last year." She put the beer can down and came back to sit on Leah's bed, looking at Leah with soft dark eyes, supplicating, almost wooing her. "I just wanted to be close to you. I was never close to a girl before, not any girl that I respected. So, don't look that way. I was just trying to get close to you. I was just showing off."

Leah shook her head.

"What?" Zulu asked.

"That's why you did it? To get close to me? To get my approval?" Leah stared at Zulu. She pushed away from her work table. "Out. Out."

"You're still mad? Well, dammit, Leah, you let it happen! I'm not alone in the blame! You get some blame, too!"

"I don't believe this is happening! What?" Leah could feel her eyes, dry, open as wide as they could in disbelief. "*I* get blame? I'm the victim, you . . . you . . ."

"No. You did let it happen. You're responsible as much as I am. As much as Carl is. You could have stood up for yourself, you know. I would have. If you had started flirting with Carl and I was interested in him first I'd have damn well put a stop to it. You know that. So don't just look so damned wounded and wronged. You let it happen." Zulu put a hand out to Leah. "Come on, let's be friends. From now on if you like a guy, just let me know. I promise I'll be good."

Leah looked at her for a moment, undecided. She shook her head, partly in disgust with herself. "Oh . . . all right. But I'm not all the way convinced. . . ."

"But you'll think about it, right?" Zulu caught Leah's hand and squeezed it. "Right?"

"Miss Knutinen, may I speak with you in my office?" Mr. Lillywhite, a PhD candidate, an instructor, called to Leah from the stairs in Folwell.

Leah nodded and followed him to the third floor, where instructors shared cramped little cubbyholes.

"Sit down. Would you like some coffee?" He had been a reader for Mr. Montgomery's Dickens course and had infuriated Leah with his comments on her papers.

Now she wondered what he wanted. She took the cup of coffee and watched him fuss with a stack of papers.

"I need a reader. It doesn't pay much, you know. But the stipend comes in useful for the penniless grad student?"

"Yes. Any kind of money helps. Which course?"

"I need a reader for my English Composition section and for my American Short Story course. It's a lot of work. What you'd do to start with is read the papers, write your comments and the suggested grade on a separate sheet of paper. I'd read the first few papers, and if I agree with your comments and the grade I'll trust your judgment from then on. I liked what you did in Dickens, and if you want it, you have the job."

"Thanks. When can I start?"

"I have the first set of Comp papers here. I'll need them back day after tomorrow."

"Okay." Leah took the papers from him. She could feel the blush of pleasure rise to her hairline. "Thank you. I'll do a good job."

"Of course."

"Leah? Walt Lillywhite here. I have a vile cold, as you can tell by my voice. So would you take over the American Short Story today? You still have your own notes, do you not? We're doing Hawthorne's 'Molineux' today."

"I've got all my old notes. But I don't know how to teach! I don't know anything about it at all!"

"You took from Monty, did you not? Just do everything he did. He was the best lecturer I've ever seen, and you must have gotten some of his technique in three semesters. Please, Leah. I can't think of anyone who has the same material."

"Oh. God. I'll be awful. Okay. But, Walt, it's on your head if I am dreadful and inadequate."

"Bless you. I'll buy you a drink when I leave my pallet. Call me tonight."

Leah put the telephone down and wobbled to her hot plate. She put the water on for tea. Oh, she thought, I cannot do it. She looked at the Baby Ben alarm clock. The class met in five hours.

She found her notes and a copy of collected short stories with Hawthorne's "My Kinsman, Major Molineux." She sat down with cup of tea, a cigarette, and her notes. She reminded herself: I was an honors student all the way through. That was thought in one tone. The other side of her, the retreating self, thought: But competence as a student is far from skill as a teacher. She read the story quickly, adding to her old marginal notes, paging through her old notebook, frowning through the cigarette smoke. She drank all the tea and made another pot. Old Moose Jaw, she thought. Guaranteed to wake you up with all the caffeine in it. Come on, brain, do your stuff! But her confidence was not to be coaxed with tea or cigarettes or with the reviving memory of classwork. I know this material. But is that enough? She closed her eyes. They have paid money, cash money, to have a lecture by an experienced and knowledgeable teacher. How goddamned awful if I cheat them! If? *If?* Oh, help!

She drank the second pot of tea. She smoked another cigarette. She thought: I have got to be good. It isn't enough to be me and just know the story and what went into it and what went on in the author's head. I have to be able to get it out of *my* head and into theirs.

She took another sip of tea. Her stomach cramped angrily and she bolted for the toilet to throw up. She brushed her teeth and took a shower, washing her long hair, toweling it dry and pinning it up on top of her head with the old tortoiseshell hairpins her grandmother had given her. She dressed in a turtleneck jersey and corduroy skirt.

At noon she made a cup of instant soup and drank it. And threw up again. She brushed her teeth, then sat down at the table with the notes one more time. She gurgled when she moved. Too much tea, she thought. She began to hiccup. "Oh, God," she said aloud. "I'm a mess. Sloshing and hiccuping. I can't drink any water, I'll drown." The waist of her skirt was tight. "Gas, too, on top of all that tea. I'll call Walt. I'm going to explode. I'm a bag of water and gas." Tears plopped out of her eyes. Grimly, she gathered the notes and books, stuffed them into her book bag, and left the apartment. "I can't do it. I'll be awful. But I can't *not* do it."

She walked the two miles to the campus, knees jellied, belly still heaving, hiccuping, gasping for air, sweating, almost sobbing, but now angry with herself and this abject terror.

She saw a girlfriend, Dee, across the street and waved to her. Dee called something, but Leah couldn't hear it. Suddenly Leah knew she had gone deaf. I won't hear them if they have a question. I won't hear the campanile when it rings for classes to change. I won't know when to start the class. I won't know when to *stop* it. I'll be up there like a drowning fish, gasping and flopping. An hour with a deaf and dumb teacher. Oh, God.

She walked up the stairs of Folwell Hall to the classroom. Then she walked away from the classroom and went to the women's room. She locked herself into a stall and sat on the commode, smoking one cigarette after another until the campanile rang. "I heard it," she muttered, pressing her head against the cold marble of the stall divider. "Thank you, God, for that."

Then it was time to do it. Strangling with hiccups, she prayed: "Oh, God . . ." But what, exactly, she wanted from Him she didn't know. She went into the classroom, stood behind the lectern for a moment, and watched the students walk in and find their seats. The terror seized her again and her bladder threatened to let go. Her nose ran. Sweat shot out of her pores. Her mouth went dry. And then the sea creature, the whale, gurgled far down within her and she said: "My name is Leah Knutinen. I'm substituting for Mr. Lillywhite, who is ill today."

Something wonderful happened to her. She looked over the lectern at the students, who looked back at her. They looked at her with interest, with attention. They looked at her with recognition and nodded, or seemed to nod, with acceptance. One or two of them smiled at her, and she felt her own smile break wide across her face. Oh, she thought, thinking under the lecture, talking about the story and about Hawthorne, watching a question rise in someone's eye or a response bob to the surface, pausing to listen or to agree or disagree; all that time, all during the hour, she thought: I really love this!

The campanile rang and Leah almost didn't hear it. But she wasn't deaf with fear, she was prattling on happily about Hawthorne's use of symbolism and color. "Oh, there's the end. Of the class," she amended herself. "Thank you, I enjoyed it." Then she blushed. She grabbed her notes and books and walked out of the classroom.

She walked back to her one-room apartment. That decides that, she thought, and hummed to herself. And the sea creature rolled close to the surface, agreeing.

* * *

The summer of her master's degree, as she was later to call it, Leah seemed to move in isolation. Her mother had written: "I am selling the farm. I don't need it and it's too hard for me. So I'm moving to California to stay with your Aunt Virginia." Leah had phoned her mother: "Mom, is there anything I can help with? Like packing or sorting?"

"No. I've got all the help I need. I'll mail your old books if you want them. You still have that Mark Twain collection of books. Do you want them?"

"Oh, yes. Isn't this all kind of sudden? You didn't write about selling the farm before, or even that you were thinking about it."

"No, I thought about it last year when your dad died. But I just now got the offer I wanted. I'll be moving next week."

Leah felt herself reaching out to catch at her and felt—knew—that her mother was once more moving away from her, eluding gently but finally the touch that Leah needed. Sighing, Leah asked: "Will you send me Aunt Virginia's address? Can I have it now so I'll know where to write?"

Leah's mother gave her the Santa Monica address. "Don't run up your telephone bill, Leah. I'll send you a postcard when I get settled."

That summer Leah read a lot. The campus with its summer school students seemed alien; her own classes would not resume until September. She had lost touch with Zulu; unaware of it, Leah had pulled herself deep underwater, hiding, attempting to recover from the abortion, from her father's death, from loneliness, to a kind of self-exile. She lived in a basement apartment that summer, lived on tuna fish and tea, saving the tea bags so that she could get a second cup from each. She walked the two miles daily to the campus and to the university library, where she stocked up on books, reading at random any title that caught her attention, pursuing authors she liked, digging away at Finnish, German, Russian, and Icelandic. She had always read, it seemed to her, learning to read English and Finnish before she entered kindergarten; and from grade school on she read all her textbooks the first weeks of classes, memorizing as she went, depending mostly on her powers of recall when the material was eventually discussed in class. She'd read her way through the school library, the town library, the county library, rummaged through church libraries and bookstores, gorging on books all the way through adolescence—gorging on books now, trying to fill the emptiness she felt.

The young men she encountered on campus, the veterans, the summer students, measured her with their eyes; something about them made her draw even further into herself. The knowing awareness in their eyes, the sureness of their moves, and the coolness . . . that's what makes me curl away, she thought. That coolness in their eyes. Even if I'd go to bed with them I'd see that coolness, that uninvolvedness. Always looking into the eyes of a stranger—I can't do it. Not lie there with him between my legs and see him looking at me as a stranger.

She sat alone in the basement apartment, reading, listening to her FM radio, not in pain, but not healing. She slept badly, waking at four in the morning, shaking and sweating in a panic whose source she couldn't identify.

"Leah! What are you doing in town? I thought you'd gone home for the summer. We don't see you in the student union anymore." Millie, one of the full-time salad workers, stood at the bus stop and waved to Leah.

"I'm here for the summer. My mom moved to California. How are you?" Leah hugged Millie briefly, smiling at her.

"Fine, fine. My vacation is coming up and I can't wait to go north and cool off. Are you working this summer?"

"No. I'm living off campus and waiting for school to start. Jobs are impossible right now."

"Do you have enough money to live? You've lost weight. I wish I could. You don't have a telephone, do you?"

"No. I can't afford one. Maybe after my grad assistantship comes through and I find another job on top of that, then I can get a telephone again."

"Oh. That's why no one got hold of you when the girls started their vacations. We need someone who worked in the cafeteria before to come in and work while vacations are on. You know, work for me for two weeks, then work for Regina when her two weeks come up. And Phyllis will be going right after. It would be full time for the whole summer!"

Leah grinned. She thought: A telephone. Coffee. New tea bags. Money! She said: "You mean no one else has grabbed it?"

"Well, we did have a boy doing it. You know the rules, if a job opens up give it to the men first. But he didn't like doing women's work, so he quit. So we've been holding off until we found a girl student. Could you come in tomorrow and get hired? Regina will be so glad to have you back!"

"What time? I'm glad to come back!"

"I start at eight-thirty. So why don't you come then? I'll tell Regina and you could probably start Monday when I leave for vacation."

"Oh, thank you! Bless you!" Leah hugged Millie and capered around her.

"There's my bus. I'll see you tomorrow morning."

That summer, once she had settled into working full time in the cafeteria, she stumbled upon a book about the Tarot. She read it and studied the cards. The designs were fantastic, she thought; so she took out her old playing cards, two used decks her mother had added to the carton of books she'd mailed early in the summer. Spraying the faces of each card white, Leah copied the Tarot designs in India ink, first in black and then filling in with jewel colors: red, indigo, purple, jade, umber, saffron. She loved the colors and the figures: the Enchantress with her hand on the lion's head; the Lightning Struck Tower with tiny people falling from it; the Hermit, enigmatic, threatening, black-robed, a crook in his hand, eyes bleak; the Juggler, bells askew and jingling, eyes wicked; the Queen of Cups, smiling, sweet, dimpled; the Queen of Swords, witchlike with long nails, thin lips; the King of Pentacles, full-chested, looking like money. They all entranced her, told her stories as she drew and colored them and pinned them up on the baize door of her closet.

"Someday I'll find you," she sang. Someday I'll find you, she daydreamed. She drew the Tarot and went to work at the student cafeteria and waited for fall classes to begin and lived under the surface of herself.

September came. Students and faculty returned to campus. Leah's assistant instructorship came through and with it her first month's stipend. She looked at the check and thought: Out of the basement and into that apartment on Knapp. A telephone. Back to the tuna and secondhand tea bags, but out of that basement with the silverfish and roaches and little worms that curl up.

Walter Lillywhite tapped her elbow and smiled at her. "You will read papers again, won't you?" he asked. "I can also suggest another part-time job for you . . . even write you a recommendation for it."

"Yes! I'll read papers. This stipend isn't going to fit me with furs. I have two monster seminars this semester and Ed Psych Methods and that research technique class. But I've read the material already and will just need to pay attention and write the papers and reports."

"Fine. Will you be living on campus? I thought you might take a place as a dorm counselor this year."

"Those got snapped up before I even thought about them. Anyway, I didn't know who to ask for references. And my other jobs are only an hour here and there."

"You must not be that retiring, Leah. You could have asked me. And I'm sure Monty, by now, would be glad to write a letter."

Leah nodded uncertainly.

"No, no. You must not cripple yourself with this lack of faith in yourself. Where are you going to live?"

"I know of a one-room apartment, if I get there before anyone else sees the sign."

"May I assist? I bought a small car this year. By all means, let me drive you to your flat and get you established." He took her elbow and led her down the stairs of Folwell Hall. "I will be living in the same hotel apartment as last year. It suits me best, for I don't do housekeeping or cooking and I have the time, thus, for my work."

His car, a Volkswagen, was parked on River Boulevard. "We have become so huge that even this street has official parking stickers required. I can, with care, afford to park my car here. Next year is another matter. Of course, I may not even be here then."

"Where are you going? Will you have your degree?"

"Oh, yes! But I must not let hubris expose me to the gods. I *think* I will have my degree." He handed her down into the little car. "Direct me."

He drove fussily across the campus and up over the

bridge. "I'll wait in the car," he said. "Will you need help with moving?"

"Books. That's mostly what I have. Maybe a box for my kitchen things."

"If you can arrange your schedule to do it this Sunday, I'd be happy to help with the car for two hours in the afternoon."

"Oh, Walt! Thank you. I'll be back in a minute." Leah scrambled out of the car and ran up the steps to the front door of the tall white house. She made quick work of renting the apartment. "I saw it last year when Dee Rupp lived here," she explained to the woman.

"Oh. Yes, she was a lovely person. I kept it empty this summer while I repaired the storm windows and put down new floor tiles. I'll be repainting it white. Will that bother you?"

"It's wonderful. Can I pay you a month today and then the deposit and the final month tomorrow when I get to the bank?"

"Yes, dear. Here's the keys. You know the rules, don't you? No loud parties or music after twelve."

Leah nodded, took her keys, shook hands with the woman, and ran back down to Walt's car.

"Of course," Walt said over the wineglass he was holding, "you know that women don't follow through on their doctorate dreams. You have done quite well so far, but I don't imagine . . . now, mind you, it isn't that you lack intelligence or intelligence of the right sort. You seem to be quite bright. But you must have noticed the dearth of women in the graduate programs. And how many women PhD's have you seen, really? I should've thought you'd be married by now; most young women find that to be what they want most in the world. Or working as a librarian. You have some of that attitude, a quietness. Almost a chastity."

Leah had invited him to dinner after she had settled into her new apartment. Now she glared as she offered him more wine.

"Now, don't be tetchy," he said, smiling at her. "Isn't it there, under all the index cards and the footnotes, the nesting instinct? Surely by now, you've felt the tiniest urge to embroider a toaster cover, to start the hearth and home?"

"I have. But if we're going to bait me, what about yourself? You live in a hotel apartment, have your meals cooked, laundry done. But still, don't you miss the welcoming smile from the cottage door, the downy upper lip of a Tolstoi woman, smelling of lace and French perfumes, the hot little body at bedtime?"

"Ah, but you see, I have my plans, my arrangements, all is controlled. When the time is right for me to choose the proper young woman, I will." He touched his lips with the napkin and sat back on the one upholstered chair in the apartment. He took out his pipe and began scraping at it with a silver penknife. "And when the time is right and I have tenure at some small but good school, we'll begin our family. And so it goes."

Leah watched him for a moment, watched his glasses reflect the light from the one candle. "You'll plan even the children?"

"The pill. I'll be sure my wife has contraceptives, and all those arcane mysteries of femalehood, well within her grasp."

This was a Walt Leah had not expected. She wondered if half a bottle of red wine always unbuttoned him so. "The pill?"

"Of course. I have been . . . uh . . . seeing a young woman for the last few months. Certainly, neither she nor I want anything as sordid as an inopportune pregnancy. She's a psychologist, not on our campus, mind you. And she is level-headed about these things."

"Hmm." Leah poured the last of the wine into Walt's glass. "You don't plan to marry this psychologist?"

"We have discussed it, but the time is not right. She has plans, as do I, that do not include marriage within the next few years."

"Well, why don't you bait *her* about marriage? Why bait me? Pick on someone your own size."

"I was making merry with you. Forgive me if I trampled upon your sensitivities. Let's be friends and give each other moral support." He grinned at her over his pipe, his eyebrows rising over the tops of his glasses. "Speaking of that. Are you able to support this flat comfortably or are you still saving tea bags?"

She blushed. She had done almost without food for three days in order to invite Walt to a dinner of spaghetti and red wine. "I'm just barely making it. But I think I have a line on another job, off campus this time. That restaurant over on Sewell might be hiring waitresses when they finish expanding. They're on the Minneapolis side and they're opening up a cocktail bar, so the tips would be great. I could do that after I finish at the student union. I need one real part-time job rather than the hour here, the hour there."

"I have a thought. Do you possibly take shorthand? The girl who has been working for Bernstein is leaving and he will be looking for someone to fill in. Now it's not many hours, but it would be on campus."

"Do I have to have shorthand? I could do speedwriting, I took that one summer vacation in high school. And I type. But, he's so famous he must have a collection of girls who'd type free."

"He also has a wife with some experience of volunteer typists. You might just drop in at his office and apply. I'll be glad to speak for you afterward."

"Oh, thanks. I'll go over on Monday. Should I just walk in? Isn't that presumptuous?"

"How else would you apply for a job? You could call and make an appointment. But I think he is relaxed about the formalities."

ം The Lovers ൠ

LEAH thought about going to Bernstein's office, of applying for the secretarial job. She had discovered since her father's death that there were two of her. One of her moved forward toward whatever it was she wanted to do. The other of her—not the whale—moved backward and pulled the first part and the whale with it. She found herself mumbling aloud as she walked away from Bernstein's office: "And I didn't have the nerve or guts to walk in there and say that I'd like to apply for the job. How did I ever teach that class when I'm so paralyzed?" Her knees were weak and her breathing was shallow. Her legs carried her back to her apartment and she sat down on the foot of the bed to smoke a cigarette and to yell at herself. But the yelling didn't help, so she put the cigarette out and made herself a grilled cheese sandwich and ate an apple.

"Nothing for it. I have to have more money." She washed the frying pan and turned it upside down on the drainer. She walked downstairs, looked to see if she had any mail, and thoughtfully, still cranky with herself, walked over to the restaurant.

"You experienced?" the woman manager asked her.

"Yes. Do you want my references?" Leah was only half lying. She thought: I don't know where I'd get experience if I didn't start somewhere, and they can call the student union. Millie'd tell them I could do anything.

"We have the girls wear uniforms and aprons. And opera hose. What size are you?"

"Dress size twelve. Fourteen." She watched as the manager dug out a short black skirt that, Leah thought, might cover the quick. And a top that was cut to it. Something prickled at the back of her neck. She was blushing.

"You'll be wearing this. You buy your own opera hose and heels. I'll pay you for them, but we don't keep them here." The manager eyed Leah. "You got nice long legs and you smile a lot. I suppose you couldn't start tonight? We got a lot of people in the bar section and they'll be good with tips."

"Um. I don't have the opera hose and shoes. And I have to finish my hours at my other job. I didn't tell them I'd be taking this job yet."

"Okay. I'll show you around the place and give you your locker key. You'll keep your uniform and things here so they won't get lost or stolen."

Leah followed the woman away from the booth and through the swinging doors to the bar section. "This is where you'd be working. We'll send you into the dining section when they're busy, but most of the time you'd be in here. The tips are better in here anyway, and you wouldn't have to share them with the busboys. And through here is the locker room and the john. We got a public john out in front, but this is for the help. The busboys change in here, too, so you'll have to watch that. Look around for a minute, I'll go get that telephone." The telephone had been ringing steadily, and now the manager picked it up.

Leah looked around the locker room, at the green metal lockers, the folding chairs, the hooks in the walls, the wire hangers, the toilet in its closet. She sat on a folding chair and watched the manager talk on the telephone.

"So look who's here!" Red-haired Helen of the dishwashing room at the university came through a closed door that Leah hadn't noticed. "College girls got to work any place they can, huh? You look pretty good."

Remembrance flooded Leah. Uncomfortably, she said, "You work here? I thought you—"

"Nah. I quit the university hospital. I work here now and get better money. And you're gonna be a waitress, huh? A cocktail waitress, I bet. Well. I suppose you found that doctor you asked me about and now you're set to get in trouble again. Fancy degree and all that and you still get into trouble. And now a cocktail waitress." She looked at Leah with such hate that Leah gasped. "Don't ask *me* for help next time. Not in the kitchen here, not help with orders. And not *any* help. You let it happen before. But next time don't ask me for nothing!"

Leah had stood up, ready to fly out of the restaurant. She was trembling. Something about Helen reminded her . . . of whom? Leah, mute, stared at Helen, saw the bright blue eyes, the fair eyebrows, the short graying red hair, the ruddy skin. But it was the blaze of blue in those eyes, the ice, the almost otherworldly impersonal hate.

"You two know each other?" The manager had put the telephone back on its hook and came toward Leah and Helen. "You better try on the uniform, this one here, and see if it fits you." She held out the black top and skirt.

Leah shook her head. "Uh, thanks but I don't think I want the job after all. I'm sorry for all the time I've taken." She stepped backward toward the locker room door. "Thanks a lot." She fled.

She didn't sleep that night, turning over in the narrow bed, watching the lights from cars brighten the ceiling: wordless, miserable. There isn't any space, she thought. It's elbows and crowding and no space. And she thought: It's a thousand small cuts. I don't know what it is, what this is. I don't know what's happening to me. I don't know how to change it. She rolled over onto her side, felt beached, gasping for air.

She went to her research techniques class and took notes in a frenzy of resolution. She paced the halls of Folwell, then finally tapped at Bernstein's door, trying to peer through the bubbled glass panes.

"Come."

Gingerly, books poking her ribs, heart poking her throat, she stepped inside his office. "Mr. Bernstein? Walter Lillywhite told me that you may be in need of an office assistant. My name is Leah Knutinen and I'd like to apply for the, ah, job. If you don't have time to speak with me now I'll be happy to come back at a better time."

He was a moderately short man with a great mane of silver and black hair, deep-set teak-colored eyes, and a gentle, pained face that made Leah want to apologize for paddling the air with her sounds. "Do you take shorthand?" he asked.

Leah, after one look at him, decided to lie. "Yes."

"Would you mind taking a few short letters now? I need to get some letters out today."

Ohmigod, Leah thought. She swallowed nothing, put her books down and looked around for a pencil and paper.

"The shorthand pad is there on that stand. And the pencils and pens are in the drawer." He was smiling at her.

He suspects I'm lying. Oh, and he's too kind to say so, she thought. She wanted to work for him. It wasn't love, she decided. But outside of pulp novels and the Gothics, which she'd read by the hundreds, she had never seen such a kind and gentle and pained face. She took the pad and a ballpoint pen and sat down across the desk from him. She crossed her legs at the knee, laid the pad on her knee, pretended she knew what she was doing. She looked up expectantly.

"This is to Miss Belle Gardiner. Seven Nine Park Place, New York, et cetera. My dear Belle." He dictated slowly at first and then more rapidly, watching Leah for a moment and then looking up at the ceiling as he spoke.

Leah thought: Ohmigod, I'll be damned if I don't get this job. She was conscious of his voice, of the pen moving along. Then when his dictation became rapid, Leah concentrated on memorizing what he said. "I'll never get it all down on paper and I'll forget what these doodles are supposed to mean." She scribbled in blind panic, conscious that he was looking at her, so she kept her face calm, confident, and above all, competent-looking.

"The next letter is to John McGivern, Associate Editor, World Publishing, Inc. Five Seven Nine Madison Avenue, New York, et cetera. Dear John: About the corrections I requested on the galley proofs, surely you of all people must understand . . ."

Leah turned the page, almost tearing it from the spine of the notebook. The ballpoint pan raced, but not in such a blind panic as before. If I can just keep his letters in my head long enough to type them, she thought.

He dictated five letters and sat back in his swivel chair. "If you wouldn't mind typing them up for me, I could sign them and get them out today."

Leah nodded and began to rise.

"Would you read that letter back to me? To John McGivern?"

Blankly, Leah nodded. She turned the page to the McGivern letter and recited it from memory. She looked up when she'd finished pretending to read it.

"Fine. Go ahead and type them, please." He smiled at her and turned to a stack of mail.

She typed the letters quickly, not daring to look around or relax even a hair until the letters, with carbons, lay neatly on Bernstein's desk, ready for his signature. She typed each accompanying envelope and added them to the stack of letters. Then she crossed her fingers behind her and waited for his verdict.

He read through the letters, Puck's grin crooking his mouth, signed them and wordlessly handed them to Leah.

She waited for a moment, then: "Um. Will that be it? When do you think you'll decide about the job?"

He took his glasses off, squinted at them, rubbed them with a tissue, and stuck them back on his nose. "I think you'll do quite well. What time of day can you work? I teach in the mornings and spend the afternoons in here working on the magazine. Do you know anything about layouts or print?"

"No. Mr. Lillywhite didn't mention that."

"Most of the job *is* taking letters." Again Puck's grin tickled one side of his mouth. "But you could help out on the magazine. We publish only quarterly, so we have a fairly leisurely pace. What I don't have time for, or don't want to take the time for, because it's painful, is writing rejection letters. If you could help with those?"

"Rejection letters?" Leah shook her head. "I wouldn't know how."

"No one does. We like to write all of them ourselves. I don't mean *like* to write them. But . . ." He sighed, turned his swivel chair toward the windows behind him and stared out over the trees. "I got enough rejection slips myself when I was starting, so I know how impersonal and killing they are. *So.* We *write* rejection letters, or notes, really. And I have this stack of them to get through. If you could help with them? Let's say it would ease pain in many directions. You don't write, do you?"

"I don't think so."

"Good. I am so glad! Writers are the most miserable people in the world." He smiled at her from over his shoulder and turned back to the desk. "Now, if you'd like the job it's yours. Can you work in the afternoons? I suppose I could leave things here and you could work in the mornings while I'm gone. But we'd still have the dictation to arrange."

"I can work afternoons. I have classes until one, and then I'm through until I go to work at the student union at five. I could be here tomorrow right after one."

"Good! I'll get you through the first batch of rejection letters and then you can see about writing them yourself. God knows, we never run out of manuscripts to send home with a little note of encouragement. Or of bland, smiling noncommittalness." He paused. "I don't think that's a word." He looked at her. "Oh, I think the pay is what the university offers as standard, whatever that is. When you want a raise, just tell me and I'll fill in that form. I don't think anyone argues about that around here. I've never known if that's because we're above arguing about money. Or if the money is not worth arguing about." He watched her pick up her books. "What are you going to be when you grow up?"

Startled, she held her books in front of her and blinked at him.

He waved at her. "Go on, go on. I'm dotty with relief over finding someone who will help with those rejections. I'll see you tomorrow."

Leah slept badly that night. I should tell him I can't take dictation, she thought. It's bad to start a job with a lie. But if I told the truth there wouldn't be a job to *start* with. She dozed until four o'clock and then awakened with a jolt of fear: He'll find out and fire me. And he'll know I'm a liar. She sat up in bed, lit a cigarette, and hugged her knees to her chest. Oh, God. Just let me get through a week then I'll tell him. I'll be honest next week. And I'll be doing a good job by then so maybe he won't fire me.

Walter Lillywhite caught her on the steps going up to Bernstein's office. "How'd it go? I haven't spoken to him as yet."

"I got the job. He's going to let me learn about the other part of the office work, magazine work."

"I do think *that's* wonderful! Will you have time for

my papers this weekend? I imagine your time is valuable now."

"I'll be able to do them. Will you want them back Monday morning? I'll bring them to your office."

"Or, failing that, stuff them into my mail cubbyhole. I must go now." He patted her shoulder and strode away.

Leah tapped on the office door and waited.

"Come." Bernstein was talking into the telephone and waved Leah to a chair. He pointed at a pile of manuscripts and nodded at her.

She looked through the manuscripts, trying not to listen to his conversation. She got out the shorthand pad, winced at it. With ballpoint pen poised, she closed her eyes for a split second: Ohmigod.

The telephone clicked into its cradle. "Women are like generals," Bernstein said. He grimaced bitterly and turned to stare out the window.

Leah wished she were invisible. She looked down at her knees and tried to dissipate into a dew. She heard the swivel chair squeak as he turned around.

"Before we get to the rejections, I have some other, longer letters that need to be done." He glanced briefly, bleakly, at her and took out a sheet of paper and his address book. "This first one goes to Aaron Smilow."

Briefly chilled, Leah scribbled and memorized. The pen jabbed the names and addresses onto the paper. She concentrated every ounce of energy into memorizing the letters as they were dictated. He dictated fifteen letters before pausing to light his pipe. Leah, glassy-eyed, refused his offer of a cup of coffee. "I'll just type these up right now," she muttered. She didn't dare even light a cigarette or do anything that might cause her to forget the content of the letters. She threw herself at the typewriter and machine-gunned them onto the paper.

When she'd finished the fifteen letters, she typed the envelopes and laid the results of her labor on his desk.

"Fine. That's fine." He signed them and handed them back to her. "Now let's get to the manuscripts and those rejections."

Turning away from him to grab her pad and pen, Leah crossed her eyes. Then, somewhat grimly, she sat down and poised herself for another onslaught of dictation.

"Now, to this guy, the name is here on the letter he

sent with the poems. He's not really so bad, it's just that he's not really so good either. I dunno, what should we say? How about: Dear Jason Whatever, we very much appreciated your poems. At this time, however, we are unable to use them. We are sure you will be able to place them with one of the other discerning publications. Thank you for sending them to us. Sincerely, and my name. Does that sound all right?"

Leah was able to write all of that down. She nodded. "It is kinder than the rejection slip. But if you write all of the letters, you'll never catch up. There's that whole cardboard box of manuscripts on your desk as well as the stack of them in the In file."

"I know. And more coming every day. We'll do as many as we can. And from now on it's your job to get some out every day whether I mention it or not. Remind me. Don't nag, though. I hate nagging. If we could work up, say, three or four model letters to suit the kinds of rejection, you could just type them as we need them each day."

"No rejection slips, then."

"No, not unless the writer is a real pain in the ass and has been persisting for years with the same old stuff. No. We'll do it this way." He dictated variations on that first rejection letter. Then he leaned back in his chair and tamped his pipe. "You go ahead with those. I've got more to do and maybe by the end of the week we'll see daylight. If I could break the mailman's legs so he'd give us a day's respite!"

Leah settled to work at the typewriter. She concentrated on the rejection letters, half hearing Bernstein on the telephone, not even glancing up when he stood beside her chair for a moment and read the words as they emerged from the machine. He patted her shoulder, mumbled something, and returned to his desk.

Someone came into the office. Leah smelled the perfume even before she glanced up. The woman was beautiful. She was slim, violet-eyed, with silver fox hair that shot silvery lights down her back.

Leah stared at her and began to stand up, to curtsy, to bob up and down.

"Oh, Leah," Bernstein said, smiling at her, understanding her. "You should meet my wife. Clara Bernstein."

The violet eyes showered ice on Leah even as the mouth curved in a smile. A long pale hand allowed itself to be touched, then withdrew to a coat pocket. The coat, a cashmere trench model, fell open and a kid glove dropped from a pocket.

Leah rushed to retrieve the glove and handed it to Clara Bernstein.

Who did not thank her, but turned to Bernstein and said: "Did you forget? We're having drinks at the club with Klavin and the others for the symphony."

"I was just finishing up," Bernstein said mildly. "I've got my coat and briefcase ready." He came around his desk, winked at Leah, and put on his topcoat.

Clara Bernstein glanced at Leah, then looked out the window while Bernstein went on talking. "I have everything, don't I? You can lock up, can't you, Leah? I'll see you tomorrow? Fine, fine."

They left the office. Clara Bernstein's scent hung in the air.

"One good thing about working in the salads," Millie said, "is the free food. You must be able to save by having dinner here five nights a week. And you should take an egg home, a tomato, once in a while. Look how much gets wasted!" She and Leah were peeling hard-boiled eggs for salads, up to their elbows in the stainless-steel pot.

"I've thought about it," Leah admitted. "But I get a good dinner every night for free, so I'd feel funny if I took anything else."

"So then I'll do it for you. You'd take a little present from a friend, wouldn't you?"

Leah laughed and agreed. They went on peeling hard-boiled eggs companionably, watching students walk past the double door. Millie said, "I wish sometimes I'd had the chance those girls have. But I got married early, and you know, if anybody was to have the education it was the husband."

"You must like working here."

"It's a job. I'm not qualified to do anything else but this kind of work. This job isn't bad. It's something to do." She looked up, eased her back with one wet hand. "I think that boy over there is looking for you. He's been standing in the doorway for the last couple of minutes. You didn't mention you had a boyfriend."

"I don't. He's in one of my classes."

"Well, go talk to him. Take your coffee break if you want."

"Oh, Millie. He isn't anyone special."

"You never know. Go on."

Leah dried her hands and walked over to the young man. "Hi, Dick!"

"Hi. I didn't realize you worked here. I was going through the cafeteria line and saw you through the glass dividers. You worked here long?"

"I've been here awhile." She waited for him to say something, to tell her why he was standing there. She smiled at him, becoming uncertain, uneasy at his silence. She looked at him and then looked away. I feel like I'm offering myself to him on a plate, she thought. Why doesn't he say what he wants?

She moved away. "Well, it was nice seeing you. I've got to get back to work."

"You wanna go out?" he asked.

She shook her head and walked away.

He followed her, catching her arm. "No, I mean it. You wanna go out with me?"

"Thanks for asking. I don't think so. I have too much studying to do." She made herself smile at him and walked steadily back to the hard-boiled eggs.

When she left the building she saw him. He was standing under a street lamp, a cigarette in his mouth. He had a short leather battle jacket open over the cotton shirt and tight jeans. "You wanna have a cup of coffee?" he asked.

His name was Richard Jacobs and he was in her Ed Psych Methods class. That much she knew about him. He took her arm and assumed she would have coffee with him at the Toddle House, which was off campus and in the direction of her one-room apartment, to which she did not intend to invite him.

He was not handsome. He was only as tall as she was. He was, also, as long as she was as they lay pinned on her narrow bed. "I don't know anything about you," she said. "Except that you're a veteran and don't do that anymore we have to get up."

"Roll over. I wanna do it from behind."

"I don't want to. I want to look at you, not the wall. I like being close this way." She smiled, soothed and purring inside, stroking her whiskers inside, full of his sex inside. "We don't have anything in common."

"This."

"Um." And, inside, she moved following his cock as he moved within her, trying with her inner muscles to hold him fast, finally holding him with her thighs and heels so that he reared above her, demanding and arrogant.

She started to say something, but he stopped her, pressing her mouth shut with his hand while he tongued and bit her nipples. Then he said: "You talk too much. Women always do." He sighed. "I'd better get going. I've got to read a paper tomorrow for Miller and I still have to type it. You good at typing?"

"I have a typing job on campus."

"Oh, yeah? Where?"

She told him, and he said, "Not bad. I'll come up sometime and you can introduce me to him." He rolled away to lie beside her, but kept one leg over her, one hand playing with her nipples. "Yeah. I'll come over and you can introduce us. He wrote some good poetry."

In her wildest imaginings, Leah could not envision Bernstein talking to Dick. Not the gentle Bernstein and this . . . person. I am a snot, she realized guiltily. And she thought: Good enough to fuck but not to introduce to your friends. What kind of bitch am I? But she could not force herself to say: Of course, come over and meet him. So she lay silent under his leg.

"Yeah. I'll come over to Folwell next week. I've got a novel I've been working on and he can take a look at it."

Worse. It was getting worse. Leah closed her eyes and prayed. Let me never speak another word, God, but take back what I said already. Dumb! she thought.

"Yeah. Okay! I'll come by next week with the manuscript and you can introduce us. I'll even take you out for a cup of coffee after." Excitedly, he sat up, swung his legs out of bed, and, rubbing the skin on his belly, laughed. "I've got to go do that paper. But I'll see you next week." He reached for his pants and pulled them on, standing to zip up the fly. "You're a swell kid, Leah. We'll come up here after I see Bernstein." He drew his boots on, then his shirt and jacket. He kissed her forehead and walked jauntily out the door.

"Oh, I hate knowing that winter is coming," Walter Lillywhite said. "It means layers of clothing to put on and take off. Vests, sweaters, undershirts, shirts, jackets and topcoats, scarves, earmuffs, gloves, galoshes!" He was walking Leah up the stairs of Folwell. "I saw you in Dinky Town last night at the bookstore. You looked very fetching in that thick sweater and porkpie cap. I admire caps."

"Thank you. It's woolly and warm and I can pull it over my ears. I don't mind winter. I hate summer, when I just turn belly up and get lazy in the heat."

"We are star-crossed lovers, then, you and I," Walter laughed. "You the snow princess and I the jungle boy."

"Alas!" She laughed with him and went into Bernstein's office. Bernstein was staring out the window; she could tell by the back of his head that he was in one of his pained, bitter moods, so she quietly began sorting the manuscripts and letters that had come in the mail.

She had gotten to know him a bit, she thought, since that first week of frantic memorizing and typing of letters. She still had not found the courage to tell him that she didn't know shorthand. And she didn't have the courage to tell him about Dick. Oi, she thought. But we work well together and even have coffee and cookies out of tin boxes at four in the afternoon, a kind of quiet time between the rush of incoming manuscripts and students.

"Women are like generals," he said. "Clara is like a field marshal. Do you know what I've been doing all morning? I've been taking the kids to see their doctors. All three kids are seeing either a shrink or a counselor. And so is Clara. She makes the appointments and I drive them over, wait for them, bring them home with instructions and prescriptions and pay the damned bills."

"Are they sick? I'm sorry. I didn't know."

"No. Well, they are. We all are sick with the symptoms, but Clara won't face it. The big truth. So she and the kids see psychiatrists to keep from facing it."

Leah absently continued to sort the mail, looking sympathetically at Bernstein, who rocked back and forth on the swivel chair.

"I don't make it easier, either, I suppose." Bernstein loaded his pipe, still looking through the window at the naked trees outside. "I leave *clues* around. I should tell her. But I'd think she'd know. I assumed she'd know." He swung around on the chair and Leah saw his face for the first time. He had a black eye.

"How'd that happen?" she asked almost before thinking.

"Yes. You'd think she'd ask, wouldn't you? But she didn't. And the kids didn't. They won't. They take their cues from her. Poor kids, no wonder they're sick. Jesus. I think even our cats and dogs are sick." He struck a match on the side of the box and held the flame to his pipe. "Maureen."

"Oh." Leah looked at him, connections being made in her head. She saw him watch her face while the connections clicked into place.

"Yes." He nodded. "Maureen. She gave me the black eye. My mistress, my sweetheart. And my wife won't ask me what is going on, what is wrong with our marriage. Jesus." He turned to the window once more. "Maybe I'm sick, too. I take Maureen to her psychiatrist and wait for her. I pay that bill, too." He looked at Leah over his shoulder. "Do I need a psychiatrist, too?"

She didn't know what to say, so she shook her head.

"I'm afraid to go to one. I'm afraid they'd take away my charm."

"Don't go, then." Leah tried to smile reassuringly. "I like you the way you are."

"I'm so relieved! You don't know how difficult it is to be the only admitted nut. They're all getting saner and saner and I just sit here being nuts."

Leah's joints felt weak. She felt the whale surface briefly and then slide under the safe waters of silence. She saw him look at her with such pain and anxiety in his eyes that she had to answer. "You're fine," she said. "I pronounce you one hundred percent okay." She didn't know how to say the rest: You are a dear man and you don't deserve this kind of pain. Sweep Maureen and her black eyes and psychiatrist, and Clara and her ice and *her* psychiatrist out of your life and just settle down into your poetry again." She couldn't say any of that, because she didn't want to step into his living space with her clumping feet. And, she knew, listening to the sea creature, that much as she liked Bernstein, much as she could almost love him, his dance, his step was too complicated for sea-bound creatures. So all she did was to smile at him and go back to sorting letters.

"She used to love my poetry, you know?" He looked at the bowl of his pipe. "She went to Bryn Mawr, and she knew poetry when she heard it. And she liked me. Maybe she was a lieutenant then or a major or even a colonel. She organized our marriage like a military operation. I see that now. I saw it then. But I loved her and I thought I needed organizing. Poets love organizing. Either being organized or organizing. That's what poetry is: the most precise organizing. And I had this vision of myself then, unbuttoned, a tie with crumbs on it, poetry and visions dropping off me, I even worked on my diction so I'd sound good at readings. And this elegant girl came along and laid a cool hand on me and organized me." He was only slightly bitter now, smiling down at his pipe. "I think I had the idea that all my poems would come out of mason jars and all I had to do was make the mason jars. What I had was a surplus of energy and ego. And when that runs down, you're stuck with . . . with General Sherman in drag." He looked at her a little wistfully. "You don't want me, do you?"

Leah felt her jaw drop. Then she blushed. "No." She shook her head at him. "You have enough problems without me. You are still loaded with ego, aren't you? Aren't you loved enough now? Your children love you. The people who save your poems love you. Clara must love you. . . . No, don't interrupt, she must still love you if she won't face what you're doing . . . what you both are doing. And you have Maureen. So don't pretend to be an orphan looking for love." She shook her head at him again. "You know it's safe to pretend with me this way because you know I'd never have the courage to be anything but what I am now. A student. A typist." She put the mail down on the work table. "I'm sorry, I think I just got myself beyond my depth. You aren't crazy or anything, but in pain and I shouldn't add my garbage to it." But even as she apologized, she could see the humor returning to his eyes. Leah was astonished at the sound of her own sudden audacity. Were all shy people like this, given a Bernstein to play off of?

"It's all right. I'll muddle through alone," he sighed. "Have you met Maureen?"

"She's hard to ignore. She's been in and out of the office or on the telephone all last week. You haven't been the subtlest of lovers."

"What do you think of her?"

"You don't need my opinion to validate yours, do you?" Leah frowned at him. "Come on, be honest."

"I admit it. I like to talk about her. I like to talk about my affairs. Why is that, I wonder? I don't like to talk about them to Clara always, but to someone, to prove that they're over. Or maybe that they happened at all. I'm bisexual, did you know that? Or ambisexual. Or ambidextrous! I went to bed once with a guy and his wife. I don't know, did that make me a fag? It was great. It was in India, so it doesn't count against me, not the fag part. I still feel the sun beating in through the windows through those funny shades they have, and the smells of cunt and some kind of peppery nuts and the wine. I didn't write that one to Clara. I told her about it after I'd been back in the country for a while."

"You *had* to tell her. Why? To hurt her?"

"No. I swear to God that wasn't it. To show her that I was back to being faithful. To show her that she was my friend, my companion, that the others didn't matter."

Disgustedly, Leah threw the letters down and glowered at him. "I'd give you two black eyes if I were Clara."

"No," he said mildly. "Why? When I'm being honest?"

Then Leah had to laugh; helpless, aggravated, weakened by his charm and even his deviousness, she laughed while she wanted to pat him on the back hard enough to loosen his lying teeth.

"What I want, what I need, is a woman I *can* be honest with and who wouldn't hold it against me—my honesty, I mean. If I could tell her everything and she'd still love me. . . . But I know Clara holds it up, holds things against me, to use against me. And Maureen too, that's why she's seeing a psychiatrist. Because of my honesty. Because of what we've done together, she can't handle knowing what we're really like." He turned and stared out the window again. "Sometimes I can't handle it either, what we're really like. What we *all* are really like."

Leah had gotten to sleep after finishing the clean copy of a report she'd written for her Tolstoi seminar. When the buzzer first sounded she couldn't imagine what it was. She sat up in the dark and then understood. Someone was at her apartment door. "Just a minute," she said, and turned on the bedside lamp. "Who is it?"

"Bernstein."

She pulled on her bathrobe, ran a hand through her hair and pushed the braid back over her shoulder. "What's wrong? What happened?" She opened the door to discover a battered Bernstein, who tottered past her into the apartment. He carried a brown paper bag and smelled of whisky and blood.

"Have you got bandages or anything for cuts?" he asked.

"Have you been in an accident? What happened?" She let him lean on her. "Shouldn't you be in the hospital?"

"Oh, God, no. Just help me, Leah. I just need some help, then I can go home. Or to a motel. Or I could sleep here? I won't touch you."

She didn't miss the glint, the devil in his eye, even as he winced with pain. "Sit down. Give me your coat." She was shocked into silence as she helped him take off his coat. His shoulders were a roadmap of tiny cuts. She could see splinters of glass still stuck in his skin.

"I couldn't stand to put on my shirt. But I had to put on some clothes," he explained. He handed her the paper bag. "I've got some iodine and scotch here."

Bitterly, Leah said: "Drink the iodine." She was frightened for him and angry with him. She wanted to hug him, she wanted to strangle him. "I get sick at the sight of blood." She begged him: "Go to a hospital."

"Oh, Leah, I think I'm trying to kill myself." He let his shoulders slump; he shook his head; he sighed with such huge despair that Leah became frightened for him.

"Should I call Clara? Maureen?"

"No. I just left Maureen."

"Did you fight with her? Is that what this is from? A fight? Did she push you through a window? What?" Leah helped him to sit down on a straight-backed kitchen chair at her all-purpose table. "Here. Do you hurt a lot?"

"No, we weren't fighting. We were making love." He held out the paper bag. "I need a drink."

Numb, Leah opened the scotch and poured some into a water glass. She watched him drink it.

"You don't know. We have to go further and further for . . . for our orgasms. She needs little flashes of pain to come. And I need to see her come before I can come. More?" He held out the glass.

Leah poured more scotch into the glass. She shivered and tied the belt of her robe more tightly around herself. She sat on one corner of the table, not knowing what to do next or what to say.

"I can stand it now. Will you put iodine on the cuts? Then I'll go on home or to a motel. I just don't want an infection. And I needed to hear a friendly voice."

"What about Maureen?"

Bernstein looked into the glass. "She always falls dead asleep after she comes. She got to bed, all right. Anyway, her boyfriend is due back today and she won't want to see me until he's gone."

Leah raised an eyebrow. "Maureen has a busy life." Then, knowing she was being bitchy, she said, "Who'd have thought it? She looks like such a dumpling. That pale Slavic complexion, those pale eyes. And thighs that sound like wet sponges slapping together when she walks."

Bernstein looked up from the glass. "You are jealous!"

"No. Not really. She just seems like such a sack of mashed potatoes. Especially in contrast to Clara. Can you stand it if I dab the cuts gently with a cotton swab?"

"Yes. Let me have my nippy and I'll be a lamb."

Leah dobbed gingerly with a swab and the iodine. "There are still some pieces of glass stuck under the skin. I'll get them out with my eyebrow tweezers if you can stand the pain." She dabbed at the tiny cuts with a cotton swab, wiped at the fine tracks of blood that crisscrossed his back, closing her ears to his involuntary grunts of pain.

"You won't respect me anymore," he said. "You won't respect me because you know about me."

"No. That's not how it is. You won't respect *me* because *I* know. And because I still like and respect you." She sighed, tired, willing him to go away.

"Is that really how it is? We aren't that bad, are we?"

She had to smile at him. "I don't know. I seem to have to validate my feelings by having someone else approve them or at least recognize them. I don't know. I'm tired. You're the poet, the one who knows." She put the cap back on the iodine bottle. "I'll help you with your coat. Should I call a cab for you?"

"You are really throwing me out?"

Suddenly she was too tired to care what he did. "I don't give a good goddamn what you do. Stay. Go. I don't have the bones to stand up anymore." She threw a pillow at him. "I'll sleep in my big chair. You take the goddamned bed, you're so determined to climb into it!"

"No. No. We have the capacity for baseness, but we don't need to act it out every time." He smiled gently at her as he buttoned his coat. "I don't need a cab. My own car is downstairs. I'll be in the office tomorrow." He went to the door and opened it quietly. "Thanks. Have a good and just sleep."

"January is the coldest damned month of the year," Bernstein complained. He was pouring scotch into a shot glass and staring out of his office window. "I like this window in the summer. When the sun shines in through it, I could fry an egg on my desk. But now it's a window into hell. Look at that icicle. Three feet long and waiting to impale the next innocent who walks under it. Christ. I'm going to teach in Mexico. If I could get a job there."

Leah glanced up from the typewriter. She had been typing from memory as usual and could not break her concentration.

"You'll have to come to see my apartment," Bernstein said. "Of course, Clara decided *now* is the time to throw me out. Literally into the snow!"

Spring semester was one day old. Leah had spent the winter break in near-seclusion, working during the day and evening at her jobs and then retreating to her apartment to sleep or write letters of application to different PhD programs. And sometimes she saw Dick Jacobs, who appeared without warning at the apartment to stand in the doorway, the leather jacket open, the arrogant shape of his smile cutting shadows in the air.

"You're rushing, aren't you?" Bernstein asked.

She nodded, trying to type the letters before they evaporated from her memory.

"I'm giving a housewarming party for my place this Saturday night. I wish you'd come. Walter is bringing his girlfriend. You could bring someone. And there'll be a lot of people you don't know. You should meet more people. You don't get out enough. Now that I'm living alone I know how important it is to meet new people. Get out. I'll get some nice faculty guys over."

She frowned and shook her head.

"So I'm a male yenta. I don't want you wasting yourself on grad students. They're only interested in one thing. And speaking of one thing. That Jacobs. Why'd you lumber me with him? I still don't know how to let him down kindly about his manuscript. It's not even bad. It's . . . Leah, are you listening?"

She looked up at him and nodded, her eyes glazed with concentration.

"Leah. I have to tell you he can't write."

Exasperated, she made a face at him and continued to type. Finally the last letter was done; she read through it for errors, found none, folded it, and placed the stack of letters and envelopes on his desk. "I will come to the party," she said. "I am sorry to rush, but I have a coffee date with a girl. Do you know how few girls there are in our grad school?"

Bernstein squinted at her. Then he walked around her, staring hard at her. "Girls?"

She pulled on her heavy coat and wrapped a wool scarf around her neck. She stuck her tongue out at Bernstein and pulled a woolly cap down over her eyebrows. "I'm ambisexual-nonsexual!" she chortled, and she dashed out.

Rennie was waiting for her, sitting at one of the Formica tables in the student union cafeteria, a cup of coffee and a cigarette in front of her. She saw Leah and waved to her.

"I'm sorry I'm late," Leah said. "But Bernstein sometimes makes it hard to get away."

"Don't worry. I got a carafe of coffee so you wouldn't

have to fight the cafeteria line. Do you like working for him?"

"I really do. He is . . . sometimes he is impossible. But mostly he's a terrific boss. Do you know him?"

"No. I'd like to meet him. I took a class from him once when I was married, a long time ago. But it wasn't what you'd call meeting him. I just sat there and took notes."

"Is this your first semester back in school? Since—"

"I couldn't come back this fall. I knew I'd never be able to concentrate that close to the divorce. But now it's a matter of saving what's left of my mind. I can't just wander around the house. And if I can finish one thing right now, I'll feel good about myself." Her hands trembled minutely as she tapped the cigarette on the ashtray. "I was afraid I'd be a freak, too, you know. All the girls seem like babies, rushing off to dates, still smelling of baby powder! And the boys . . . men, even the grad students seem just to have started shaving or they're cock-happy. And I can't just be alone anymore. All my married friends put me into isolation the minute Donald announced that I was asking for a divorce." She looked at Leah. "Married women don't talk to each other. Or they don't once you decide *you* aren't going to be married anymore. Like I had gotten a contagious disease. Or worse, that I was going to go after their husbands." She brushed her hair back and sighed.

Leah nodded. "It isn't much different in school. But . . . well, I guess I'm used to isolation."

Rennie sat back on the chair, crossed her long legs, and sighed again. She was, Leah thought, one of the most beautiful women she had ever seen. Almost as tall as Leah, Rennie was Junoesque, deep-breasted, small-waisted, with the head of a Greek statue, deep-set almond eyes, a straight, modeled nose, a sweetly curved mouth that dimpled at the sides. And she did not seem aware of her beauty, seemed instead to be a tall, calm child who could chuckle and bubble over with genuine laughter even while pain tracked around her eyes. "Let's have dinner together tonight," she said. "I'm still living in the house. I lost custody of it and I haven't moved out yet, but I can't stand it by myself when the girls have gone to sleep."

"I wish I could, but I have a paper due."

"How do you *do* it? You work and go to school? And I think I'll have trouble without working."

"I didn't know you had children, that makes it even harder, doesn't it? I'd be in a coma of fear."

They looked at each other over their cigarettes and nodded. Leah said: "It's the little wars."

"Oh! I know! What a relief to talk to someone who *knows*. When you talk to other women, do you hear the sound of doors closing in their heads? Of shades being pulled down?"

And they both said: "How come you—"
Rennie finished: "Didn't get married?"
Leah finished: "Did get married?"
Leah said: "No, you first."

"Oh, well, you know, lots of reasons. Everyone *was*. And I was scared, you know, of what would I *do*? I missed that first wave of getting married right after high school. I mean, my girl friends had engagement rings for graduation presents and some of them . . . had to get married. So, I went to college. You know, at five feet eleven inches, a hundred and sixty-five pounds, I was something of a misfit in high school, so my parents—my mom, anyway—thought I stood a better chance at college. And I got good grades and it was fun living in a dormitory and doing the cute things girls do. But I was scared. What if I didn't make it? I don't mean graduate. I mean find the right person. But then Donald was always there, and he was . . . safe. And then I got interested in school. That surprised me. That I did get interested. And Donald said I could go on with it. He was going to be a psychiatrist and we'd have enough money so I could go on with it. So . . ." She lit another cigarette, chain smoking now. "What about you? I envy you, you know." She pulled a fleck of tobacco from her lower lip. "Not that you are anywhere near the spinster stage."

"I guess I haven't met the right person, it's that simple." Leah glanced at her watch. "Rennie, I have to get to my salads. But would you like to come to Bernstein's party Saturday night?"

"I'd love to. Thank you. It's like being in Siberia, living in the burbs and not getting to meet people. I thought I'd have to . . . one: join a church; two: get into politics; three: start hitting the bars; or, four: all of the above."

Bernstein, crossed-legged on a footstool, seemed to be cast adrift in an exhibition. The white walls were hung with painting after painting, some hugely out of scale with the small rooms. The bedroom was dominated by an eight-by-ten-foot-tall painting that Bernstein said "is the headboard for my bed. When I get bored looking at myself in the mirrors on the ceiling, I can look at my painting. It's of me, don't you recognize the old cockmaster there? What I need now are more mirrors so I can look at me looking at me." He wore burgundy trousers and a matching velvet jacket with quilted satin lapels and a lily in the buttonhole. "Am I anyone you'd like to know?" he asked, watching Leah's eyebrows settle back to normal. He took Rennie's hands in his and drew her into the apartment, saying: "You are welcome, indeed, to my parlor, said the spider to the fly." He seemed to want to stroke her arms, but restrained himself, satisfied to hold her hands and to gaze up at her. He brought her a glass of wine and sat her in a tall crimson-and-gold chair. "Take the throne, let me put this under your feet." He brought the footstool to her and stroked her ankles.

Leah watched him for a moment, then saw Walter Lillywhite standing with a very steamy-looking woman. "Hi," she said, hugging Walter and nodding to the woman. "I'm one of Walter's tots in the English department."

"Leah. I'd like to introduce you to Esperanza Rose." He smiled with an avuncular air at Leah. "You are doing well, I hear, in the Tolstoi. And Bernstein is quite respectful of your typing prowess. Indeed, of your stenographic supremacy!" He mocked himself and bowed to Leah.

"Thank you. And I owe it all to you. Do you like his little apartment?"

"He might have subdued his paintings a bit, but other than feeling the need for red velvet ropes, I think it's suitable."

Bernstein insinuated himself between Walter and Leah, whispering, "She doesn't look in the least like a lesbian."

"Who?" Leah was utterly ignorant. "Who doesn't look like a lesbian?"

"Your friend Rennie. She doesn't give off the vibrations of a lesbian."

"Who ever said she was one? Where did you get that idea? Are you smoking something?"

"You did. When you left in such a rush that day to meet a *girl*." He grinned at her.

"Oh, really! That's not even funny. You're carrying craziness a little far. She is not a lesbian. I am not a lesbian. Do I conjugate it all the way before you . . . agh! You are impossible—but isn't she terrific?"

"I'm in love with her. She is a Picasso classic. She has serenity. She's calm. Is she single or what? She's got a ring on. I stole her glove. I'll keep it by me forever." By this time Bernstein's black-and-white hair was standing on end with excitement.

"She's divorced. But why don't you ask *her?* Or don't."

"Oh, Leah. Don't tell her anything about me. You know. I want her to think only the best of me. I'll tell her the worst when the right time comes." He pressed her hand with his, his teak eyes pleading.

Leah wanted to go home to her own apartment. The air was thick with the breath of predators. Even Walter Lillywhite, with his wire-rimmed glasses and leather elbow patches and incipient potbelly, was a carnivore, she thought. "Bernstein, I didn't invite her here for your sensual delectation. She's vulnerable and I like her. I like you, you know that. But you scare me." Leah hated herself, hated the way she sounded. "Talk about closing doors," she said aloud to herself.

"I know," Bernstein said sadly. "I'm a sensualist."

Aggravated by this shift, Leah said: "No, you're a sexualist." She regretted it instantly. "No, I'm sorry. I'm being a bitch to you and you don't deserve it." She hugged him. "I won't say anything to her."

"Oh, my angel of discretion and help in my need!"

The party moiled around in the small apartment, closing together at times, falling apart in pairs or small clusters, a breathing thing that shifted back and forth, watered at the bar, smoked in corners, laughed and muttered, hummed in fragments, gradually blended into a stew of jokes, gossip, revelations, and open secrets. Leah and Rennie talked when they were within earshot; mostly,

Rennie was claimed by Bernstein, who was falling in love with her right there in front of everyone.

Walter Lillywhite said: "Your friend has certainly conquered the literary lion. She has him caged without even the bristle of a chin whisker." He was about to say something more, but thought better of it, looking at Leah with a loaded glance over Esperanza's politely curious eye. "Ah, Leah, we can give you a lift home if events . . . ah, well, we can give you a lift home."

"Oh, thanks. I'll check with Rennie. It is getting to be that time."

"*Who* is that?" Esperanza asked.

Walter and Leah looked at each other. They knew who had just walked in. "Maureen!" Walter mouthed silently.

"I think I'll go and see if Rennie wants to leave," Leah said hastily.

"Who *is* that?" Esperanza pinched Walter's arm.

"The Queen is dead. Long live the Queen," Walter said. "Go ahead, Leah. I think Bernstein will be spending this night alone. By choice." He winked at her and whispered into Esperanza's ear. "The ex and the current. Tact is called for. I'll get your coat."

Leah touched Rennie's arm. "It's a little hard to be subtle or delicate, so pretend I was. Blink once for go get lost I'm doing fine. Twice for don't leave me here at the mercy of passions I wreak not of."

Rennie blinked twice. " 'Wreak not of'?" She touched Leah's arm. "Something changed in the atmosphere. What is it?"

Before she could bite her tongue, Leah said: "The Ghost of Orgies Past." She bit her lip, cursing herself silently for a bitch and a blabbermouth. "Come on, I think we should go on home."

"Oh, are you really anxious to go? I'm having a wonderful time. I'm a little in love with your friend Bernstein. Could we stay just a few more minutes? I want to let him know I like him." She blushed. "I feel about twelve. Isn't he nice? He's so beautifully boned. Like Michelangelo's David. And he's . . . Leah, I like him and I don't want anything to spoil it. Feel my hands, they're ice cold. I'm all clutched up inside and . . . shy."

Leah listened to her and watched Maureen's progress around the living room. Bernstein was two people behind her, trying to catch her, trying to herd her away from meeting Rennie, vacillating between salacious pleasure-seeking and genuine apprehension. Oh, God, Leah thought. She was aware of Walter coming to stand beside her as Maureen, pursued by Bernstein, came toward them.

"Do you feel what I feel?" Walter whispered. "A kind of fascinated dread? Are we two birds being hypnotized by the same snake?"

"Please. I am going to have to go home. Should I take Rennie with me?"

"Yes. Maureen's been drinking, from the look of her, and she was quite ready to start snatching people bald before. If she sniffs out even the possibility of a new interest for Bernstein . . . You take Rennie one way and I'll stand Maureen off at the bridge."

Leah, without waiting, took Rennie's arm and steered her to the alcove where their coats were deposited. "I really feel kind of rotten, Rennie," she lied.

"That came on suddenly, didn't it? Who's that woman that just came in? She's a sight."

"Oh, some old drab from the nether regions of the English department. We have one or two of them that surface every year or so. Here's your coat. And mine."

"I want to say good night to Bernstein first." Rennie put on her coat and looked at Leah. "You can wait at the door. I have my keys right here, okay? Oh, Bernstein, I have to take Leah home, she's not feeling well. But I want to thank you for a lovely evening." She let Bernstein kiss her hands, smiling down at him. She bowed her own head slightly and kissed him firmly on the lips. "Thank you again. I'm so glad I got to talk with you for a bit."

"You aren't *leaving*? You tear my heart out. Please, don't leave!" Bernstein turned to Leah.

"You ass!" she hissed. "Maureen's here. Walter is holding her off until we leave."

Bernstein, still holding Rennie's hand, seemed not to understand Leah. "The party's just beginning. You'll miss the fun. We didn't play any of the games I'd planned." But he winked at Leah.

"Games?" Rennie looked at Leah, then at Bernstein.

Leah stopped dead in her tracks. She thought: What am I doing? Everyone here is of age. Rennie, too. I'm the only one who clumps around on fishy feet while they do some kind of fandango. Smiling, she said: "Games. Thank you for the evening, Bernstein. Thank you, Rennie, I'll go on home. I really am tired."

"You wouldn't leave me, Leah?" Bernstein said.

"Yeah, I would. I am. Good night." She kissed Rennie's cheek and walked toward the door.

"Leah!" Bernstein trotted after her. "I was joking about games. I wouldn't do anything, you know that."

"I don't care. You don't need me as your spectator."

"Oh, Leah." He hung on to her arm heavily, keeping her from opening the door.

"Bernstein. I saw that look on your face. Mischief. Sex games with Maureen and Rennie. Or at the least, an embarrassing scene for Rennie with you as the . . . not so woolly lamb!"

"I swear that was not what I was thinking! Since the instant I met her—Rennie—I have been pure. I have been saved! I have been washed in the blood of the lamb, saved from myself." He clung to her arm. "Believe me!"

"Oh, God, Bernstein." Grimly, Leah opened the door and hauled herself through it. Bernstein came with her, still clutching her arm. "Will you let go?"

"No. I know, it's hard to conjure, but I did, I fell in love with her tonight. Oh, I know, you are right. I did . . . entertain . . . but flashingly! the notion that it would be fun to go to bed *à trois!* But only for an instant did I think that. Leah, I'm not lying to you, I did think it. But one more look at that face, the neo-classic nose, that calm repose of hers and . . ." He stopped to look at Leah. "You do believe me? I have a rapture, a passion for her. I don't know what to do with it, with . . . my passion." His voice faded.

"Hang it out the window!" Leah went home alone.

ℰ Seven of Wands ℰ

AND I look at the Seven of Wands, remembering Bernstein's passion. And the road maps on his back, the blood inching along the pale flesh of him, the . . . goathide of him, the ramhide of him, and think of you, Ben, and what may be trembling and hot passion with you, that erect and throbbing rod of yours, trembling, whetted, wet with desire. Oh may it tremble and burn, that rod, that *wand!* And as I look at this wand in my hand I pray, I invoke all my sick gods, and my witches, that you spend this night with a rod that will not be damped, a wand that will wave and wave and find no rest, no nook, no cubby, no red and waiting wetness, no dark and sucking place. I would that your wand, Ben, find no entrance, but only the closed, the clamped, the locked sphincters, the clenched teeth. Not for you tonight, I pray, the solitary place, the joint, the split, the hot wet where slides the seeking rod.

So, my dearest love, if Hecate reigned tonight, you would not ride, not hump, not buck, not slide into, ram through, no, nor any way at all find entrance for your prong, your little cock, your large rod, your long and knobby root.

Wands again. And I am aware that as Bernstein had locked rooms, his secrets, those he did unfold to Rennie when the time was right, his words, his promises made to me that spring when he was proclaiming his huge love, the certainty of his redemption in this cleansing love, this lamb's blood love he'd found with Rennie the moment he met her; just as Bernstein had his secret room, secret losses, just as my mother had her buried children, her buried heart, I see that Ben has had his locked room. And I rattle my bones outside the door, my tears a chain mail on my breast; the tears grow cold and weigh me down now as I sway through the watery light of near-dawn. And wands waver on the cards like sea grasses, and I, weighted with tears, swim through the swirling colors of what was, what may be, what is, and down farther along the maze to where the darkness is solid with shapes and sharp jagged edges.

For they did marry, Bernstein and Rennie. As Walter said a year later, it was the Jewish American Prince of Poets and the White Anglo-Saxon Princess, the fairy-tale ending. "Oh, he'll be faithful," Walter told Leah. "He has been adventuring over the vast bellies of the world, had his taste of light and dark meat, and, according to the American way, has paid his dues as a man and an artist, has repented, and now comes to the high plateau of his life with the prizes: reputation and beautiful wife."

"You sound hostile," Leah said. They were walking together after the commencement exercises, Leah now hooded and capped, her still wet PhD in her paws.

"No. I love the man. As you do. With a grain of salt, in fact, a sack of it. And I wish him well. But I am glad that he is going to New Mexico to teach. It is too wearing. I am only thirty-two, and he at fifty wears me out. I dodder!" Walter pressed Leah's arm. "And you, dear child, did well, despite my teasing. And, if I may say so, your penchant for loutish lovers."

"Oh. Well." Leah felt her face prickle with heat.

"Tush. It's over, I know. But now you must begin to live your life. Enough of self-abuse!" He gravely touched her cheek, not smiling. "You must begin to live now. You used this time well, I know, but you spent too much of it observing and equivocating. Don't plan to spend the rest of your life in half flight, watching. You must not retire. He smiled. "What I do best—instruct. Let's not say goodbye. We are friends and constant, are we not?" He kissed her and rushed off, his gown and hood bannering, his second PhD scrolled in his hand.

Now they come, the apparitions, coruscating, sparkling, whirling. No longer dim or hesitant, they come from the ceiling and the corners: slashing hooves, nightmares, daymares, frights, gap-eyed hags with dugs that flap-flop, astride the skeletal mares of dying desires, of wombs tipped and torn, scraped out, wounded; and with them these screeching harpies drag the one-eyed, the ruined, the toothless and silent babes of abortions past; and they come slanting their eyes at me, I who am the ummother of them, the conception gone sour of them; and I draw back from them, disowning them if I could, aware that they are all tied to me with knots of blood, that still-winding, still-wounding string tie of blood from years ago.

ᙠ Page of Wands ᙣ

PENTACLES, Wands, Cups and Swords—the Wands had won. And then she was teaching, her degree framed neatly, her hood packed in tissue, her cartons of books trucked to the first apartment financed by her new position as assistant professor of English at the small college in Nebraska, Jefferson; and the year there had been a splendid daze of discovering that she was blissfully happy in the classroom, that the lecture notes she prepared, stewed over, memorized, were in fact all right, they were no more boring than any other lectures she'd heard, that her classes did indeed sit down and take notes and look up like owls watching the very words drop from her lips. And she unashamedly loved her students. She loved teaching. The first summer after that first teaching year, she bought a small used Dart, a car that seemed constipated, was ugly, but did not let her down. She argued her landlord into painting her apartment, upholstered a chair, bought a couch that would turn into a bed if Esperanza and Walter Lillywhite, now married, ever came to visit, bought herself an Icelandic daybed that was firm in the mattress and chaste as a nun's cot, but could and eventually did contain two busy bodies. She was happy. She wrote haiku that summer, knowing she was not a poet like Bernstein, but knowing also that she could organize seventeen syllables into a pattern that made small happy spaces for her.

Esperanza and Walter did come to visit. They encompassed Leah in a joint hug, insisted on seeing her cubbyhole office on campus, her classroom, the bookstore. "And?" Walter said, looking at her through his wire-rimmed glasses.

"He's being circumspect," Esperanza said. She sat on

Leah's couch, feet up under her, her black hair dramatic against the porcelain white of her forehead. "We want to know if there are any men—a man—in your life."

"Oh. Ah."

"Translates into no, doesn't it?"

"I haven't met anyone to be serious about."

"I don't think she wants to settle here, Walter," Esperanza said. "It's small town, this place. She really can do better. Do you see her married to a farmer or to a small-business man? Really? Didn't you notice there is one major street in this town? What do they do here at night?"

"It's really a nice university town," Leah defended it. "They have a community theater and a small symphony orchestra. And the university theater does five plays a year in addition to the laboratory plays."

"And football. I could hear the football squads running and yelling as the taxi brought us from the airport. Really, Leah."

Walter tapped his wife on the knee. "You may not be fair, Esperanza. She may like it here. It seems a quiet place, but one might say the backwaters suit her."

Leah made a face at both of them. "You came all the way from the East Coast to nag me."

"No. We really did want to see you. And this made a convenient break on the way to California. But you must not plan to die here, Leah." Walter pulled an envelope from his jacket. "I have here the dates for the next MLA, and I hope you will allow me to introduce you to a few people. If you publish a few things here and there, you'd be in a good position to move onward and upward." He smiled, content with his own tenure at Merrimac, in New York State.

Leah sighed. "I wish it were enough to be a good teacher."

"You know what they said about Christ. A wonderful teacher, but he didn't publish! It's the same for us. I would hope you'd have more ambition than to lie here in the shallows. I don't mean that you must become a chairperson. But, Leah, a small cow campus! Even our Merrimac is larger, more cosmopolitan."

Leah equivocated. "I don't think it's so bad here. I love

the students. And what makes a bigger or more well known school better?"

"Let her live her own life," Esperanza said. "You love giving advice. And it's a bore! Now, I have a present that's coming for Leah and I want a nice dinner, a glass or two of wine, and then let's go out somewhere for a drive."

Walter coughed and nodded. "I saw the delivery van drive up. Leah, I do hope you won't think us presumptuous! But I give advice, and Sper does things on impulse. And I hope this impulse of hers will not offend you." He went to the door and opened it. He glanced out, nodded, and took a large carton from the delivery man. "Yes. Here's a . . . amazing, Sper! He didn't take the tip. It isn't all bad in small towns!"

He handed the carton to Leah and kissed her. "It goes to you with our love, please remember that."

The carton yowled and shook. A curved claw stuck out through one of the air holes in the cardboard. Leah looked at the glowing eye that glared at her. "What is it?"

"A kitten. Siamese. Esperanza has always had Siamese, and she insisted that you be lumbered with one."

"Close the door, Walter. Leah, I know you will like the kitten once you get to know it. Let it come out of the carton by itself."

"I don't *dare* touch the carton." Leah put it on the floor and stepped back, watching as the carton continued to shake and howl. The sound of cardboard being shredded made Leah take another step backward.

"Isn't it darling?" Esperanza asked.

"You should see her with our Siamese," Walter said to Leah. "She has scars in the most unbelievable places! She lets them bite and claw her in ways that if *I* even attempted would get me incarcerated for life!"

"Open the box," Esperanza said to Leah.

Leah tried to open the top of the carton, but a claw slashed at her fingers, drawing blood.

"It's getting to know you," Esperanza said.

Bravely, Leah opened the top of the carton. She flinched, expecting another slashing claw, but when nothing happened, she looked inside the carton. A very small blue-eyed kitten stared back at her. Its eyes were slightly crossed. "Something is wrong with it," Leah said. "Come and look."

"Pick it up."

Leah shook her head. "You pick it up."

"No. These first few moments are vastly important. It's up to you to shape this cat's personality and his sense of belonging. So you pick him up and he'll understand that he's your cat."

"What do we do, establish a blood tie?" Leah still looked at the kitten, but did not venture a hand toward it.

"Oh, pick him up! Look how frightened he is, poor baby." Esperanza crooned to the kitten and pushed Leah toward the box. "He might sputter at first, but if you gently but firmly hold him in your hand and address him directly, he'll adjust magnificently."

Leah took a deep breath and gingerly offered her hand to the tiny creature, which instantly struck at it while its fur stood on end. It seemed to bounce on its tiptoes, to send off small sparks of ferocity; even when Leah gently grasped it, it struck at her hand with tiny barbs that drew blood.

"Ouch!" Leah gasped. "It really does not want to make friends." She held it gently and tried to pat it. "I can feel it tremble." And with that, Leah became the possession of a Siamese cat.

Esperanza told her how to feed it and water it. "It will keep itself clean if you get a box and kitty litter. You have to empty that once a week or you'll notice a bit of odor."

"She understates, Leah."

They watched the kitten inspect Leah's hands and arms and lap. And watched it climb down Leah's leg, clawing a trail down the hide. "Did I ever say I was a masochist?" Leah asked, pulling the kitten's claws out of her skin. "But thanks, anyway."

"We do our best," Walter said. "You can't live alone forever. And once you start with one cat you are bound to have another, and then kittens and so on and so forth, with jolly trips to the vet and the drugstore. And if you get status-conscious you'll want to enter the baby in shows."

He smiled at her, then asked casually, "Have you seen Bernstein's new book of poems?"

"No, I haven't. Is it out yet?"

"They should be in the stores this week or next. He

kindly sent me an advance copy. I would have thought he'd send you one too. Ah well. I brought my copy along. Would you like to see it?"

"Oh, yes!"

Walter took a slim book out of his briefcase and handed it to Leah. "If you want to read it at a quiet time, why don't you keep it overnight? We can discuss it tomorrow morning."

"Um." Leah was reading. "Excuse me, I think I'll just skim them now." After she had read four or five of the poems and gone back over them, wondered at them, she looked up at Walter and Esperanza. "I wonder if I ever will feel my own life. My own emotions. He does, crazy as he seemed to me then. . . . It's a talent, or a gift, or what he called his charm . . . bearing witness to your own life." She shook her head. Then she smiled at Esperanza. "You only knew him a little bit but didn't he seem more *there* than most other people?"

"He did," Walter said. "But he had disciplined himself, too, to be *there*." He sat down beside Esperanza and put an arm around her, looking to her for agreement.

Leah, watching them, suddenly felt the prickle of awareness: they had been discussing her, worrying over her; and she knew that they were going to, had already started to try to move her life around for her, lovingly, of course. She balked. She went underwater. "What will I name my cat? And what will we do for dinner?"

Esperanza looked at her, comprehended. "And what will we not talk about? We won't talk about you. Walter and I both are so fond of you, but I can see, if Walter can't, that you are not ready for the helpful advice, the loving tramplings of feet on your sensibilities."

"Thanks."

"I am outnumbered," Walter said. "Well, I submit. Shall I run out for some wine with dinner, or shall we all go out as we'd discussed?"

But they had moved Leah's life. Leah bought a copy of Bernstein's poems and read them to herself and to the cat, whom she named Psi. How could Bernstein be so sensible in his sensitivities? And he made use of everything; Rennie's feet in the dust became for him a whole Bible story. She sighed enviously, wistfully, then put the poems on the shelf with her other special books. Walter's right, she thought. I'm not living my life. But how do I do that?

Four o'clock in the morning. Her best and worst time. When she would awaken, beached on the shallows of night-not-yet-over-and-day-not-begun, half in dream and half in reality, the waters of her life ebbing away from her so that she lay gasping, drowning, drowning in the air, feeling—as she pulled the winding sheets of her cot away from her legs—the shroud, she thought, of her grave. And then she'd light a cigarette, make a face in the dark, wrestle with the fears that smothered her, fears she could not name, guilts she did not want to name even as she saw the single accusing eye in the dark, heard again the wail and scrape of her unmothering, and felt again the knotted thread of blood that tore from her flesh and even now left her ticking and quivering with grief.

"And there's something lacking in me," she said aloud in the dark. I can't seem to make that living connection with another person. I missed it somewhere.

And she stubbed the cigarette out, musing: Bernstein with his sexual morbidity, his burlesque passions, was able to make the connection at last with Rennie. And Walter and Esperanza. My aunts and uncles and cousins. People I don't even know. It isn't sex. It's . . . that connection, that tie of caring. I can't keep jumping into bed with men because I'm looking for love.

And she had to blush in the dark because that period of teaching a year in a place and then moving on to another college town, that time before thirty, she did go to bed looking for love, approval, assurance that she did indeed exist, if only for that moment of spasm.

And who was there? Leah sat up in bed at four o'clock in the morning on her thirtieth birthday, alone finally, having danced the slow, erotic, but technical dance of sex. Psi came disapprovingly out of the kitchen and jumped up on the bed. He yawned bad breath at her and waited for his scratch and cuddle.

"Oh, Psi. I'm thirty. And not in love. And not loved. And what I wish for me is to love someone worth loving and caring about. And what did I do tonight? Dinner out. A drink at his place. And the 'Let's go inside' line, which means go to bed and neither of us much wanted to, but what else is there to do but screw when you don't have that much to talk about and loneliness is breathing down your neck. And I hate to think that this is going to be the total of my life. If it is, then I think I'll go back to being shy, modest, and . . . I guess I didn't fall in love and no one loves me—and, Psi, I'm half lying: it's all right. I have the blessed students and a job that I'd do free, but I'm glad they pay me. So I can settle for this. It is perhaps pale, perhaps that's what sea creatures have, the gray equivocating life, watching other people feel their lives.

"But I'm doing it again, that slide into my swamp of self-pity. So shut up, Psi, and so will I and in an hour we'll get up."

That's what she said then. That's what I say now, and I make a pot of Morning Thunder tea, sip it, the domestic ritual soothing me, making me peaceful. I go outside, all harmless, to pick up the paper, to greet Psi, who swaggers down the back lawn, whiskers warning me that he'll have none of my cuddling and cooing today. The juniper has pink among its needles, fall is about to crisp the edges of the trees. A juniper ball, bright-beaded with dew, catches the light and I think of Christmas. Not too early, I grin, to think of Christmas cakes and puddings. Of how to fill Christmas this year; I'll not be desolate, I say. My teaching Christmases began by accident a tradition that I will not break: the warm wiggling bodies of students! That first Christmas here in Leicester, I made in my apartment an open house, inviting a few students who hadn't gone home to come and sing and eat with me. And that party of candles and wine and lies about ourselves, fables of work not yet done, of sitting under the tree and reading the Tarot, of reading poetry and rimes, of mashing candies into the carpet, of dribbling cranberries onto the tree, that party seeded into my teaching years and sprang up every year, growing in all directions so that it began the afternoon that classes ended: nibbles, snacks, sandwiches, coffee, jugs of wine, bales of cakes, carols, wassailing, snow people, snowball fights, forgotten sweaters, lost gloves, mended hearts, and continued into the humming Christmas Eve picnic and journeys to church, the ringing Christmas mornings, with the turkey enormous, rambunctious under wraps in the oven and dishes soaking, washing, lost, lost, and I'll do it again this year. And the telephone ringing for whom? Yes, she's here somewhere, I'll tell her. I forgot to tell you. Never mind, are we out of plates? And Christmas night, finally, when all have fallen asleep, all have toppled in heaps on the floor to nap, to daydream, some of them have gone, finally all have gone, and I with the tree and the lights can sit snug in my robe, knowing that I have been touched, have touched the gentle hearts of the young.

I carry the teapot and my cup to the study. As I pace along the hall I hear the silence of the house, it seems to move with me, that silence that is almost a presence. I am silent, too, drifting around, an apparition that I see dimly in the hall mirror, a revenant, I am there and then I am not. And then there is a sharp tap, a finger-tap, almost a tick, against the window in my study. The wind, I think, it will make great sea sounds in the trees, it will make waves in the grass, it will make the casement cloth whisper like a shroud, the whole house will shift under that great sea sound, the sky will shift with the sea sound, the stars will sweep up into new shapes, new constellations, new patterns; it will, that wind, make a clear space, it will bring back the silence, it will wash away the apparitions.

But the wind cannot wash away the apparitions. It stirs them into voice, and now they fill the rooms with wild and whirling songs, lamentations, accusations, hag voices out of a past, voices that whine from behind locked doors, voices that gibber at me, tongues lisping suggestions that wrinkle along my flesh in the patchy blush of morbid sexual jealousy.

"I assumed you knew," he said. "There's been someone all along."

O false Ben! A fury grips me. It sweeps up from the soles of my feet, scorches along my nerves; I sweat; my breasts, the nipples shoot flames. I wish they could. I wish they had. That while you were sucking at them, lighting them with your tongue (that lying tongue), the blue flame had spurted like milk from my breasts and scalded your face, boiled your eyes out of the sockets. No words, no thoughts can contain this heat, the damned heat of knowing you had "someone all along." And that heat, melting at my belly to chortle and welcome you still. Still!

I cannot contain the truth, it seems. Cannot accept this killing fact.

Too much has happened; I cannot contain the explosion of lights, facts, information of yesterday's "I assumed you knew." The Lightning Struck Tower, yes. The explosion has blown me empty, vacant; my mind opens and closes in a shock. A rape. The horrid intrusion of an unwanted cock, a brute forcing itself past my sex and into my center: my feelings, my perceptions. Now the oily sickness, the nausea, wells up in the bottom of my throat. I am abused, injured, to the very tick of my viscera, where a trembling begins, the long painful trembling that will wail and moan in anguish and grief. O I will haul this blood trail with me down to the bottom of the sea, O there is no help of understanding, of comprehension, only the shudder of the wound.

O Ben. What have you done? What horrors have you spawned upon me with your "I assumed you knew"? You fucked me with those words and leave me to the conception and labor as I track you down the trail you marked in the maze.

I want to stop thinking. But there is a murderous fascination here, a self-wounding fascination as well as the hope for understanding, for that clean break of resolution. So I go on and turn up the next card.

ಶಿ Queen of Pentacles ಳಿ

SUDDENLY Leah thought, Of course, that's where I met Zulu the second time.

The Town and Gown Club in Leicester. Leah, newly contracted to teach at the University of Leicester, went to the club for a dinner the club gave for newcomers. Leah walked in, tall, timid, wishing to God she knew one face. And there was Zulu, looking as if she'd sprung newly born, like Venus on the half shell, more than half naked in a dress that was cut to the quick in front, up to the hip on the side, her raging red hair licking in flames around her face, loop earrings that dangled to her bare freckled shoulders, the nipples of her breasts upstanding beneath the sheer fabric of the dress or whatever it was, the fancy weave of her fanny as she walked across the ballroom toward Leah on her high follow-me-home heels. She was independent, as much a statement of herself as an act of God. Leah, not at all sure that Zulu would remember her, hung back for a moment until their eyes caught and held; then Leah stuck her hand out but encountered, instead, Zulu leaping for a hug. "Dammit!" Zulu's low voice had been honed to a resonant sound Leah could not quite classify. And her smile!

"What are you doing here?" Leah asked, hugged breathless, inhaling the musk that was almost visible on Zulu's hair. "Teaching?"

"What would I teach? Dontcha remember? I didn't finish Minnesota? I got ah . . . well, they frowned a bit upon me and my Greek prof and his divorce. *You* remember. So I went on acting. And I got on television. After all those damned beauty contests I entered. Homecoming Queen candidate! Aqua Follies Queen candidate! Snow Queen candidate. Sweetheart of Sigma Nu candi-

121

date. And never won one! Even if I was the only one with any kind of talent other than baton twirling. I was the only one who could swim, ski, water ski, ice skate. . . ."

"I know, I know. But that got you to television?" Leah thought: It makes sense. That voice. That . . . confidence.

"I am the darling of the tube hereabouts. I do commercials like crazy. I did that bank commercial. And I work for a couple of stores and ad agencies, so I am dolly on the spot with everything. Garbage cans, china, paper towels, detergents. And now I sell for a foreign car dealership so I get my own car."

Leah and Zulu sat together at one of the long damask-covered tables, switching their name cards and giggling. "I'm really glad you're here," Leah said.

"Me too! Say, let's do our social thing and impress whoever it is we're supposed to impress. Then let's sneak off, just us, and go have a beer and talk about old times. And the good old days. Gawd!" Zulu laughed and shook her head. "A lot of changes for both of us, I bet." Her bracelets jangled for a moment and then subsided. "Did you get married? I suppose you did."

"No. You?"

"Almost a couple of times. But it's hard to get married and keep the act going. So. I'd have thought you'd be married by now. You were so quiet and . . . straight . . . I mean not free like I was . . . am. But you didn't either, hah?" Zulu turned a searching look on Leah. "You still look so serious and considering. And that shyness or whatever it is. Listen, let's get together and I'll help you pick out some clothes that are a little more lively. And I'll introduce you to my hairdresser. You haven't ever done anything to . . . embellish yourself, ya know?"

"Oh, thanks. I'll wait a while for the changes. I don't really want to spend a lot of time with my hair and all that salon business. I teach and—well, I can take care of myself."

Zulu lit a cigarette. "Okay. But I'm glad to help when you wanna fix up."

Leah was about to say something more, but Zulu had begun to smile over Leah's shoulder. Leah recognized the smile: the bitch-in-the-bush smile. She looked around and saw a man approaching. Leah murmured something about bathrooms and slipped away. Zulu has not changed all that much, she thought.

And Zulu would call on a Friday afternoon. "You can't fool me, Leah. You don't have a date tonight. So I dug up one of my nicer men, he sells surgical instruments, and we're coming over to get you and we'll go eat and drink. And I'm bringing you one of my smashinger outfits so's you'll look alive. For Chrissake, move."

It did help, Leah had to admit. "I'd sit in my apartment and read papers and feel cobwebs growing if you didn't haul me out. But I can't go out all the times you call. Besides, I feel a bit like the second choice on some of these evenings when both men are feeling your knees under the table."

"Well, dontcha know? I can't always take two guys at once. Much as I love the attention."

"It's just that you have such an appetite." Leah would grin at Zulu.

"Well." And Zulu would look at Leah, quizzing her for a moment: "Was that a stab? Humph."

But watching Zulu and her appetites, Leah found herself thinking: Maybe I'm undersexed. Or lack vitality. Or enterprise. Or curiosity. I don't seem to have that need to leap into bed so often. Maybe I'm short some hormone.

But the truth was that she simply was no longer interested in sport fucking. Like shooting fish in a barrel, she thought. Or what? It's too easy? Means nothing? Oh, God. At thirty-umpty-um I am dried up sexually?

And try as she might, she could not force herself to beguile herself into bed. Not even a good companionable fuck, she said ruefully to herself. Or, yes, a *companionable* fuck, if it came with a cuddle, a bit of real affection shared. But what I've experienced recently has not been that. And here am I! I'll be bald, forty, warts growing, a whisker or three on my chin and that funny pinky flab on my butt and belly.

But the threats of warts and whiskers did not move her, either, so she became, much to her surprise, peaceful and chaste.

She taught. She wrote haiku. Made a small pond life for herself at the university; bought herself a green Pinto; found herself an apartment with windows in every room;

painted the apartment and fixed its back door, which led to a small walled-in courtyard with a cat-sized door for Psi, who came and went at will, once bringing her a very tiny dead rabbit that he seemed to think would suit her, but it didn't and she flushed it down the toilet; bought a sofa that turned into a bed, white and blue; discovered cookbooks and began to cook for her students, who then began appearing at any hour for an omelet and a talk; invited her mother to come and visit, and was refused; found one day while hanging a Wyeth print that the wall masked a fireplace; tore the wall down and then got the landlord's permission to let her clean and use the fireplace; celebrated by having students come over with marshmallows, hot dogs, pork chops, potatoes for a living-room cookout; saw Zulu come and go with assorted men; listened as Walter and Esperanza called to announce the birth of their son; taught, read, and wrote more haiku, and still woke at four in the morning, but now always had a stack of student papers and red pencils beside the bed, beguiling the hour with muttered curses and gurglings at the oddments her students thought were presentable work.

Then she read a theater review in *The New York Times* by a person who seemed actually to understand what the play was about. She was so impressed that she wrote him a letter of approval. And forgot about it.

Then a small publishing house that had held fifty of her haiku for ten months wrote to her to say they would be publishing the collection.

She read the letter twice, sitting cross-legged in front of the tiny fireplace, while Psi rubbed his whiskery face against her arms and buzzed. Then he sat back on his haunches and scratched his ears so hard that he toppled over against Leah. She absently reached out to hug him, but got in the way of a scratching hind claw. "Psi, I'm thinking. What would you do to celebrate if your haiku got published?"

Psi margled at her and scratched the other ear.

"Of course! New York City!" Leah stuffed the rest of her letters into her handbag and called the airport. Then she dug out her suitcase and started packing for a weekend or three days in the city. Psi jumped up on the bed, mewing accusingly at her.

"Oh, okay. Fleas." Leah found the can of flea spray

and loosed it liberally on Psi. Then she went on packing, humming to herself. The cat rolled over and over playfully on her neatly folded and packed clothing, leaving small gifts, a sort of bon-voyage tickle in the suitcase.

Leah flew to New York City and stayed at the Plaza, posh, old, too expensive, but grand for three nights. Standing at the marble reception desk, she searched through her handbag for a Kleenex and found the letter from *The New York Times*. The critic she'd applauded had written to her: "If ever you are in New York and have a moment to spare, do call me for a drink."

And because what in Leicester appears to be a good idea, may in the lobby of the Plaza suddenly stretch into lostness, Leah became shy and all her strings were untied and she knew no one. He's probably a dear little man of sixty or so, she said to herself. And writes reviews and wears a sweater vest and nurses his expense money between paychecks. I'll call him and maybe we can have coffee sometime while I'm here.

So she called him. And can a PhD from the Midwest find happiness in the Plaza at four-thirty in the afternoon? She can fucking well try, Leah thought, burbling happily in the bed on the seventeenth floor with the critic. They did try, striving energetically to discover every nook and cranny, every unexplored crevice, wrinkle, dimple, navel, crack, nostril, ear, every toehold, every knees-up-motherbrown, your-turn-to-come-my-turn-to-watch position they could think of, and others that just happened. As it resolved, however, they were not the only animal life active on that bed. Her drama critic left, bitten by more than one kind of love bug.

The next morning he called from his office not happy. "I'm embarrassed as hell, but I may have some kind of disease, Leah," he said. "I've called my doctor for an emergency appointment, so when we meet for lunch at MOMA I'll be able to tell you more."

"You sound terrible. When did you discover it?"

"After I left you and came to my place to shower and shave, I started itching. And I have these marks that itch."

"Oi. I hope it isn't serious. They have medication that cures all kinds of bug." Leah tried to sound reassuring.

"Well. Lord, Leah, I hope I didn't transmit it to you,

whatever it is. But I'll know by lunch and then if you've been exposed we can get you to my doctor." He sighed. "I'll see you at twelve-thirty."

"Do you want me to go to the doctor with you?"

"No. But thanks. If it were anything else but this, I'd love to have you come along and hold my hand. Until lunch." And he hung up.

Leah had planned to find her way to the Cloisters by subway. But now she paced the hotel room and smoked. Then because she was smoked out and it was only eleven, she decided to wash out her underwear and panty hose. Idly, she sloshed the nylon hose around in the basin and scratched herself. An itch moved from place to place. As soon as she'd scratch her right underarm, her thigh would begin to itch, then behind her knee, then . . . "What the hell did he give me?" And she stripped to examine herself. Small red bumps like a pox rose on her skin. And itched. Chicken pox? Smallpox? She couldn't think of any venereal disease that appeared within twenty-four hours, but what did she know? She showered for the second time that morning and washed her hair, scrubbing herself with vehemence.

Her hair in a towel, her robe tied around her, she sat down with a cigarette and tried to think. Well, they do have shots, sulfa, penicillin, miracle drugs. . . .

A bang on the door and it flew open. Earl strode in and looked at her. His face made her think of stop-action filming: an expression would form for a split second and be replaced with another: rage, shock, hysteria, rue; finally he laughed, a great roaring laugh, and grabbed Leah. "A fine thing," he hugged her until her eyes watered.

"What?" She tried to push him away far enough so that she could look at him, but settled for staring up at his chin. "What?"

"You have fleas!"

"*I* have fleas!" Then she remembered. "Oh! Psi!"

" 'Oh sigh!' You are too literary. 'Oh sigh.' " He laughed. "My lady with the literary—*Ouch!*"

Leah had dug her fingers under his shirt and pinched him. "No. Not 'Oh sigh.' My cat's name is Psi-Psi. So I said . . ."

" 'Oh, Psi!' " He hugged her again. "And for that I

went haring off to my doctor convinced I had some kind of thing that would guarantee I'd be cockless in a week."

"I'm sorry."

"Hum. Well, are you hungry?"

"Not really."

"Good. You wanna see my calamine lotion?"

And she would remember, smiling, the little red bites along his buttocks, and grin aloud at the calamine lotion making pink crusts on his tender cock.

She'd been uneasy in the conscience about his wife, his separation. "I couldn't miss the wedding ring," she said to him on the last night in the Plaza. "I find that I am not a happy adulterer, or whatever it is that the . . . that I am right now."

He kissed her ear. "You are a special and dear person. You did not cause the separation. Truth to tell, I don't quite know myself what caused it. I don't know many married people who are living together right now. It seems to be the thing to do—living apart. The women have lovers or house fairies. The men have secretaries or mistresses. Parties have gone out of style or become too dangerous, with emotional land mines. . . . You know, you can't invite a couple anymore because they might be separated and show up with their lover and then there's the long dull embarrassment. No, don't worry about it. But that's not what I want to talk about right now. Listen, Leah, it's not that far, Leicester. I can fly up there. Or you could fly back down here. What I'm saying is, my dear, I've grown accutomed to your fleas."

It wasn't love as in *Jane Eyre* or *Wuthering Heights* or the somewhere-I'll-find-you genre, it was better; it was fond sex, cuddling, trusting, discovering that she could let her babbling gabbling rollicking tender kidside surface; she could let the sea creature surface, holding her breath, yes, but still surfacing for a peek, to return to the underside of herself, singing the wordless sea song of the whale.

There were the telephone calls from New York. "Are you coming down for the weekend? I have tickets for another Simon play. And Chekhov." Or: "Bring something slinky. We're going to Lincoln Center and then to a cocktail buffet, and after that we're going barhopping." And he'd come to Leicester, flying up with his briefcase full of reviews he was writing, once the galleys for the book he'd done, and he'd take over her apartment, the length of him making the rooms small; the bed seemed made for pygmies, the tub and shower for sardines; the fireplace a toy he said, for cooking toy chops and itty bitty things; and he'd befriended the cat: "You lousy fleabag! Give me fleas even before we'd met!" And he thought she didn't keep enough big towels, so he sent her some from Bloomingdale's and a case of Taylor wine for the nights it was too cold and ass deep in snow and no one, not even he with his six feet four, would venture out for wine. But he did venture out to push her little green car out of snowbanks when she thought once they should go out to a movie he'd missed in New York and it wasn't that good anyway! And they read her students' papers together; he agreed someone should teach kids how to write, someone should teach Remedial English Comp: so she asked to, and she did; and he laughed at the filthy limericks her students wrote, insisted on sending one student an asbestos folder for the "hot dirt" he was writing.

She had worn her Elvira Madigan dress, her hair piled up in a knot that, for once, went with the outfit she was wearing, and they'd had an afternoon with some Baizerman sculptures that they both liked at the museum, had walked uptown holding hands and talking until they came to the restaurant where he'd made dinner reservations. She had thought once while they were walking that she should utter some small three-word sentences; but somehow she held back; rather, the sea creature drew away, while she, Leah, wanted to say it; the sea creature rolled under the deeper waves, anxious, cautious, a not-quite-moan, not-quite-murmur of "Wait, wait" sighing in her ears.

He poured her a second glass of wine and watched her drink it. His eyes, his face, did that stop-frame expression shift again, catching her attention so curtly that her breath clotted. "We've had some wonderful moments," he said, taking her hand, something very like pain in his eyes.

Clichés, she thought. He's rarely done clichés. Then all thought stopped and she watched him, watched his lips form what would come next; she tried to guess at it, tried to accept it before it was said and therefore final.

"And I know you'll understand if anyone can understand."

She said, or thought aloud: "Your wife."

"She doesn't know what a bastard I've been. I mean she doesn't *know*. I hope she only suspects, because I can . . . Jesus. I'm going to go back to her and this time give it more than half of what is asked. You know? Marriage is supposed to be fifty-fifty. Or sixty-forty. I've hurt her in ways she hasn't faced yet. I know that. And I want to save the marriage, save her from facing those hurts. Before she even has to start examining them. Like: I don't want her to realize she has the capacity for suspicion or doubt. I know what suspicion feels like. And jealousy. I feel jealousy about you. When you go back to Leicester I want to break your face so no other man will look at you. And when I've called you late at night, after midnight, and you answer sounding like a cuddly kid, I have the hots for you and at the same time I *know* you've got a guy in bed with you and that's why your voice sounds like that. Even though I *know* you haven't been dishonest with me." He let her hands go and turned away for a moment, then he poured more wine into their glasses. "I want you. But I want Sally, too. And because I can't pretend I'd ever be able to be faithful to Sally if I thought you were still around, I have to say . . . goodbye and I love you."

The candlelight flickered on the table between them. Leah, looking at him, saw a door close behind his eyes, shutting off all the light in them. She swallowed dryness.

The Moon

A major arcane card, the Moon tip to the surface of my pattern. The Moon: deception, disappointment. O we are approaching the dread center. And the Moon is in the arms of the New Moon. I know the moonlight is deceptive, tricking the eye as it does. And you, Ben, Juggler, Magician, you have that same talent for misdirection. But how could I have been so deceived? The Moon touches the subconscious, fractures the light to hide what chooses to be hidden. I look at the card again. The Moon is in the arms of the New Moon.

And staring upward is the crayfish, struggling with his water world: the light there is wavering, the moonlight shatters surfaces; he cannot see clearly. I can almost hear the scrabble of the claws as they tear at the water and the shore; the crayfish sinks, the weight of his armor bearing him down even as he reaches eternally for that betraying Moon.

So it is with you, Ben, in the arms of a new love. You have scarred the sky with your deceptions. Like the crayfish, I sink with the weight of my armor, my chain mail of tears turned hard; like the crayfish, I am craven and follow your spoor across the sky, tearing at myself, at my world, my body moving to find yours.

The scroll here on this card is the testament of unconscious knowledge, the knowledge that comes from Hecate and the underworld, from ancient Mu, knowledge that comes from the Hall of Osiris, the center of the maze, where beasts wait to destroy the truth seeker.

It is not to ancient Mu that you have flown, Ben, Orion, Old Moon, keeper of my tenderest whims, but to Los Angeles. And there you betray me.

A sigh of pain and I remember how I have saved even

the smallest nail clipping, kept a snippet of your hair that you let fall on the dressing table, fondly picked up after you in the bathroom and smiled at the crinkled pubic hairs in the tub; I remember how Psi and I, both abuzz with content, would sit on the edge of the tub and watch your ritual of shaving; the shaving brush *en chemise* with foam, your soap mug, the hallowed concentration as the blade passed over the so-alive flesh: but you grew cross with our attention and forbade us the bathroom. I saved those hairs and nail parings, skin scrapings, and now, lover, I'd squinny my eyes over 'em, I'd throw the bones skyward, squat in the dust and draw patterns, invoking Hecate for the subtle vengeance.

ᓫ Ten of Cups ᓬ

LATE September, and the opening days of the fall term. Leah's office, silent all summer, now hooted, bellowed, harangued, was a hullabaloo of students who sat cross-legged on the floor, clung to the window ledge, sat one-cheekedly on her desk, held registration forms out to her to initial, waved papers at her: "I completed my incomplete for you!"; "I wrote this story, will you read it?"; "I need your okay to take eighteen hours this semester"; "Can I ask how come you gave me a lousy C-minus in Dram Lit?"

Leah, beaming, nodding, shaking her head, initialed, accepted, filed, took down appointments, frowned at the "lousy C-minus," said: "You probably really ruined yourself on the final exam."

Eventually some of the mob wandered away and Leah was left with five boys and a girl who waited, looked at each other, and then pushed to say: "Having taken your Remedial Comp course last year, we were wondering Miss Knutinen, if we could take another writing class with you. Not just remedial, you know, but to do other kinds of writing like poetry and fiction."

Leah, pleased, tickled, about to leap, said: "Does the catalog list a course like that?"

"No. You know it doesn't. But we'd work hard. We got a lot out of Remedial Comp." This was Mr. Wiesel speaking. He was thin, serious. "We thought if you could arrange a time, we'd be glad to find out where we could have a little class, you know, some room not already in use. So all you'd have to do is okay it and we could get started right away."

"You want to take an extra class and do the extra work? What about credit? You wouldn't really stick with something for a semester for no class credit."

They did have the grace to blink and shuffle their feet.

"If you really are serious and won't let me down by pooping out halfway through, let's do this. . . ." And she explained how they could create their own writing class and get it accepted by the powers in the Dean's office. "So, let me see, the only afternoon I have free this semester is Friday. You wouldn't want to have a class from two till five on Friday."

"That would be fine," they said, nodding to each other, smiling at her.

"Well, then I'll file a request for an add sheet and you all sign it this Friday when we meet. What'll we call the class? And what will I say is the intent? You know, at the end of the semester I'll have to write out a report on how well we met the intent I file now."

"Creative writing?"

"Expository writing?"

"Writing techniques?"

They went silent, watched her for a response. She nodded encouragingly, "It's your class. You should name it."

"Experiments dot dot dot—I mean, colon, writing?" Wiesel said.

"Experiences: Writing?" Another boy, named DeWitt, asked.

The others nodded equably.

"Votes?"

"We all vote for that one," Wiesel said. "We can live with that."

"Oh, Miss Knutinen. I have a friend who wants to take the class, too, but he couldn't be here for the meeting. Could I sign him in anyway? His name is Barry Freeman and he writes a lot." Miss Insalaco blushed.

"Fine. So that makes it six for Fridays." Leah made a note on her desk calendar. She looked up at them. "I hope you won't object if I use the Friday class for experiments myself. I'd like to try some assignments on you, get your opinion on whether they work or not and then use them on the remedial class." She saw their acquiescence and went on, "How about a first assignment? Due this first Friday. The use of subjective time. A nightmare."

DeWitt grinned at her. "Length of assignment, however many pages it takes to do it right?"

The others chorused: "Flabby writing! Weak! Awk Syn! Rep!" And gathering their book bags, they filed out of her office, stamping their feet in time to: "Awk syn! Rep! Circular!"

They met in a seminar room that had one window. They immediately opened that window, found an ashtray, set up the coffee jug and paper cups, and by the time Leah settled herself in a chair, they had sorted through their papers and decided who should read first. Leah said, "Before we start, where's Insalaco?"

DeWitt said: "She'll be late. She's still getting organized with her work schedule."

A young man came to the door of the room, looked around, came in, and sat down next to Leah.

"Mr. Freeman?" Leah asked. "A friend of yours told me you'd be taking this class with us."

"I have no friends," he said harshly.

"Oh." Startled, Leah asked, "You are Barry Freeman?"

"Yes. Here's the first assignment, the nightmare." He thrust pages at her as if they were tainted, then turned away and looked around the room from under his eyebrows, glowering. "I'm not a writer, I'm in pre-med."

Leah thought: What a sullen little poop! She looked at the other students and saw the thumbs-down look in their eyes. Wait, she thought at them.

Insalaco came in, saw Barry Freeman, and blushed. She sat down at the far end of the table, almost hiding behind her book bag, glancing at him from under eyelids that trembled. "I'm sorry I'm late. Here's the nightmare," she said breathlessly. Every word brought a fresh wave of color to her face.

"Thank you. Now, DeWitt, will you read yours?"

Mr. DeWitt read his nightmare of waiting in Grand Central for the train that would carry him home, of the vagrants who urinated on the floor, who sat with gray gums exposed as they dozed, snored, stirred fitfully, stared at him, and judged him because they knew him. "And I never got out of the station. That was the nightmare, that I spent all my eternity there because of what I had not told my parents; because of what I was myself, I would sleep on those benches, wear a dirty overcoat, be rootless, homeless, in that grubby, scuzzy station." DeWitt finished and looked up for comments.

"Yea!" Whitney cheered and stamped his feet.

The others agreed, nodding and smiling at him.

"I like how that works," Whitney said. "The whole thing happens in that flash, that second while the sweep hand of a watch goes around once. I've done that kind of instant sleep and nightmare, too, but you *really* got it."

"Pshaw, it was nothing," DeWitt said, grinning with pleasure.

"I think you will have your work cut out for you to beat that," Leah said. "This promises wonderful things for the rest of the semester. Now, can I ask one more thing of you all? If you'd be so kind as to type your clean copy on a stencil, I'll have the office run off copies for us. Then we can read along as the writer reads along and make notes to turn them over to the writer for his/her edification."

They nodded at her.

"I also think, DeWitt, that that is good enough as is to submit to the campus rag. The magazine."

DeWitt said simply, "Thank you." But he swallowed hard, and Leah and he shared a silent cheer.

"Now, before we go on to another nightmare, next week's assignment is erogenous zones. I do not want the usual. Not the breast or the buttocks or the crotch. But the nose. Or elbow." Leah looked for the ashtray, found it, and tapped her cigarette over it. "Questions?"

"Do you mean an erogenous zone on my body? Or is this what turns me on to someone else's body?" Nicholson asked. "My elbow or her elbow?"

"Hers."

"Can we do personifications again this year?" Miss Insalaco asked. "I loved doing that last year and I've thought of another one I'd love to do now that I'm a better writer."

"Of course. Whenever you have something you want to try, tell me and we'll put it on the schedule. You realize of course, that we have only twelve weeks to work in— no, ten! So we'll have to decide which ideas to write."

"Can we do another big project?" Wiesel asked. "I

know last year it was like pulling teeth because most of us weren't in that class by choice. But now we are and I'd like to work on a long story."

"That's what you were working up to, isn't it?" Leah asked. "I think it's a good idea. Not just the weekly exercises, but a long project. If you want to tackle a story or even a one-act play!" She lighted another cigarette. "Now, let's see, Miss Insalaco, would you read?"

Monday, Wednesday, and Friday mornings at eleven she met with the Dramatic Lit 133 class. Thirty faces, she thought, looking at them over the lectern. "Othello, was he a pawn?" she asked. "And Iago, certainly a magician, a trickster. In the sense of misdirecting attention, he was a magician, wasn't he?"

A hand speared up at the back of the room. *"Why* was he so evil? I read the play in high school and reread it here and I don't ever see a reason."

"Does anyone have a suggestion?"

"He wanted to be the general?" a male voice, Mr. Fish's, said.

"He was in love with Desdemona?" Miss Cortez asked.

"He was lacking something that Othello had? And if he could destroy Othello, that made him the stronger?"

Leah nodded. "That's good, what is it that Iago lacked, or thought he lacked?"

"He seemed the worst when he watched Othello and Desdemona," Mr. Fish said. "He lacked love? But he had a wife."

"Or perhaps he lacked the capacity to love," Leah suggested.

"And so he wanted to destroy it when he saw it in someone else?" Mr. Fish eyed her skeptically.

"Oh, I think that's true!" Miss Cortez said.

The campanile sounded the quarter hour. Leah began gathering her notes.

"This class always ends when we get a good discussion going," Mr. Fish complained. "But when you are doing your lecture . . . that dictation with the long yellow pages, it's the pits, and it goes on for *hours.*"

"See you Monday. Think about magic, think about the imagery of the magician, the trickster, how Shakespeare uses that imagery." Leah waded through students and out into the hallway.

"Erogenous Zone: The Hunchback's Hump," Mr. Whitney read. "I saw him in the park, sitting on a green bench. His hump loomed above his shoulders, hard, throbbing, dwarfing his shoulders and head with its thrust." Whitney grinned over his cheekbones and went on, a chuckle rasping the underside of his voice.

When he had finished reading, he sat back, his seal-black eyes bright with mischief.

"Oh, that's gross!" Miss Insalaco said.

"But it works!" Wiesel said, nodding at Whitney. "Mine isn't nearly as imaginative. Elbows! Someone else read."

Nicholson handed out the copies of his erogenous zone piece and began reading aloud. "My love's belly button is a wineglass wherein I quench my thirst." He glanced up at Leah, saw her nod, and continued: "I sip from that goblet the dark Burgundy, the dusky taste, and bite the edges of the cup."

"Wow!" DeWitt said. "Sounds like her belly button is deep enough to hold a quart."

"Burgundy!" Wiesel said. "How about Mogen David?"

"It kind of fizzles out after that line," Nicholson said. "There isn't a hell of a lot you can say about a belly button without getting into the belly and its environs."

"I think it's a matter of spending time with the belly button," DeWitt said. "You know, firsthand experience."

"And then writing about it in calm detachment," Leah said. She looked around. "Mr. Freeman, we haven't heard from you. Are you ready to read?"

"I did bring something. But I want to explain something about it first."

"No, we don't allow prefaces or introductions. Each writer submits his work without any apology here because the work must stand alone on its merits," Leah began.

The rest of the class chorused raggedly: "No prefaces, no apologies! You couldn't escort your work to an editor!" They grinned at Leah and chanted: "Awk syn! Split in!" Wiesel said: "You weren't here for the first course we took with Miss Knutinen. We learned the hard way not to apologize or preface. And she has a lethal red pen!"

"I wrote about hair," Freeman announced, and then

read: "Hair is a directional sign pointing to the center of love's intent. The down-pointing black arrows on my lover's head." He looked up, saw the attention of the whole class fixed upon him, blushed, and took a deep breath. "The down on my love's upper lip shades that soft place where I would lay my smiles." He stammered and put the page down. "I guess I'm not ready to read anymore."

"But that's terrific!" Wiesel said.

Miss Insalaco blushed and looked proprietary. Leah saw that look. "Oh, dear God, she's in love with him. Well, maybe it'll work." But something felt askew there. "Miss Insalaco, would you read now? I think we have to hear from the other side."

"It's hard to find something on the male," Miss Insalaco said. "I mean, everything is erogenous."

"Whoo!" DeWitt burlesqued a wink at her.

"Never mind the lower class, read what you have," Leah said.

"Wrists." Miss Insalaco's breath fluttered the edges of her pages. "Wrists, the intricate turning of nerve and bone, the quick skin, the dark prickle of hairs . . ." She stopped. "Please, I think it's . . . well, could you just read it to yourselves? I feel . . . overwhelmed by the guys in this room and you'll laugh because when I read it aloud to *you*, it sounds suggestive and I didn't mean it that way at all." She laid the pages down on the table. "I'll be better with the next assignment. But I can't read this one aloud."

"All right. We'll make our notes on the copies and hand them back to you next time," Leah said. She smiled at Miss Insalaco. "I'd like you all to write transitions for next time. A short third-person narrative with transition. I have more stencils here if you need any."

"Listen," Zulu rasped over the telephone. "It's the last party we'll be having on the terrace this fall. I was at dinner there last week and the chrysanthemums are something to see. So, come on, let's go for a couple of drinks."

Leah hesitated, turning the pages of her desk calendar, looking for an excuse not to go. "I'm not in the mood," she said.

"You could be. You've been sitting around like a goddamned *nun* ever since you and that Earl broke up. Jesus, I know you haven't had a date since then. Come on, it's free gin and tonics."

Leah mumbled a faint denial, thinking: I barely survived Earl. I can't think about him even now without a groan. I'm pulled together now, humming off pitch, safe underwater, undetected in my vulnerable center.

"You know all the people at the Town and Gown Club anyway. So how are you gonna meet anyone and get hurt? Come on!"

Leah looked out the window at the late-autumn sun, at the brown grasses dappled gold and bronze, at the leaves just tipping from the trees.

"So I'm coming by to pick you up."

"No, I'll meet you there. Five?"

They met at the bar and carried away their drinks, Zulu tan and barbarous with a red wig, swinging loops of plastic pearls, her freckles lighting her face, her fox eyes bright with malice and vitality. They sat at a small round table. Zulu said: "My gawd."

"Your eyes always get a little bit of a spark when there's something male in the room," Leah lit a cigarette. "Who is it this time?"

"I'm pointing," Zulu said, cocking her head to the right.

Leah looked. "Not my type."

"You're so goddamned smug." Zulu turned her profile to the room, aiming.

"Oh, I see who you mean. He's probably available again. His name's Phil. He's in the Eco Department. He and his wife are separated. He has a following among the female students." Leah added, wickedly, "You know. The two wineglasses, the locked office door."

Zulu crossed her eyes at Leah and turned to smile at Phil, who responded, glanced at Leah, and came to stand at their table.

"Hello, Leah," he said. "How are you?" He let his hand touch Zulu's shoulder. "Hello."

Leah watched the male-female exchange of looks and pushed her chair back. That was when she saw Ben. "Oh damn!" She bit her lip. "Phil, do you know Zulu? Why don't you join us?" She muttered the introductions. "I know you'll excuse me. I'm really tired. I'll talk to you tomorrow." She grinned at Phil and kissed Zulu and left.

She planned to leave. But as she turned away from

Zulu and Phil, she walked into Jake Solomon, who held on to her with both hands. He was staggeringly drunk. He held on to Leah until he regained his balance. "Oh, I got a friend I want you to meet over here. He's new to the club and I want him to meet some of the people. Women, you know what I'm telling you?"

"No, Jake. I'm just leaving." But Leah was helpless. What is it with drunk people? she thought. They cannot be embarrassed. And somehow they manipulate the sober victim so that the victim tries not to embarrass the drunk. She didn't know what it was, but Jake had done it to her. She found herself helplessly holding him up as he lurched across the room. To Ben, who watched their progress with an enigmatic expression.

"Leah, I wanna innerduce Doctor Ben Calloway. He's over at University Hospital researching. Pathology. Ben, this tall lady is Leah Knutinen, one of our two English professors who are also women." Jake stood between them, lurching from side to side, seeming to pull against an anchor, smiling with accomplishment.

Ben smiled at her and took her hand briefly. Leah smiled and backed away as quickly as was decent. "Nice to meet you," she said. She had her car keys in her hand; half of her mind was plotting how best to escape. The other half, the sea creature, was burbling: O yes! She was beaming, nodding at him, all her edges softening and opening out, once again vulnerable. "I've got to be going," she said. And stood on one foot, caught. What was the song the mermaid sang as she danced on bleeding feet? Leah sang that song then. Ben Calloway was that song. He, his face, was tattooed on her wrists, tiny dots of him penetrated her flesh and went to the marrow of her bones. She was caught as surely as the mermaid, and even while she shuddered with gladness, she already longed for the sea, the underwater self, the safety of being undetected. All this, and he hadn't said a word.

Jake Solomon, his narrow shoulders and hippo hips swaying, his harum-scarum beard already a bird's nest of crumbs, his sweater vest stained, began a sentence, waving his gin and tonic right onto Leah's blouse front, following the drink with his other hand, pawing, apologizing. "Aw, hell, Leah, I'm sorry. Lemme wipe it off."

Leah backed away from the two men. "No, that's all right, Jake. I was going home anyway."

Ben, his handkerchief out, steered Leah out of Jake's range. "Here, it won't stain, will it?" He had her elbow.

She, melting at the joints, was led to a small table near the tall windows.

"Sit here a moment and catch your breath. I'll bring us both something to drink. What would you like? Another gin and tonic, or would you like something else? Waiter!" He held out the chair for her, seemed to tuck her into a protected place, and seated himself while creating a waiter from thin air. "I'd like some white wine." He looked at Leah, who nodded. "A carafe of the Chablis, please. And something from the cheese tray and some fruit."

He looked at Leah and said, "How *are* you?"

She could still feel his touch on her elbow. She had, of course, gone mute. She nodded brightly at him then began to search her handbag for a cigarette, turning her eyes away from him, digging terrierlike through the jumble of odds and ends—car keys, pill box, address book, small notebook, wads of tissue, lipstick, eyeliner, hairpins, scissors, pliers, mascara, tweezers, pens, stamp book, throat lozenges, calorie counter, dead lighter, matchbooks, she knew she could grub endlessly before the cigarettes surfaced.

He laughed far down in his throat and offered her one of his cigarettes. He lit it for her and handed it over.

"Thanks. I know I've got some in here somewhere." But now she could concentrate on the cigarette. She couldn't look *at* him. She couldn't look at *him*. She did look at the end of his cigarette, at his wrist, at the buttons on his jacket sleeve. Shyness, she thought. My cursed shyness. She waited to see which way she would go: a sodden lump of silence or a gabbling twit.

"Jake thinks very highly of you," Ben said. "You're permanent and full-time on the staff?" He took her hand and turned it over, palm up. "You've got a star in your hand."

She was going to be mute, she could see that. She raised an eyebrow at him and began to draw her hand away.

"No. See, there just under the third finger, there's a star." He ran his forefinger up and down her palm and her fingers curled. "Good reflexes, too." He smiled. He leaned over and touched her forehead with his.

She jumped.

"Are you always this nervous?" he asked.

She looked around, shaking her head. "I think I'm a little tired."

"Well, let's have that glass of wine and some cheese. Did you drive, or may I see you home?"

"No, thank you. I have my car." The wine arrived, Leah watched while Ben poured two glasses. "What kind of research will you be doing?"

"Histo-pathology. And I'll be teaching a research methods class in the spring. But histo-pathology is my specialty. And choriocarcinoma."

"It sounds complicated. Even arcane."

"It's . . . maybe it is arcane. I'll have to give you a tour of my office and lab one of these days." He touched his glass to Leah's. "To the arcane in our lives."

Later he walked her to her car. "Did I get your last name correctly? Knutinen?"

She nodded and climbed under the steering wheel. She turned the key in the ignition, hoping that for once the contrary automobile would not stall here, still within his reach, hoping that for once she could shift the Pinto into reverse and actually travel backward.

"I'll call you, may I? You're in the blue book?"

She nodded and released the clutch. The Pinto, treacherous as a cat, purred and reversed smoothly. She watched him step back and make a kind of salute. Then she concentrated on driving home, scolding herself: "I eroticize disaster. I am patterned for disaster!" And yet the sea creature bubbled, chuckled, unfolded the tender edges with sensuous pleasure.

"Do not call," she muttered the next afternoon. "You are nothing but a fantasy. I hang my lusts and juices on the cock of fantasy, so do not call."

"Do not call," she said aloud at four in the morning, falling out of sleep to stare at the ceiling, rolling to look at the clock and light a cigarette, sitting up in bed and dragging a folder of student papers up onto her lap, a red pen ready to slash and stab: "Awk syn!" "Dangling prep!"

Do not call, she prayed silently in the shower. It is not to be wasted, this long discipline I have had of teaching, this long self-enforced chastity that leaves me calm at the center. She said to herself in a factual voice: He has a cruel edge to his upper lip. His philtrum is too deep. And the sea creature whispered: Just right for kisses, hmm? And she stood silent under the water for a moment; then: I am eroticized for disaster, that's it. A tall, dark-haired man with a cruel cut to his lip and an obsidian eye . . . and all my patterns shift. The part of me that does not wish me well, the dead or dying part of my heart seeks the silhouette that contains riddles. I think I will find completeness in the fantasy he cuts in midair. I don't know him and so I will not play the fool.

She scrubbed hard with the washcloth. Liar! laughed that humming heedless self. But she said: Do thy worst, blind Cupid, I'll not love! and turned the shower to cold.

৬৯ Six of Cups ৫৯

THE Six of Cups: love affairs that turn out not so well. Am I repeating a pattern? How then, had they gotten married? Decided to marry? They had begun going out, if that was what it was called, to plays, movies, the symphony; those tense, attenuated evenings that stretched into two in the morning and he couldn't seem to leave, and couldn't seem to stay, at least not long enough to take his clothes off and get into bed with her; instead he tortured her with perfect kisses, holding her against him so that she thought the zipper of his trousers would burn her flesh, and yet it always stopped short of fucking. It was worse than rape, because she was so desirous, so baffled. And she'd ask him, "What? What's wrong?" And he'd leave, but not until she was on the edge of assaulting him, whether to rape the hell out of him or to beat him with her fists; she didn't know. And she'd pace the floor and wonder, What? What? If he hadn't had an erection, she'd have known what-what. But he'd had an erection, it would press and bulge against the fabric of his trousers, she'd feel the tender thing there between them. Was there such a creature as a male prick tease? Whatever! At four in the morning, alone, she'd wrestle free of her tangled sheets and walk through the dark to the kitchen for a glass of ice water and then pad back to her bed, her feelings bruised, wondering, What? What?

She had tried to talk to him about it. It. They'd gone to dinner at the Winterset, a favorite restaurant out in the country, and the whole evening had been threaded with tension. He'd had that bitter, pursed look around the lips, the avoiding eyes, she knew that look by then; even though she could not fathom it, nor understand what brought it about, she could recognize it. So she said: "I'd like to have a talk tonight."

And he'd said, "I won't be forced into an either/or situation."

Which, of course, had astonished her. "I don't know what you mean. Either what or what?"

"The great American nightmare. Marriage."

Had she gaped? She wondered. She knew that her temper had begun its slow burn up the fuse. "I wasn't thinking about marriage," she said, not quite honestly. First things first, she reminded herself. "I was thinking about this tension we have every time we see each other." Her voice had gone down an octave, but was increasing in volume. She'd seen his covert glance around the restaurant and had tried to diminish the sound.

"Are you going to be hysterical?" he'd asked, and signaled the waiter for the check.

"D'you mean, am I going to make a scene? Right here?" She'd suddenly, terribly, wanted to make a scene, the palms of her hands itching for the plates, the muscles in her forearms fairly twitching to start throwing things. But she'd only folded her napkin and put it on the table.

He'd taken the check from the waiter and left the tip under his butter plate. And with a gesture of despicable courtesy, he'd taken her elbow and led her out of the restaurant. Once in the car, he'd said, "You know this is my last night in town before I go to California. It would have been nice if you'd let us enjoy it."

She'd watched his profile. He drove, as always, efficiently, smoothly, his meticulously kept hands grasping the steering wheel, his body relaxed, the sexy thighs long and muscular on the car seat.

"I do want to talk tonight," she said. "I don't mean to be unpleasant or to quarrel." She'd wondered: Why am I apologizing? What is this pacifying? The next thing I know I'll be saying I'm wrong. And what the hell am I wrong about? I'm the one who feels wronged. *Wronged!* Because, sonofabitch, there is something askew about the way we end our evenings.

And she'd heard herself say: "You know, I care about you a great deal."

"That's what I mean. I'm not ready for that kind of thinking," he'd said.

"I'm not talking about marriage."

He'd glanced at her, briefly, that bitter look in his eyes.

Then they'd become silent. He'd driven direct to her apartment building and parked the car. "I won't come up tonight."

She had watched his profile in silence, had become resolved. "Yes. Then it's better done now. I don't want to see you anymore. It's just as well you're going to California tomorrow. We'll both have the two weeks to get used to the idea. Or, *I'll* have the two weeks to get used to it. I just don't want to go on seeing you."

He'd sat silent, with a look she didn't understand; he'd washed his face clear of expression, even of bitterness. And he'd blushed. A curious blush of—what was it? Radiance? She had not been able to understand it at all.

She'd nodded to him and gotten out of the car. And before she could waver, she'd gone into the lobby of the building, let the heavy door lock behind her, and walked up to her apartment and let herself in, slipping the chain on the door, kicking off her shoes, making herself a double scotch on the rocks. Then she had sat down in the dark and begun to shake. Looking around the apartment, gulping the scotch, shaking. But she had not wept! She'd felt shock. Her hands were clammy and cold, her stockinged feet were icy. She'd made another scotch and showered. Then she'd put on a fleecy nightgown and gotten into bed with a sleeping pill. And, amazingly, slept.

The next morning, a Friday, she'd awakened, looked into the mirror at her face. "So much for the visible damage," she said. "I look fine. No bloodshot eyes, no bags. No tears making my nose red. Just like the loss of virginity, it doesn't show."

She'd been lying, of course; she knew that. She had suffered the damage underwater, as usual. And the whale, the great soft female whale, was making its undersea sounds of distress; the mermaid self, that creature was silent. Only the whale self moaned, made soft cries of distress. But no one else could hear them; no one else could feel the undersea tremors that made her knees unsteady, that dislodged the detritus of old griefs, shifting and tearing away the tenuously balanced world of her self.

She'd dressed and gone to her classes, bright, determinedly bright. And stayed on campus until after six that night, taking her briefcase, loaded with papers, to the library, to remain isolated, busy.

That weekend she'd gone out with Zulu and two commercial pilots. She had been fondled, had said, "No, thank you." She had not drunk too much, had, instead, been vivacious, funny. Until Zulu said: "Listen, what the hell is wrong with you?"

"Oh, nothing. Well, something is, but I'll get it straightened out myself."

"It's that Ben, isn't it? The one you met at the Town and Gown Club. He struck me as cold, you know? Not even good for a hate fuck."

But Leah had frowned and closed her eyes.

"Well, if it is him, it isn't worth all this. You've been doing a star turn all evening. Like you've taken some kind of pill. Listen, d'you wanna go to bed with Phil? No, huh? Well, I kind of do wanna. So, we'll drop you off and I'll call you tomorrow when I get up. You wanna do something, just us girls tomorrow?"

Leah had agreed and gone home alone. And, amazingly, she'd slept well that night, too. That Sunday morning she went to church and sat quietly looking at the banners and the statues, letting the silence fall over her, wishing she could break the silence she felt toward God. I want to have more than faith. I want to *know* that You exist. That You aren't a grotesque fantasy created by a needful humanity. I had this sense of an active silence, of an active listening, and I thought that was God. Now it is the silence of absence.

Impatient with herself, she knotted her hands together, not sure that she was praying, not entirely apologizing. Oh, it isn't because of Ben that I feel this way. I've somehow gotten out over the abyss, have gotten cut off from that active listening, and now I'm in a silence from all directions. I know Ben is not the answer to me, or the completion to me. I know I am drawn to disaster, I seem to have that appetite, even that pattern. So it is best that Ben, too, is silent. And absent.

She'd gone to Zulu's for the rest of the day, spent the bright fall afternoon roaring around the great lake in Zulu's boat, coming home that evening with windburn and the sense that she had avoided a very painful involvement with Ben Calloway. She showered and washed her hair, taking the time for once to sit in front of her bedroom mirror and brush her long hair a hundred strokes. I feel the way you feel after a tooth has been pulled, she told her reflection. Shocked but healing.

Monday she'd gone to her classes, looking marvelous, freshly tanned; had bubbled and gabbled, as normal, as happy as she could expect to be. And the whole week had gone that way: students clustering around her, laughing with her, or brooding at her because of test grades they'd hoped would be better, groaning at the prospect of term papers and the long-term view of grizzling away at Dram Lit 133. So she'd been surprised that next Friday afternoon when she was stuffing a fresh batch of papers and blue exam books into her briefcase and Ben walked into her office, looking like hell.

"I really need to see you," he said.

ᘛ The Hanged Man ᘊ

FREEMAN laid the last page of his manuscript on the table and looked around.

DeWitt, Nicholson, and Whitney sat hunched together at one end of the refectory table. Leah waited, blowing smoke rings.

Wiesel finally said: "Is this a palpable silence? I think you finally shut off the famous Whitney gusher." He doodled on his copy of Freeman's manuscript. "You certainly shut me off."

Miss Insalaco said, "Is there such a word as nakidity? It's the nakidity that takes my breath away. And the shockingness. I don't know if I like you for writing this way or even feeling this way about yourself. Or if I like you for . . . confessing."

"Miss Knutinen always talks about firsthand experience as the best," Freeman said defiantly.

"But we're a writing group," Wiesel said gently. "Not a therapy group."

"Cheap shot!" Freeman said, ready to withdraw, ready to walk out of the class.

"Oh, wait a minute!" Leah tapped the table with her lighter for silence. "I wonder why everyone is so exercised. You all are reacting very strongly."

"I think Linda's reacting because for once it's real sex and real pain," DeWitt said. "Not her ladies' mag pink stuff. I for one think this was valid, if rough and raw. I get tired of us listening to the Miss Teen America crap we get every week from the distaff side of the table."

Miss Insalaco opened her mouth, but subsided, content to glare at him.

"I'd like to make some comments," Leah said.

They sighed and waited while she made red slashes on her copy of Freeman's script. "I like a verb here and there, it activates the sentence." She circled a sentence fragment. "You seem to need a pamphlet to remind you that 'of' is not 'have.' But then, Mr. Wiesel is attempting to change the language in that direction, too." She used the red pen a lot. The black and white pages sprung leaks and dribbles as she worked her way through the piece.

"Do you have a special pleasure in bloodletting?" Freeman asked her. "You seem to get a kind of sex kick, I can see it while you are sitting there now."

She nodded and went on.

"No comments about the content? You didn't react to anything but the awk syns?" Freeman tried to read past her red pen marks.

"Well, yes." Leah laid the red pen aside and leaned back in her chair. "Like the rest of you, I was a bit taken aback by this script. To see oneself tied up in a plastic garbage bag and left on the curb by one's parents is not what one expects from 'How I Spent My Thanksgiving.' Although, I know we all have had some searing moments with our parents, their expectations for us."

"I thought it was disgusting," Miss Insalaco said. "No one does that to a turkey! No boys that I've ever known. It's . . . ugh."

"We all know about your sensibilities," DeWitt said. "You miss the important part—his pain."

"Well, he turned me off any sympathy I'd have felt when he did that to the family turkey!" Miss Insalaco was blushing in spasms, in waves, in violent upheavals of color that merged into tears that pelted her cheeks. "I thought we were here to learn how to write! I don't know if this is what I want to learn. I *know* it isn't."

Wiesel said, "But isn't part of learning to write actually learning how to read? And to expand our understanding?" He touched her hand gently. "You can't be a writer with depth if you stay in the safe areas that you already know."

The other young men nodded agreement. Freeman looked vindicated and lit a cigarette.

The campanile, muffled by the snow, tolled five. Leah pushed her chair away from the refectory table. "Wiesel, next time I want to hear a rewrite of your shofar story. That's too good to let drop because you are afraid of rewriting. Nicholson, you still owe me that Halloween thing.

The end of term is nigh and you all owe me one or two rewrites." She stood up, smiling at them, stuffing papers into her briefcase. "I think we should tackle nightmares again, now that you are looser."

"What about suicide notes?" Mr. Wiesel asked. "We all loved them last year. I can really get into the mood this year!"

"Mmm. I'll think about it." She walked out of the classroom and headed toward her office. The students followed at her heels, hauling on their coats and scarves, dropping books, retrieving them, bumping into each other and Leah.

"Miss Knutinen?" Miss Insalaco said. "Will you be having open house again this Christmas? We all could come over and help trim the tree."

"We could help you get the open house set up," DeWitt said. "You know, we could get the tree and bring it over for you. And generally . . . help."

"We'd bring stuff, too, not just come to eat," Wiesel said.

"Okay." Leah unlocked her office door and stepped inside. "I'll plan on it. The last day of classes, right?" She was about to go on talking when Emily, the department secretary, pushed through the students. "Leah, look what came for you! What gorgeous man sent them?" She held a florist's box out to Leah. "I couldn't resist, I know you wouldn't mind. They're beautiful! Pink and ivory roses! Two dozen!"

Leah looked up and blushed. She felt the blush start somewhere under her brassiere and burn its way in patches along her throat and face. "Thank you, Emily." She took the box, laid it on her desk, and opened the card. "Waiting to be with you tonight. Ben." She read silently and put the card back into the envelope.

"This man must be brought around here," Emily said. "I cannot imagine anyone sending two dozen roses!" She patted Leah's shoulder. "Is he the one that sent you those spider mums this fall?"

Leah nodded.

Miss Insalaco touched one of the roses. "Gosh! I wish someone would send me *one* rose."

"Maybe if you are very very good, like Miss Knutinen

must be!" Mr. Whitney said. "Then someone will send you flowers!"

"Out! Out!" Emily herded the students out of Leah's office. "Your class is over. Go home." She closed the door and smiled at Leah. "You really must bring him around. How did you ever catch him?"

"I didn't catch him. I haven't caught him. I don't even know how women go about doing that. It isn't anything serious."

"One rose is sweet. One dozen is a lot of liking. Two dozen is serious! I've been married five times, I should know." Emily waited for Leah to say something. Then, nodding at the silence, she said: "Well, I'll let you go on home. You must have a date with him this evening. Have you been courting long?" She touched a pink rose. "Romance." She waved a kiss at Leah and left.

"A romance," Leah muttered. "Courting." She replaced the cover on the florist's box, gathered her books and briefcase, locked her office, and, burdened with the flowers and briefcase, walked thoughtfully to her car. Old-fashioned words, she thought. I don't know what it is we are having. I do a lot of sighing and moaning and wondering. And swearing. I hope this is not going to be another evening like last Friday. Please, God, don't let it be.

She opened the Pinto door on the passenger side and placed the box of roses on the front seat, throwing her briefcase and the rest of her things into the back. Walking around the car, she swept snow from the windows. She climbed in on the driver's side, starting the motor, buckling the seat belt, lighting a cigarette, waiting for the car to warm up. He does not have a sense of humor, she thought, that's all there is to it. I should just stop seeing him. He is a mystery to me. And when I'm with him, I'm a mystery too, going insane, falling apart, wanting to throw him backward on the bed and rape him, and yet I'm so goddamned shy and modest that all I do is writhe around on the inside, listening to my sea voice hum and bubble. He doesn't have a sense of humor and that is one reason I should stop seeing him. I know he will make some reference, some chiding reference, to last week and I will be apologetic. Sonofabitch. This is asinine.

She inhaled smoke and let it drift from her nostrils, listening to the Pinto motor grumble unevenly. "I know, time for a tune-up," she conceded aloud as she tapped the accelerator and the grumble smoothed. But I'm in the wrong mood, dammit, she told herself. We should sit down and have a long talk. But it's off to another cocktail party, I'll bet on it, and that is not the time for a talk. We never did talk. He came back from California and said he needed to see me. And I thought we'd talk then. But no.

What had happened then. . . . He'd stood there in her office doorway, looking like hell, white and strained around the mouth, his eyes dark with what she realized was pain. "I really need to talk to you," he'd said.

She'd lied. "I'm sorry. I'm not free tonight."

"Please." His voice had been rough at the edges, as if he hadn't slept. And the lines around his mouth had become even whiter.

She didn't care, she'd told herself. "I don't even like him," she'd muttered to the sea creature, who was not helpful.

"I . . . Would you just come out and have a glass of wine? A cocktail? I won't keep you from your date." He hadn't attempted to touch her, but stood tiredly in the doorway, one hand still on the door.

She'd tried looking at him squinny-eyed, to get a clear fix on him. But she'd seen the shape he cut in the light, the dark eyebrows, the ash-colored hair, his knuckles, white, on the door. Grudgingly, "I suppose I could take that much time."

His look had turned warm.

She'd refused that look, that warmth; yet it'd made her knees go into orgasms. Yes, I know, she'd thought. With him it is eargasms. Kneegasms. She'd kept her eyes hooded, avoiding him, while she packed papers into her briefcase. "The Faculty Club?" she'd asked.

"Le Gommeut Caneton?" he'd suggested. "It would give us a chance to talk if we didn't stop on campus."

"I'll meet you there." She'd found her keys and planned to edge him out of the office, but she felt his eyes on her; her knees betrayed her deliciously.

"I'll follow you to your place and then you could ride over with me. We'd have more time together." His breath had touched the nape of her neck as she brushed past him to the hall.

"Um." She'd locked her office, briskly walked down the hall, heels clicking on the marble floor. He'd held the heavy double doors open for her and she rushed past him, knowing she looked as if she were fleeing demons.

His long black car had followed Leah's Pinto to her apartment. "He does everything in such a way that I see sex in it," she'd muttered to herself. "Even his damned car!" She'd parked the Pinto. Or is it me? I'm cock-eyed, that's what I am. Oh, Jane Eyre! Oh, Jane Austen. Oh, Cathy galloping over the moors. I'm in love with a man I don't like. No, I am not in love with him. I am and I'm not. Shall we take a vote on it, us who slosh and gurgle around in here. Only the nays need speak.

She'd watched Ben walk toward her. He'd opened the Pinto door and helped her out. He'd held her elbow (elbowgasm) while he walked her to his car. He'd tucked her inside, drawing the safety belt over her hips to fasten it, his hands brushing the tops of her thighs. She'd felt that touch through the heavy fabric of her coat and skirt, felt it light and smoulder, felt a sparkle under her skin. Her breath had stopped and then started, but at a deeper pitch. She'd turned her face away from him and lighted a cigarette silently while he got into the car on the driver's side.

In the darkness of the restaurant, Ben's eyes had been shadowed as he watched Leah sip at her wine. "You're so quiet tonight," he'd said. "Thoughtful." He'd waited for an answer. Then he'd said, "I missed you. Can we still be friends?"

She'd drunk that first glass of wine and nodded. "I think we could be friends." Then she'd been stricken by such pain that she forgot about Ben entirely for a moment. "Oh," she'd heard the sea creature wail. And she'd moaned herself, thinking, Oh. Now I will have to work at containing myself again. All the damned emotions and impulses to put my arms around you, around people, all the sharing ideas that surface, all the urges to care, all those gratuitous tendernesses have to be caught, contained, muted. Damn.

She'd held her breath, closed her eyes, concentrated on containing the pain. She'd nodded again, this time to herself, then opened her eyes to smile at Ben. "I think I can handle that, being friends." She'd felt something like relief begin in her chest, a releasing of the pain, a subsiding of emotions. And she'd felt she had escaped. That she would recover. Escaped Ben. Would recover from Ben. She'd nodded to herself.

Feeling safe, she'd watched him pour more wine into the two glasses, watched him as he relaxed, as he stretched his legs out, ankles crossed, beside the low table. She'd watched his hands, the long fingers with the spatulate nails, the fine hairs on the tops of his hands, and then she'd stopped watching, aware that he was watching her, smiling at her. She'd looked away, taken out a cigarette and tapped it on the table.

"I know what you were thinking," he'd said. "I could feel your thoughts."

"Is that one of the things involved in being friends? That you think you know my thoughts?" Annoyed by her own transparency, she'd put the cigarette down and found her handbag, hitched herself out of the banquette. "I really do have to get going," she'd lied, knowing it was visibly a lie.

"Now you're angry. I was teasing, Leah." He'd stood beside her.

She'd found her coat and hauled it on, ignoring his outstretched hand.

"Be reasonable, Leah."

He'd taken his own coat and followed her out to the street.

"I don't feel like being reasonable." She'd glared around the street, looking for his car, looking for a taxi. "I was damned dumb to come out with you."

"Where are you going? The car is this way."

"I think I'll take a taxi."

"Don't be an idiot." Roughly, he'd taken her arm and wrestled her to the car. "Sit!" He'd slammed the car door and gone to the driver's side. He'd glanced at her as he started the motor, but didn't speak.

She'd sat silently, the anger fizzling out through her toes. Before she'd said them, she knew what the next words would be. "I'm sorry." And she'd felt the giggle rising upward, bubbling up to bang against the roof of her mouth. "I'm sorry," she'd repeated, almost inaudibly, trying to swallow the giggles.

He'd glanced at her, eyebrow arrowing down in what she

knew was anger, bafflement. He'd driven carefully, smoothly, direct to her apartment without speaking.

She couldn't speak. She'd kept saying, "I'm sorry," then dissolving into helpless giggles, waving her hands, trying to get past the "I'm sorry" part to the explanation of why she had become angry: One, I'm shy and didn't know I was so transparent. And I didn't want you to know how you affect me, but you affect me and that doesn't affect you so I was angry and embarrassed, and first of all you came bounding back from California looking miserable and all you want to be is friends.

Of course, she could say *none* of that. Nor could she add: And I'm giggling now because giggling is crying, every woman knows that: the giggles turning upside down into small sobs that hurt the insides of the eyelids.

When they reached her apartment building she'd allowed him to walk her to the entrance. He'd taken her key, opened the heavy door, stood aside for her to enter, followed her inside, and walked her up the stairs to her apartment, where he unlocked the door.

She didn't know what she was feeling. There had been too many emotions running in crosscurrents, she could only nod her thanks and step inside the apartment and close the door, closing him out, closing herself away from him. She'd stood there for a moment, forehead resting on the white painted door; then, sighing, shaking her head, rubbing the tears away, she'd gone into her bedroom and sat on the bed. She'd shaken her head once at herself and undressed, stood in the shower, dried herself, put on her ratty old flannel "penance" nightgown, and hauled out some students to read and grade.

"I'm my own worst enemy," she'd said to the red pencil in her hand. "I was nothing but a bag of waters and vapors and teapot tantrums."

She'd said, "Of course, he could have smiled and asked me why I was laughing. A friend would have done that. But no. He became stern, grim, adult, faced with . . . with this spouting whale, this faucet, this spigot, this ululating waterworks!" She'd thrown the pencil down and gone into the kitchen for a glass of ice water.

The buzzer had sounded.

She'd opened the door six inches, keeping it on its chain.

"Ben!"

"You didn't go out," he'd accused her. "Open this door." He'd stepped through as she released the chain. "You didn't . . . You aren't dressed."

She'd goggled at him.

He'd put his left hand out, touched her breast through the nightgown.

"Oh, no," she'd said. "We aren't back to that. You know how I feel, what I think. No." But her breast had tingled. The nipple had betrayed her. She'd crossed her arms over her breasts, backing away from him. "I'll put on a bathrobe." She'd grabbed her robe from the closet and yanked it on.

"I do want to be friends. That's why I'm still here." He had followed her to the bedroom door.

She'd pushed past him. "Well. I'd like to be friends too. Would you like some coffee?"

"Would you?"

"Yes." She'd gone into the tiny kitchen, rattled around in the cupboard until she found the coffeepot and its works. She'd run water into it and measured the coffee into the metal basket. She'd plugged the coffeepot in and turned around. Ben had been immediately in front of her. He'd put his hands on her upper arms, stroked her arms to the wrists, and then taken her hands, kissing the palms, the tips of her fingers. He'd held her palms to his lips and stared at her, his eyes dark with pain.

"What? What is it?" she'd asked his eyes. She'd opened her arms to him, responding to the silence in him, the pain that made his eyes bleak. "Oh, what is it?" she'd asked, holding him now in her arms, holding him tightly to her, patting his shoulder, patting the back of his head, murmuring: "Oh, dear love, what *is* it?"

But he hadn't spoken. He'd put his arms around her, stroking the small of her back, her shoulders, running his hands over and over her body, her breasts, her ribs, moving his hands over her belly and up between her breasts, never speaking, blocking her questions with kisses; he did not speak, he moved her body to his, he gripped the small of her back and forced her body to his, moving her thighs apart with his, drawing her nightgown up, touching her thighs, his hands demanding something from her, drawing a pattern in flames all down the center of her belly.

He said against her mouth, "I want you, Leah."

They made love in her bed, the student papers hastily brushed to the floor, along with Ben's clothing, Leah's nightgown. He was wonderful. He was tender, solicitous, the "perfect lover," she thought, gasping with the sheer pleasure of a cock well placed. But it's his hands, it's his mouth, she groaned to herself. "Ah, no," she said aloud. "Ah, please *yes*." She had fleetingly wondered, as her nightgown fell: Why does he want to make love now? and had not been able to answer. And what if it doesn't work with me? What if, after all my lucubrations and lustings, I am lumber? He'd be able to tell."

But the moments of doubt were lost, dismissed. He was, she thought, like a practiced host. He waited for her responses, watching her, somehow a technician but not cold and distant, but rather, she repeated to herself, solicitous. She worried, even as she felt his hands caressing her again, about this lovemaking, *why* was it? And because she worried about that, she worried about not being what he wanted, what he needed from her. She saw him watching her and blushed. She was gasping with pleasure, at the same time knowing she was partly acting, acting to please him, to soothe him. And what if what he needs from me is an orgasm and I don't have one? What then? But he continued to caress the small of her back, down between her buttocks, between her thighs, the hand moving between her labia, and somehow he triggered her clitoris so that she yelped and tried to move away from the hand; she always had that preliminary jet of fear, the fear that she would die if brought to climax; but the hand stroked the now wet and throbbing clitoris, the mouth sucked at her breasts, she was mercilessly pinned by this man's weight, her legs spread, vulnerable, first moving to avoid the deeper fierce penetration of his cock; then, when he moved inside her with a kind of demand she recognized, wanted, dreaded, she turned her face away from him, then turned back to meet his mouth, struggled to envelop him, wrapping her legs around him, wanting to lock him forever in that precise place that sent long bursts of heat and delicious agonies along her nerves and muscles; and she heard herself making sounds in the back of her throat, felt the first not-to-be-denied shudders of climax; the thrusts of pain-pleasure began deep in her body, the flesh on her belly and breasts goosebumped, the tiny hairs on her skin stood straight up, chilling her, tickling her, and she gripped him with her thighs, heard herself cry and laugh, drummed his back with her heels and let it happen to her over and over again.

At last she began to falter, the clenchings of pleasure lightened, she wanted to rest, to stop. Her legs began to ache, the muscles of her thighs went slack, then cramped for a moment. She felt him still watching her; he brushed sweat from her eyebrows, the tempo changed: he bucked up inside her, he touched her body in a different way, thumbing her clitoris even as he moved inside her, then drawing thumb around her anus in a rub that sent new thrusts of heat and desire through her; he seemed, almost, to sit back on his heels to watch her, lifting her pelvis so that her knees seemed about to hit her ears. And then he buried his face in her neck, thrusting hard and groaning, and she felt his orgasm, the tattooing of sperm, the quick hard jerks of his cock knocking at the inside of her body.

Then he relaxed and lay on top of her for a moment, kissing her eyelids, cupping her face and smiling into her eyes. He eased over to lie beside her and grinned. "Cigarette?"

They laughed and looked around for cigarettes. "Hold still," he said. "I found some." He lighted two and gave one to her.

"Ah, God. The best." She snuggled beside him and watched the cigarette smoke drift over his chin. She reached around behind herself, found the sheet and pulled it up over them. "Warm enough?"

"Mm. You?" He slid an arm under her shoulders and smoked over her ear, blowing into it, then kissing it.

"We forgot about the coffee," she remembered. "Are you hungry?"

"Carnivorous! But coffee will be fine."

"I'm hungry. I'll make something." She got out of bed, pulled on her robe, and went to the kitchen.

"You wouldn't, by any chance, have a robe or something for me?" he called after her.

"Oh. Of course." She took Earl's robe out of the linen closet. "I do have one." She handed it to Ben and went on to the kitchen to raid the refrigerator. "Omelet?" she asked. "I have eggs, cheese, English muffins, some Canadian bacon that looks okay."

"All of it. I'll toast the muffins. Do you have ice cream? I'll make milk shakes."

"Milk shakes?"

"You have to have a milk shake after sex. That's protein. You don't want to be a burned-out case and good for nothing."

"Don't you get fat?"

"No. You burn up a lot of calories in bed."

"The wonders of medical research! There's chocolate and a dab of vanilla in the freezer compartment." She held up the small electric mixer. "Will this work for the milk shakes?"

"Yes. We just want to soften the ice cream so we can drink it. You wouldn't have cream?"

"No. But I'll put that on my list."

And she had. The next morning, a Saturday, she'd made a list, finishing with "bathrobe for Ben." Because she felt the old fantasies of Earl still present in his old blue robe. And when she hung the tobacco-brown velour robe in her closet, moving the old blue one to the back, she could hear Zulu saying: "You'd better settle down one of these days or accept the fact that you could open a shop: used robes . . . used you." But Zulu was not there to roll her eyes at Leah. Only Psi, who came tumbling down from the shelf above the clothes rod, dragging sweaters, plastic bags, scarves, mittens, woolen socks, glaring at her for waking him.

And Ben, what had he done that day, that Saturday evening? He had told her, kissing her forehead: "I have something I have to do tonight. But I'll call you, okay?"

She, too replete with pleasure to do more than purr, had smiled, and kissed him.

Their courtship—if that was what it was; and Leah then, Leah now, sitting in the Pinto with two dozen roses, didn't know if that was what it was. Or friendship. Or moods and sulks, unexpected hostilities and dislikes. She ground the Pinto into first gear, stamping hard on the accelerator. What is it with him, with us? she wondered. We can be happy for a matter of days sometimes. He calls, we go somewhere together, even play bridge with some of his doctor mates and their wives, go to dinner, go to his place or mine, go to bed. We did get into that pattern after the first time he came back from California. And I'd be browsing, grazing along the peacefulness of it, the calmness of browsing along the silence, nibbling here and there at his chin, at his lips, touching him on the back, almost in a doze of delight, and then I'd look into his eyes and there he is suddenly disliking me, suddenly I am intruding upon him.

And he has no sense of humor! Dammit, I hate that in a man. He doesn't laugh with me, at me. And God forbid I should ever smile at him about him. I don't ask that we become a nightclub act. But dammit, a laugh, a joke here and there along the way, what would it hurt? But, then I say to myself: Look at his good qualities, how kind and caring he is, how solid he is at the center, what a rock he is of . . . maybe stoicism, but calm, strong. So he is a little more Heathcliff than I had thought. More Rochester with the glooms, the unexplained sulks. Maybe it's a good balance, me with my overload of exuberance and liquids. I knew, there in my deeps, that if I stopped equivocating I'd be tipped into excesses, extravagances. So, perhaps it is a good balance. I'll gabble and chuckle for the two of us and keep my distance. We are best at being friends, I think. He was right to limit to that. And he need never know that I am lurking here underwater, weaving designs with seaweed. For that is what I am doing, the warp and woof of my dreams, I weave with green water-weeds. They are tenuous yet tough, as gritty as my sensibilities, and as contradictory as my common sense, my sense of disaster's cutting edge.

But again, looking at the roses, waiting for the light to change, she thought: I admit it. I am in love with him. But what is it that I love? Once past the lust—and I am not yet past that—what will there be for me, for us? I have studied him from angles, tangents, head on, nose to nose, knee to knee, been in close juxtaposition, have gazed at him across the sudden ice of his glare, and what is it, precisely, that is beloved? What is it about him—what peculiar and dear quality about him—that keeps me here, keeps us here, delicately poised as we are, seemingly caught within the membrane of a tear, I know I cannot change him; he will not be my bonny laughing lover; he will be, I know, always there and I will be always here held at arm's length, caressed at the distance of a glare. And why do I stay, yearning over the distance at him, cutting my feet upon the ice? Do I have a morbid taste for pain? Or is it something more, something simple; of course, it is something mysterious and complete: he answers the me of me.

"And, of course," she muttered aloud, stamping on the accelerator when the light had changed to green. "Of course, it is best that we maintain the distance, the friendship. Closeness, more intimacy with swords, would probably kill me with delight."

When he came to her apartment that night, he brought a bottle of wine and a bottle of champagne. "Did you understand the roses?" he asked, putting the wine on ice.

"I thought they were lovely. See, I've got them flourishing in two vases." She hugged his arm as he stood in the middle of the living room, and smiled up at him.

"I want to have a talk, Leah." He put her away from him, took her hand, sat her on the couch, brought the wine and two glasses, poured the wine, and sat down across the fireplace from her. "I've been thinking about us," he said, smiling at her, smiling *approvingly* at her. "We get along well together, we're comfortable together. I care a great deal about you. You are attractive, beautiful at times. You deserve to be cared about. In fact, at times, it seems to me, capable and competent as you are, it seems to me that you need to be taken care of. You know, your impulsiveness, your occasional excesses." He was going to go on.

Leah swallowed some wine, listened to him, went deaf, heard him, went red from head to foot, began to tremble, wanted at first to hug him, then fought the impulse to throw the wineglass at him, to throw the roses at him, to throw the table and chairs at him.

He said, "I think we should be married."

She thought: I'm going to give myself whiplash with all this overreacting. Because now she was swinging wildly from one reaction: joy; to another: dismay. She could hear the sea creature wail: "Wha-at?" And she could hear it, "Yea!" She said, "I'm appalled." And wished she hadn't said that.

Because the warm look of approval disappeared. The eyes went from candlelight to obsidian.

"I'm appalled because I'm so surprised," she modified, she placated. "We were doing pretty well as friends, that kind of distance. You seem to need distance. And I could live with that." She bit her lip, annoyed with herself. "A closer intimacy wouldn't work. We are too different. I do crazy things and you don't find them in the least amusing or forgivable."

"Now you're bringing up old crap. I thought we'd agreed last Friday not to do that. You don't stick to agreements."

"Oh, Ben! You weren't amused or able to forgive that cocktail party thing. It wasn't old crap, it had happened the week before and you were still brooding about it."

"Look. I admit at the time I did not think it was funny for you to pour a daquiri into my jacket pocket because I was talking to what you called a sex limpet."

"Hmm."

"But, later, when I got to my place and thought about it, I did laugh."

"You did? But you breathed ice at me right up to the door here. And went home, directly home, still icy."

He did not warm now, either, but continued the obsidian look.

"There. You're doing exactly one of the things, one of the reasons I don't think marriage would work."

He raised an eyebrow.

"Disapproving of me," she explained. "Disliking me."

"I don't find a reason to like your behavior. Is this how you handle a marriage proposal? Digging up old quarrels. I don't find that charming."

"So how can you ask me to marry you when you find so much not to like, so much to disapprove of?"

"I told you that you deserve to be cared about. You are warm, somehow sturdy, I suppose." He looked at her, contemplated her.

"What are you thinking *now?*" she asked.

"I would like an answer."

She felt herself resolve. "I don't know you well enough. We don't know each other well enough. We are antagonists too much, and I don't always know why."

He sighed, shrugged, stood up. "I had thought the evening would end differently."

"You're not leaving?"

"I think it's best." He nodded to her and walked to the front closet for his coat.

"Oh, Ben! Don't be angry! I didn't mean to hurt you or rebuff you." She tried to hold his arm, but he put her away from him and took his coat from the hanger. "Can't we talk? You did take me by surprise. I'm no good with surprises." She could see anger and hurt in his eyes; anger won. "Ben, I didn't mean to trample on your feelings."

"No. I am going to my place. Or for a ride. I have to think about it all over again. To you I may seem to be a difficult person. But I am not, I assure you. I have not offered you anything I could not afford to give. I have not deceived you. I am a private person. I do like my, what you call it, distance. I had thought a marriage would be suitable, workable, between us. I would have respected *your* privacy. Your need for time alone." He had put his coat on and settled his scarf under the collar. "I'll call you in a few days. Perhaps I'll have thought it out again."

Remorsefully, prayerfully, she clasped her hands under her chin. "Oh, Ben, I am so sorry. I truly did not mean to hurt you."

He put one hand on the doorknob.

"Oh, God. Will you, anyway, come to the open house I'm having for my students? You said you'd like to meet them. It's informal, you know, and you could come in anytime and there wouldn't be any . . . tension, pressure."

"I'll see. Friday, is it?"

"Yes, the first day of vacation, before Christmas."

"All right." He opened the door, nodded to her, and left.

"Miss Knutinen?" Marc Wiesel said on the telephone a week later. "We got a tree, and if you don't have any other plans this afternoon and evening we could bring it over."

Leah sighed. "I don't have any plans at all. Come on over. I'll start a fire and put the hamburgers and potatoes on the ready."

Shortly after, a Christmas tree ascended the apartment-house stairway.

Miss Insalaco, piloting, came first, and the tree, propelled by the bang-footed students, careened through Leah's open apartment door and stopped in the center of her living room. "I brought mistletoe!" Miss Insalaco said. "I'll hang it up for you."

"Where's your tree stand?" DeWitt asked. "This tree is heavy."

"Here." Leah put the metal tree stand down and watched while DeWitt and Whitney maneuvered the tree upright and straight.

"Whoo!" Wiesel huffed. "It was a job getting it up the three flights. "How did you do it yourself last year?"

"I'm strong," Leah laughed, taking coats, gloves, scarves from them and putting things away in the closet. "I got the decorations out. Do you want to eat supper first or decorate?"

"I brought some wine and wassail stuff," DeWitt said. "I hope Linda brought it upstairs. Did you?"

"Yes." Miss Insalaco opened a large shopping bag and pulled out bottles of wines, brandies, cranberry juice, apples, cinnamon sticks. "Is this going to be enough?"

"For starters," Nicholson said. "Shall I start the wassail? Or the hamburger?"

"I'll do the wassail," Miss Insalaco said.

"You won't put enough foo-foo in it," DeWitt said.

"Then I'll start the decorating," Miss Insalaco said. "You want to help with the trims?" She looked hopefully at Freeman, who was silently unknotting the strings of lights and testing the bulbs.

"Yes. Do you have spare bulbs, Miss Knutinen?"

"I do. For once, I got my lists made early. I have extra bulbs, one whole extra new string of lights, new decoration hooks, a box of decorations to replace those that smashed last year. . . ." She paused to eye them all reproachfully. "You do remember helping to put the tree away and the consequences of trying to dribble a glass decoration?"

"That was not our fault," DeWitt protested. "You let Fish spike the punch."

Leah poked at the fire. "I've got the potatoes baking

already. I'll put the hamburgers on now. Who wants a salad?"

The tree decorating advanced through the evening; the hamburgers were broiled over the open fire, wassail made and drunk, salad tossed, the meal devoured, and the kitchen cleaned up. Then the candles were lighted and they settled on the floor in front of the fireplace to toast marshmallows.

Leah, watching the students, was grateful to them for their cheer, their prickliness, their toughness, their noise, their sass.

She saw Freeman glance at his watch.

"I hate to be first to leave," he said, standing up, avoiding Miss Insalaco's eyes. "But I've gotta get back early."

"Oh, I wish you'd stay," Leah said. "It's not ten!"

"You never said you were leaving early," Miss Insalaco said, uncrossing her legs, getting up.

"Yeah. Well, I gotta go now. I'll see you for open house, though. Thanks." Almost guiltily, it seemed to Leah, he grabbed his coat and rushed out the door.

Leah followed him, saw him dart down the stairway. When she returned to the fireplace she saw a flicker of complicity between Wiesel and DeWitt. Miss Insalaco, staring into the fire, was fighting tears. "Well, I'm sorry he had to leave," Leah said. "But that needn't spoil the rest of the evening."

"True. He gets into these moods," DeWitt said. "We share a suite with a guy who's a really good friend of his and he said Barry is moody a lot. You know, drives around a lot by himself. Goes out after hours and just drives. And gets into a mood for no reason. He just gets into them," DeWitt looked at Miss Insalaco. "It isn't anything to worry about."

The next night, the twenty-first of December, the party took on a life of its own, a pulse beat of candles, lights. DeWitt, Nicholson, Wiesel, and Miss Insalaco came early to help; they set the mood: tomfoolery, hijinks, swamping Leah with hugs and smacking kisses under the mistletoe. The other students from Dram Lit and Rem Eng and Eng 101 came singly or in gaggles, entering shyly, dropping scarves and gloves, munching on the candies, sandwiches, expanding in the warmth of the tree, the candles, the older students, the fireplace; even Psi did his host-cat dance and purred, rubbed ankles, finally sat regally on the fireplace mantel.

Zulu, arrived at the party, took one look at Wiesel and said to Leah: "I'll take a dozen of that to go!" She cornered him and offered him a view of her spectacular shoulders, leaving him gaga with wistful lust. She came back to Leah. "No wonder you like teaching!" She wore a purple knit thing that left her breasts more naked than clothed. A nipple peeped out.

Leah, nodding to the nipple, said, "Lady, if you're going to drown those pups, can I have the one with the pink nose?"

Zulu, tucking her breast back in, hitching the leopard spots around her hips, burning in the bush, bitchery, lechery lilting from her eyes, winked at Leah and launched herself again at Wiesel.

Miss Insalaco, the punch bowl in her hands, said: "Who's that?"

"One of my oldest friends. Is that in need of a refill? Here, let me." Leah took the bowl into the kitchen. "I've got the hard stuff in that big bowl. Don't let me confuse them."

"Have you talked to Barry today?" Miss Insalaco asked.

"No. He should be here somewhere."

"No. I knocked at his door and he didn't answer."

"Well, it's early yet. Don't worry about him."

"Um. Uh. Miss Knutinen, if he isn't here by ten, could I use your telephone to call him?"

"Of course." Leah carried the refilled punch bowl out to the living room.

Ben had come in and stood with his coat on, talking to Zulu. He nodded to Leah, but continued to talk to Zulu. Zulu, turning around, saw Leah and waved to her. And took a firmer grip on Wiesel, who blushed visibly and stammered something.

"Hello, Ben. I'm glad you're here," Leah said.

He kissed her on the cheek. "I can't stay long."

"Would you have time for a cup of wassail? Or punch?" Leah stood on one foot, then the other, felt her breasts prickle and the nipples rise just at being near him.

"Would you like to be introduced to some of my students?"

"I know Mr. Wiesel here. Zulu introduced us."

"Then this is Linda Insalaco. Doctor Calloway." Leah, Ben's hand on her elbow, his breath on the nape of her neck, walked on jellied knees among the bunches of students, singling out a face here and there for Ben to smile at. He touched the back of her knees with his once; she was horribly aware of him. She glanced at him. He is conscious of what he is doing! she thought. He knows what he's doing to me. He had placed a hand on the small of her back; the heat of the hand chased chills up her spine and into her scalp and then down to the undersides of her breasts.

She moved away from the hand. She was able to glance at his face. He avoided her eyes. She thought: A tease. And no smile. The cheer of the party left her. She felt her shoulders slump, felt her face go slack. Then: The hell with him. This is my party!

She drank a glassful of the vodka punch, lit a cigarette, and turned to smile at Miss Insalaco, who was tugging at her sleeve. "What? Are we out of something? Why don't you stop the waitress business and let me do it? Come on, have a cup of wassail, stand under the mistletoe and see what happens."

"Miss Knutinen, it isn't that. It's almost ten."

"Leah, I'll be leaving now." Ben smiled at Linda Insalaco. "It's a good party."

"So early? You're the early Doctor Calloway. And we are wondering about the late Mr. Freeman. Excuse me, Linda, I'll call Barry. Ben, I'm sorry you want to leave so early." She could not offer her hand to him. Nor her cheek for the obligatory kiss. She went ahead of him to the apartment door, opened it, held it between them, a shield, a barrier. "Good-byé, Ben."

"Will I see you over the holidays?"

"If you choose to."

"We have a lot to talk about."

All her tides were running in his direction; she could feel herself being dragged along sea bottom and up onto the rocks. She shook her head, laughing at herself. "Oh, Ben. Call me when you want to. I'll be here." She closed the door, leaned on it for a moment, then turned back to the party and Miss Insalaco. "Yes. I'll call him right now." She went to the telephone, dialed. "No answer." She put the telephone back into its cradle. "He might be on his way here."

Mr. Fish, of the Dram Lit course, came up to them. "Linda, we're starting some dancing. Would you dance with me?"

Leah gently shoved Miss Insalaco at Mr. Fish. "Go on. Barry will turn up eventually. Have some fun yourself, for heaven's sake!" She glanced at her wrist watch. I think I'll call him again, she thought. She made sure Miss Insalaco was dancing, then she dialed.

"Hullo." It was Barry's voice. But muffled.

"Barry? This is Leah Knutinen. Some of your friends are here waiting for you at the party."

"I have no friends." And he hung up.

Exasperated, Leah put the telephone down. She poured herself a glass of white wine and lit a cigarette. Automatically, wineglass in hand, she moved around the living room, pausing to smile and nod at a student, handing around the trays of candies, nuts, sandwiches, cookies, little cakes, fruitcake, plum pudding and hard sauce, the relish trays with celery, cauliflower, broccoli, pickles, olives, cheese things on toothpicks, and all the time she kept hearing, "I have no friends." And that odd muffled voice.

"Listen, Leah," Zulu said. "The party is gonna go beddy-bye soon. I think I'll be on my way while I can do it without hauling that gorgeous boy with me. It's been a nice party, but let me know when you're ready for adults."

"Oh, Zulu. Didn't you like it at all?"

"Of course, I did. But I'm gonna leave now." She had her coat over her shoulders. "Kiss me." She smacked Leah on the cheek. "I'll call you in a day or so."

Zulu's departure was like a tear in a grain sack: the students began to leave in dribbles and spurts, hugged Leah, dropped gloves, scarves, stumbled over each other at the door, flowed down the stairway, shushed each other, called up to Leah, waved, smiled, subsided finally as the downstairs door slammed.

The last to leave was Miss Insalaco. Mr. Fish had taken her by the hand with an air of proprietorship, had led her out the lobby door. She had looked up at Leah and shrugged, blushing.

The candles snuffed, the tree lights out, Leah began clearing away the debris. Pensively, she emptied ashtrays, gathered plastic cups, dumped napkins and paper plates into the trash can. "Oh, damn," she muttered. "That boy is—I'll call him one more time just to ease *my* mind."

The telephone rang nine times before he answered. And she *knew*. "What is wrong, Barry? Would you like to come over here for coffee?"

"No." But he didn't hang up. She could hear him breathing, hear something under the breathing that frightened her.

"What *is* it?" she said. "Tell me. Let me help."

"It's too late. You can't help." Silence. Then, "He dosen't care! You can't help." And he hung up.

Leah grabbed her car keys and handbag, threw her coat over her shoulder, and bolted out the door.

When she opened the door to his dormitory suite after pounding on it and getting no response, she had to close her eyes for a moment. Blood spattered the beige carpet, the ivory walls were charted in blood, the door to the bedroom was tracked with blood. Leah followed the blood trail into the bedroom, cringing with each step, knees melting with horror.

"Barry," she called. The bedroom was dark. She touched the wall switch.

Barry sat propped against the headboard of the bed, his legs over the side. He seemed to be watching Leah with tired eyes while he nursed his left arm to his chest.

"Barry!" She felt her own clammy hands wringing each other. Then she was touching him, shaking him, trying to restore light to those glazed, lightless eyes. "Barry!" She looked for the wound and found his left forearm opened from elbow to wrist. Sickened, she looked around, stripped a pillow of its case, which she tied roughly, angrily, around his arm. She heard herself swearing at him, crying at him, heard him finally murmur something in response.

"You have to go to a doctor!" she said. "Is this the *one* cut?" He seemed to have bled too much, she thought, for one wound.

"My leg." He had opened a blood vessel, a vein, in his

left ankle. The carpet under his feet was slick, almost slimy, with blood.

Leah found a pair of scissors in the bedside table drawer and slashed another pillowcase. She tied his ankle as best she could, using a washcloth to pad the wound.

Breathlessly, seeing spots before her eyes, Leah scrambled for the telephone.

"No!" Barry said. "I won't go to the student health service! They'd call my folks. I'll finish the job, I swear, if you make me go there!"

"You have to have a doctor. Oh, God, let me think." She couldn't remember Ben's telephone number for a moment, but then she dialed it. Just as she was about to wail with hopelessness, Ben answered. "Ben? Leah. Listen, please, could you help me? My student, Barry, has cut his arm and ankle severely. Please, could you take care of him?"

"Why can't you take him to the student health service?" Ben asked, reasonably. "They take care of students there twenty-four hours a day."

"He won't go there. He says he'll kill himself if I force him to go there. Please, Ben."

"Where are you now?"

"I'm on campus. But I don't think he should stay here. Could I bring him to your place? Your hospital?"

"No! I won't go to any hospital. I'll get out of here on my own." Barry was standing up, sliding a little on the bloodied carpet.

"Oh, sit down. Ben, I'll bring him to my place. Could you meet us there?"

"I do not approve, Leah. You are taking on too much responsibility. No one will thank you." Ben sighed. "All right. I'll be over in a minute."

Leah let the telephone fall and turned to Barry, who had sat back on the bed. "Now. Where's your coat? You just sit still until we're ready to go. I'll help you downstairs to my car. Is there something I can put on your feet? Not those high boots." She hunted under the bed and in the closet, found a pair of sneakers and a pair of socks, which she pulled over the bound ankle. She tied the sneakers, noticing that when she touched him, Barry's skin was clammy and cold. She found his bathrobe, wrapped him in that, tying the cord around his injured arm to support it.

She buttoned his heavy winter coat over the robe and lifted the hood up over his head. "Now, you lean on me. Let me take most of the weight and we'll just skedaddle back to my place so Ben can sew you up."

Ben was waiting for them in front of Leah's building. He handed Leah his case and carried Barry up the stairway to her apartment.

"What can I do?" Leah asked, setting Ben's case on the low table in the living room.

"Boil some water." Ben helped Barry to unwrap and sat him on the couch. "And bring out a couple of sheets and towels. No reason to mess up your place too."

Leah obeyed. She spread a sheet on the couch, tucking it under Barry. "The towels are next to your case. Why do doctors want boiling water? Even nowadays when you have better means of sterilizing things."

Ben glanced at her and laughed. "You're babbling. I want some coffee. And a pot of it will do this young man a lot of good, too." He made a face when he peeled the pillowcase away from Barry's arm. He looked at the wound, and then he looked appraisingly at Barry's face. "You must really be hurting to do this to yourself." He reached for his case, opened it, and without looking selected a vial and a hypodermic. "Leah, I think you'd be better off in the kitchen with the coffee. And make us all some milk shakes. With eggs in 'em." He glanced at her. "Are you all right?"

"I'm fine!" Leah backed away, went to the kitchen, and sat down until the whirling spots disappeared. She made the coffee, strong. Then she took out the ice cream and made the milk shakes. She sat down again and waited for Ben to call her into the living room. She could hear him talking to Barry, a steady monologue, no questions, a kind of patter that made even Leah, sitting on edge in the kitchen, slacken and relax. Who'd have thought he has so many words in him, she mused. She found herself smoking one cigarette while another fumed in the ashtray at her fingertips.

Finally Ben came into the kitchen. He washed his hands at the kitchen sink and dried them with a paper towel. "I think he'll be all right now. Don't worry about the coffee. He's in shock right now. I found a blanket and put that over him. Let him sleep as long as he can. Now."

He sat down across the kitchen table and accepted the coffee she poured for him. "Thanks. Now, what you must do tomorrow morning is call one of his friends or roommates and tell them that he hurt himself accidentally and that he is seeing a private doctor. And that he'll be back for classes after the holidays. I don't know what he'll tell his parents, but that's his problem. I don't see you bearing any kind of legal blame for this if he screws himself up anymore."

"He won't. He just is terribly hurt about something."

"Mm." Ben sipped his coffee thoughtfully. "You go too far, Leah, with this mothering business."

"I don't mother my students."

"Perhaps not. Is that my milk shake?" He took the large glass of milk shake and dolloped some of it into his coffee. "I'll finish this and then I've got to go. I think he'll be all right tonight. I'll come by tomorrow around lunchtime to look at him. If you want my advice, and I think you do, let him stay overnight, maybe two nights. Then I can put a final dressing on him and he can go back to campus. I'll take the stitches out within the week. And that's that." He looked at her, assessing her. "I'm telling you that you have done all you can for the kid. And you should let go now. But, on the other hand, I know you. Whatever brought him to this point is his problem. I seriously doubt that *you* can help him. Or if he even wants, really, your help."

She didn't know what he was talking about at first. Then: "Oh. You think he should see a psychiatrist?"

Something closed behind Ben's eyes. He said, "I don't know if he wants a psychiatrist. But it is *his* problem."

Leah nodded. "Okay. I hear you. I won't delve. But I do thank you for helping. You should be in general practice. You're so calming. Besides knowing exactly what to do, you were able to calm him just by talking to him."

"Thank you. Well, time." He stood up, put the coffee cup and milk shake glass into the sink, kissed her forehead, and went to the living room.

Leah, following him, watched him touch Barry's forehead for a moment and listen to his breathing; then Ben nodded, picked up his coat and case. "I'll be back tomorrow." He spoke softly. "You get some rest too." He smiled at her and left before she could say anything more.

She left one lamp glowing. "If he wakes during the night he'll know where he is," she whispered to Psi, who rolled, belly up, on Leah's bed. She turned the bedroom light off, climbed into the bed, pushing Psi over to his side, and listened for Barry. Don't be dumb, she scolded herself. He's too tired and worn to do anything more to himself. Still thinking that, she dozed off, but she wakened at intervals during the night to listen.

"I guess I owe you an explanation," Barry said. He was sitting up on the couch, sipping the coffee Leah had made.

"No, you don't. Can I scramble some eggs? Toast?"

"No, thanks. I don't know if I'm hungry or not." He looked wobbly, vulnerable, tired, and frightened.

Watching him, Leah thought: He looks skinned out. His eyelids are the same blue as skim milk and he blinks too much. She made a cup of hot milk and set that down. "Drink this, I think you need it."

"You know what I'd really like? Soggy cornflakes."

"Like you get at home, right? I don't have cornflakes, but will Wheaties do it for you?"

He nodded. He followed her to the kitchen and sat, hard, on a kitchen chair. "I am sorry for causing you all this trouble."

"Don't worry about it." She poured milk over the Wheaties. "You judge for yourself when they're soggy enough."

"Thanks." He scooped four teaspoons of sugar over the cereal.

They sat in silence for a few minutes, Barry stirring his cereal, Leah sipping coffee, Psi washing his paws on the kitchen counter. Psi, whiskers out to the sides, jumped from the counter to the table and, staring Barry in the eye, helped himself to the milk in Barry's cereal.

Barry, startled, laughed. "Uh. No, let him have some. It's the least I can do."

"Stop flagellating yourself. You can't go on with that. Eat your breakfast and go back to sleep."

But they were edgy with each other. The unsaid words made a sensible pressure in the room.

Barry ate his cereal. Then: "I'd like to talk about it. I feel better now and . . . could you tell about me before?"

"I thought you were disturbed about something. The story about going home and being wrapped in a plastic garbage bag."

"No. That I'm gay."

"Oh."

Barry was fighting tears so hard that Leah's eyes teared in sympathy. "And the . . . other person . . . well, he shits on me all the time. I walk around like I'm stuck in a revolving door, I can see other people, but there's always glass between us. But I could touch him. Feel him." Tears spilled down his face. "Oh, it was always difficult. He'd only see me after he'd seen this other person he's seeing. A girl. But then he started not keeping our times together. I'd wait around and he wouldn't even call. Or he'd call up and want to see me immediately. And then he just stopped." Barry took a paper napkin from the holder and blew his nose. "It's . . . I don't know. I wanted to come out of the closet. And I don't know *how* I'd tell my parents. But I thought I'd be open here at school and that would be the first step. I'd get strong about myself here and then I could go home and somehow get it out in the open with my folks. But Donald, he doesn't want to. He's got this girl, too, and she'd shit if she knew about us." He smiled, a thin bitter smile. "As it is, I'm being shitted on, because he dumps me whenever she's around and then he comes into my room at night and insists on sex no matter how I feel about it. And then I feel like a whore when he won't stay the night."

Leah watched him pick at the soggy cereal. "I think you'd better get back to sleeping," she said.

"Penguins, huh?"

Baffled, she looked at him. "Penguins?"

"The story about the little girl. One day a guy came to lecture with slides about penguins. And he lectured and showed slides for over an hour. After he was done he looked around and wanted comments. He looked at the little girl and asked what she thought. And she said, 'I think I learned more about penguins than I wanted to know.'" Barry cocked an eyebrow. "Penguins?"

"No. Of course not. But I do think you should hobble back to your bed and at least nap."

" 'Kay. Thanks. Did he say when I could shower or anything?"

"He'll be back today and you can ask him. I'll get some pajamas out and he'll probably let you wash up tonight." Leah watched him move carefully back to the couch, helped tuck him in. "I'll turn on the tree lights. Would you like a fire?"

"Yes, thanks. It's really nice of you."

Leah puttered around the apartment, lighting the fire, washing dishes, glancing at Barry from time to time, watching him slide into a doze. How terrible love is when it costs that much, she thought. She went back to the kitchen and began making a grocery list.

The buzzer sounded once. Leah sped to the door to keep the buzzer quiet. It was Ben.

"Sh-sh," Leah whispered. "He's just dozing off."

Ben nodded and stepped inside. He followed her to the kitchen and closed the door. "How's he been?"

"He slept pretty well. And he just ate some cereal." Leah lifted the coffeepot. "Want some?"

"No, thanks. Did he talk at all?"

"Yes, a little. Oh, Ben, he's in terrible pain!"

"I saw that. He'll get through it."

"Do you want to wake him up?"

"No, not yet." Ben looked at Leah with an intensity that caught her off guard, surprised her. "Leah. I think we should get married."

She blinked at him. Her whole head went empty.

"We could do it. It's the twenty-second now. If we get our blood tests done at my hospital they'd rush them through for me. And the license could be done today. We could be married five days from now. And go somewhere before you have to be back for the beginning of the next semester. It's intersession. Finals are over. You have a week off."

She heard his words from underwater; they were like stones being dropped, falling through the water to the sea bottom where she drifted and gazed upward at him, at the light behind him.

Then he took her hand, drew her to him, seemed to draw her through her bemused silence, through the watery light, to him. He kissed the palm of her hand, the soft sensitive pads of her fingers.

She must have said something, she could feel the words press against the inside of her mouth, feel the sibilants whisper against the back of her teeth. But what had she said? "Yes." She couldn't hear herself. She couldn't hear what he said in response, could only see the flash of despair in his eyes before he closed them and kissed her. He held her close, almost too tightly, she could feel something shake inside him—was he laughing? Or, no, he was smothering a kind of grief. But then he put her gently away from himself, kissed her cheek, and led her out of the kitchen.

"How're you feeling?" he asked Barry. "Can we leave you alone for about an hour or so?"

"Um, yes. I'm fine. Kind of dozing and resting." Barry yawned and rubbed his eyes. "I can't seem to get any energy going."

"That's all to the good. Leah and I have some things to do downtown. I'll bring her back and check on you this afternoon." Ben smiled at Barry, then took Leah's coat from the closet. "Here. My car is just in front." He helped Leah with her coat. "Take your handbag. You'll need some identification."

Barry watched them, his eyes brightening with interest, but he said nothing.

"We'll be back in a bit." Ben led Leah out of the apartment.

The cold air made Leah blink, drew her up from the bemused silence. "But, Ben, we have a lot of things we never talked about! Where we'll live? Children. You do want children? I think we should *not* rush into this." But the look he gave her sent her back to silence. She allowed him to place her inside the car, hitch the seat belt around her hips, tuck her coat around her knees. She felt . . . what? She didn't know. She looked at him from under her eyelashes. "Ben," she said. "We must talk."

"Do you not love me?"

"It's not that."

He had turned the ignition key and the motor hummed a rich multicylinder sound. "I don't intend to force you into anything, Leah. But it is simple. If you love me, as you've said, then I think we should marry. Otherwise, not." He took his hands from the steering wheel and folded them over his lap. "I don't think you want to complicate it," he added. "We are adults. Certainly, we are both past the youthful unrealities of romance and yearnings, are we not? We know each other at certain levels of honesty that perhaps other people do not attain. You, I assume—know what I am and what I offer you in marriage. I also know you, and you must know that you are the only woman I could ever love. He lighted a cigarette and offered it to her, taking a second for himself. He touched her face gently with his right hand. "I understand, of course, second thoughts, this panic of indecision. I confess, I have had them too. But I would like to share a life with you. I think you love me and I find great peace and content in that, as I hope you do."

She felt his words calming the surfaces of her mind; he was right, of course, she thought. She did love him. And as he spoke she could see through his eyes the distances of his thoughts, of peace, of reasoned calm, of a life that moved in patterns measured out almost musically. She nodded to herself, to him. "Yes," she said. "I think so."

They were married two days after Christmas at five-thirty in the evening. Barry, the black stitches out of his arm but wearing an Ace bandage on his left ankle, insisted that he be allowed to serve as best man. "Either that or maid of honor," he whispered to Leah. "I feel a definite responsibility about this marriage. I was there when it happened." And he was, in fact, helpful. He surprised Leah by knowing a chaplain on campus who would perform the ceremony, and he arranged for Leah's flowers. "I know. Violets!" he grinned at her. "Let me exercise my imagination and money. If I don't make it as a doctor I intend to open a flower shop in Miami or Saint Pete." He had recovered his vitality in what, to Leah, seemed an amazingly short time. So the flowers were violets; Leah was almost afraid to touch them, fearing to crush them: her panic had returned on the wedding morning. Barry came to fetch her, wearing a tweed jacket, jeans, and buckskin sneakers. "I don't have regular pants," he apologized.

"You look fine. Come in, I'm having trouble with my hair. With my hands!" She could not get her topknot to stay put. It slid off to one side or the other, the pins drove straight to her brain. She had already broken a bra strap and pinned it, had had to sit with her head between her knees for the toppling dizziness that swept over her, had thrown up her morning tea, and walked on jellied knees.

"I'll stay with Psi," Barry reminded her, watching her poke three more hairpins into the knot atop her head. "You won't have time for a long honeymoon, will you?"

"No. We'll stay in town. He's on call until New Year's." But that's all right. Ben says we'll go somewhere for spring break. Do you know what his big surprise is? He's been smug and superior all week."

"He's marrying you. Isn't that enough?"

Leah thanked him with a smile. "No, I don't think that's it. Well, I'll find out when he thinks I should. There. Let's go."

The flowers came out of their box, the chapel door did open. The chaplain shook Leah's hand and smiled. Leah went deaf, walked down the aisle with Barry muttering or humming something in her ear. She let Ben take her hand, nodded to him, hoped she smiled at him. She was sinking under the waterfall of words around her, the sea creature dragged her down past levels of light and pressure so that she was sealed in the blue deeps of silence.

Eight of Cups

THE Eight of Cups: the home and extravagance; lavish spending. Ben had bought a house. That was his surprise. And he led Leah, the bride, the mute, Leah the paddler of air; Leah out of water was led through the front door of this house to totter through the empty echoing rooms, through the endless echoing rooms. A chandelier dripped ice from the dining-room ceiling; the naked windows opened to snowscaped lawn and faced the white echoing rooms: There is nothing but white inside and out, Leah thought. The house was antiseptic, unnaturally clean. Perfectly clean. Leah longed for one fingerprint on the white high gloss paint, some homely dust! She would have cherished a cobweb. But even the fireplaces had been sucked barren of ashes, there was no comfort there.

She looked at Ben and saw his fantasies dance ahead of them through the rooms, laying carpets, hanging the windows with fabulous draperies, placing furniture. She could see through Ben's eyes the fireplace, a leap of flames, a chuckle of warmth. The dining-room table, damasked, snowy, iced with silver. The chandelier glittering to conversation. And she, Leah, was touched by Ben's eye; he placed her before the fireplace, she could feel the dangle of an earring; or he fitted her into the space at the head of the table, she felt her hair smooth unnaturally into a helmet; then she saw Ben's eye decorate her, she was the chandelier, twittering and alight at the ceiling; she floated, was mounted over the fireplace, or sat before the fireplace in perfect unnatural elegance.

"What do you think?" Ben asked her, his fantasy billowing around them thick as fog.

"I hardly know what to say. It's incredible."

"I did buy one piece of furniture," he said, taking her arm.

A bed fit for a king, Leah thought, looking through the bedroom door. A bed that could bed an entire court! A whole country of bed, she thought, and sat on the edge. She lay back and made angel wings on the snow-white spread. She looked up at Ben. He had not joined her, but stood in the bedroom doorway. "What?" she asked. She wondered if she should have waited for an invitation. But then he smiled and came to lie down beside her, carefully taking off his shoes, taking her shoes, letting his hands warm the soles of her feet, then grasping her ankles, stroking her calves, the inside of her thighs. And with that attentive, commanding look, he moved his hands under her clothes, cupping her breasts so that they grew heavy with heat, solid as fruit, ripe and painful under his sucking mouth; and his hands moved to stroke her body into a sullen and demanding heat, his thumb and forefinger circling her vagina, stroking, insisting that she open until she did open, gasping with a painful need for him; it was pain he gave her, pain because she wanted him and pain because he held himself away from her, rubbing the head of his cock against her, teasing her so that she struggled to grasp him, always his mouth and hands and body driving her further and further in pain and desire until she moaned; and then slowly, deliberately, he entered her, drove into her, thrusting himself through the bruised lips of her vagina to the painful desirous center and then holding her in thrall while he deliciously, deliberately murdered her.

They fell apart. Leah, nursing her bruised mouth, felt tender, felt ravaged, felt wonderful; Ben, his mouth still at her breast, reached around for cigarettes and held them out to Leah. She took two and lighted them. She began to get up, but Ben held her back, leaned his weight on her, imprisoned her with his body, and exhaled smoke over her head. "Comfortable?" he asked.

"Mm, yes. But won't we get cold? Wouldn't you like the sheet or something?"

"In a minute. Just lie here." He moved so that he was leaning on her and on an elbow, one arm under her shoulders. Idly he stroked her body, tracing the outline of her nipples, the faint blue of a vein on one breast, a mole under the other, the whisper of belly hairs, the scrub of pubic hair, the place he had so recently bruised; his stroking hand slipped into her vagina, fingering, exploring, exciting, so that Leah's body reluctantly warmed and responded. He put his cigarette out, took Leah's from her and put that out, put the ashtray down on the floor, and pulled the pillows out from under Leah's head.

"Oh, Ben, I don't know . . ." she began, but he kissed her and slid between her legs, his cock heavy and warm, demanding, thrusting against her buttocks, thrusting into her vagina; his hands cupped her buttocks and raised her, turned her over, his cock slipping out so that she groaned and reached for it, but he kept it from her, thrust it between her buttocks, then into her vagina, then up along her belly; his hands were hard upon her body, he moved her to his will, his cock first on her belly, then at her lips, then his lips on hers and the hot searching cock sending the small shots of pain, the pain of wanting him, up from her burning cunt. He would not enter her, but used his cock as a toy, as a tease, as a device to send those burning fuses of pain and desire up along her body, so that her breasts ached and tingled, became unbearably tender to the touch, and yet she wanted his touch, wanted the harshness of his sucking mouth, her voice surprising her now with small sharp cries, and yet he would not enter her, but stroked her clitoris with that cock, with his fingers, with his tongue, and again with the glowing red knob of cock, and wrapped his body around her, imprisoning her, turning her around under him, controlling her and driving her, caressing her beyond her own body, so that there was no such thing as body but only this world of sensation and her own final cries as she came and came, the orgasms rocking her, convulsing her, the tiny hairs on her body standing up in showers of electricity as her skin blushed in patches, as her very pores climaxed, and he drove that cock into her, making her weep and cling to him as she died, was drowned, and then her muscles lax, her body falling away from him, falling onto the white rumpled spread, beached. And he, thrusting once more, groaned, sobbed, shuddered with his own coming, and then he, too, was beached upon the whispering sheets, the tangled bedclothes.

It was Psi, the cat, who made the house possible for Leah. She brought him to the house in his carrying case and let him out in the living room. He eyed her once, rubbed against her boots, and stalked across the bare floors to disappear around a corner. He was invisible for a day and a half, his voice coming through the walls. "Mm-mow! Mow!" she heard him in the wall of her workroom, saw the glare of his blue eye through the grid in the air vent. She heard him grumble in the wall that separated the kitchen from the laundry room; she heard him in the master bedroom wall and caught the blue flash of eye again in Ben's study wall.

"He can't get hurt, can he?" Ben asked.

"I don't think so. He's just investigating."

They had eaten supper at the kitchen counter, where Leah was unpacking the stainless-steel flatware and sorting through their joint pots and pans. "He'll come out when he's ready. But he thinks he establishes territorial rights this way."

"I see." Ben took his plate and coffee cup to the kitchen sink, where he rinsed them. "I'll be off now," he said setting the dishes in the drainer.

"Again? I think you're working too hard. You spend too much time on those slides."

"No, it's that we have some stains coming up that I want to look at. I have a consultation tomorrow morning early. A young girl came in a week ago with what looked like a pregnancy. But she swore she wasn't. And her doctor said she was still intacta, so they brought her in for tests. I'll know tonight if it's carcinoma." He sighed. "It will be hell if she does have cancer. Her parents are nice and she's just fourteen. She's barely out of training bras."

"Oh, God."

"Yes. I'm not going to think about it until I see the slides. Don't wait up. I'll hang around until the slides come up. And then I have the report to write." He kissed her forehead and went out the back door.

She watched his car move out of the garage and around the curved driveway to the street. Absently, she washed her own dishes and the pots and pans and made tea. Then she took the tea and cigarettes into her workroom, the only room besides the bedroom that, in her opinion, was habitable. She got a fire going in the small fireplace and sat on her Icelandic daybed, feet up, cuddling into her old raggedy bathrobe. The radio played Sibelius's *Swan of Tuonela*; the fire stuttered; the house, still a stranger, seemed to settle into a watching silence.

The telephone rang. Zulu. "Hi! Are you gonna be home? Why don't I come over and have a housewarming drink? I'll bring the drink."

Leah laughed. "Okay. I'll put a light in the window." She put the telephone down and went into the living room, where she got a fire going, arranged her old corduroy hassock and some cushions on the floor, and made a picnic on the hearth.

"Not only happy homemaking, but happy birthday to us!" Zulu barked, hugging Leah, shaking snow from her coat, kicking her boots off. "This is going to be an eventful year for us. Pisceans have been in mud for a while. Now the sun is entering Pisces and we're gonna see some big times, big changes, unexpected happenings. Although, you got going early with this getting married right under my nose and not telling me and now this house. What is it? A modest mansion?" She strode around the living room in her stockinged feet, her hair flaring in the firelight, her eyes snapping with interest and curiosity. "I didn't think, really, you'd marry the ice man. But . . . hell, I want you to be happy, old girl. Are you?" She didn't wait for an answer. "Gawd, you need furniture and drapes and stuff!" She squinted her eyes. "Let's see, you must let my Bruce help you. He did my place and you gotta admit it's class!"

Leah shook her head, remembering Zulu's black furniture, the black draperies, the stainless steel, the glass, the stage lighting in the bedroom. "Um, I'll do it in stages. You know, slowly. We already have the bed. And Ben's study is almost furnished. And my workroom. So it's only the big rooms and draperies we need."

"But Jaysus! All the white. You could perform surgery right here. Listen, at least get some colors. Here's the champagne anyhow, let's have a glass for the house and then a glass for us and then a glass for any reason you care to name." Zulu thumbed the cork from the champagne bottle, managing to spill nearly one third of the wine on the floor.

Leah rushed to find a cloth, wiped the spilt wine, and then laughed. "Do you want to see the rest of the house?"

She suddenly felt close to Zulu, grateful for the noise, the color, the life of her.

"Yeah, let's have a tour." Zulu carried the champagne bottle and followed Leah through the house, remarking: "God, it's empty. You gotta get some stuff in here."

Then, back in the living room, Psi came out of somewhere, his whiskers and ears wreathed with cobwebs. He walked partway across the living room floor and then fell over on his side, washed his forepaws vigorously, purring, and smiled at Leah.

"Where's he been?" Zulu asked, watching the cat. "In all this white he managed to find some dirt and dust."

"Underground. Under the floors, under the white." Leah heard herself say that and asked: "How fast do I get drunk on champagne? Is this just champagne?"

"Yah. But you probably lost your head for drinking since I saw you last. Come on, let's see the house and I'll give you my helpful hints. You know," Zulu continued, talking as she followed Leah into the dining room, "you could use some red draperies on gold or brass rods in here. And in that entryway you could put a tree." She poured more champagne. "I saw a great idea in one of Bruce's magazines. A house with a boulder in it. Well, it was part of a wall and it made the fireplace, but I loved it. I wish I could do that with my place."

"Um. Here's Ben's study. Isn't it nice? He brought those file cabinets over from his office."

"Yeah. Listen, will I get to see him tonight?"

"I hope so. He had to go over to the hospital for some work."

"Well, I can't stay late. I hate to admit it, but nowadays I have to get my sleep or I'm nothing."

It was eleven when Zulu left, and Ben had not yet come home. Leah, locking the front door behind Zulu, glanced at the dark street, then turned lights off as she moved through the house, bumping against Psi, who accosted her in the dark and bit her ankles. "Down!" She nudged him aside. She bathed and went to bed with a book and a glass of white wine, falling uneasily asleep with Psi knotted on her stomach.

"Sh-sh, go back to sleep," Ben whispered. He had turned off the bedside light and kissed Leah lightly on the forehead. "Talk to you tomorrow." And he turned his back to her.

She let herself fall back into the darkness, thinking she would see him in the morning.

But February had brought a nighttime blizzard, and when Leah's alarm rang she could see the snow shawling the fence posts and trees, blowing almost straight across the driveway and dumping a drift that looked house-tall. She scrambled out of bed and rushed to the kitchen, where she turned on the radio for the news and the weather report. The teakettle went on high while she listened to the radio: "Ten inches of snow expected and fifty-mile-an-hour winds. Travel advisories are out. School cancellations follow." She muttered to herself, pouring Morning Thunder tea into the tea ball and setting the time. "Damn! And of course the university never closes!" She crabbed at the snow for a moment, then took her teacup and cigarette to the bathroom. She showered and dressed in record time, stuffing her legs into corduroy pants, wool socks, and her ancient boots. She braided her hair, pulled on a turtleneck sweater, and ran outside to dig the Pinto out of the garage.

The snow was drifted close to the garage door, a drift hip-high, and she wallowed through it wondering if the Pinto could possibly get through. She warmed its engine, then backed to the very rear of the garage, planning to make a running start and bull her way through.

"I can take my car through, I think," Ben said. He had come to watch, dressed, gloved, his topcoat and scarf blowing rakishly in the wind. "My car is heavier than yours."

"Um." Leah got out of the Pinto and held her arms out for a hug. Ben hugged her, kissed her forehead, and said: "Are you sure you have to go to school today? I can get out to the hospital because the road crews have been working all night on the freeways. But perhaps the university canceled classes?"

"No. They never cancel. I'd have to get a dog team if all else failed. Or skis."

Ben got into his car and started the motor. Leah watched him, leaning against the side of the car. Glancing in, she saw a beer can on the floor of the back seat.

"Why don't you let me see if I can get through to the

street?" Ben asked. "Then the Pinto can plug along the beaten paths." He rolled up the window, waved, and drove slowly through the drift at the garage door. His heavy Ford LTD moved sedately, heavily, without pausing, through the drift and went on down the driveway.

Leah saw Ben wave as the car turned onto Hawbrook and away from home. She gathered up her book bag, closed the house for the day, and herded the Pinto through the snow to the university.

"Miz Knutinen, uh, Miz Calloway," Barry said, grinning at her from her office doorway.

"Oh, hi, Barry, what can I do for you?"

"I wanted to see how you're doing. Since you got married you've been a little scarce around campus."

"I'm sorry. Do you feel neglected?"

"It's understandable, I guess. The honeymoon isn't over yet. What I was wondering, is, well, we were all wondering if you're going to have the annual, the regular new-semester party, or if that's off now that you went and got married. I'm the elected asker of that question. The writing classes want to know. Also, the girls say they'll bring stuff."

"I don't have any furniture!"

"Do we care?"

"I don't suppose you do. Well . . ." Leah knew she was smiling. "Fine. Let's have the party. What day did you plan?"

Barry cleared his throat. "We're not that brash. Almost, but not really. Would some time in May be all right?"

Leah looked at her desk calender. "It's fine with me. But let me check with Ben. I can call him now if you'll wait a minute."

"We don't have to be so definite right now."

"I'll call him. Otherwise *I* might forget." She glanced at her wristwatch. "Four-thirty. He should be in his office or the lab. Just a minute." She dialed and got his secretary. "Is Doctor Calloway there? This is Mrs. Calloway."

"He's not in his office right now. Could I take a message?"

"Has he gone home? Or to the lab?"

"I don't know. You could try the lab. Do you have the number?"

"Yes. Thank you." Leah dialed again. "Pathology? Yes, is Doctor Calloway available?"

"Pathology One. Doctor Calloway? No, we don't expect him anymore today. Can we have him call you tomorrow?"

"No, thank you. I'll speak to him at home." Leah replaced the telephone. "I'll have to let you know about the party tomorrow."

"Okay. We didn't mean to push, anyway. So. Oh, I had something I wanted to tell you." He came into the office and closed the door. "Can you tell I'm different?"

"You seem to have more color. Are you feeling better?" She glanced at his arm, but the long sleeve covered any scar.

"I'll say. I'm over Shithead, if that's what you mean."

"I'm glad. You don't need that kind of trouble."

"Well. No. Uh, Leah, I know you don't think I'm depraved or anything because I'm gay."

"Yes. I don't think that." She sat back in her chair, offered him a cigarette. "What?"

"Well, there's someone. He'd been around before, but I couldn't seem to get Shithead out of my head so I didn't pay any attention."

"Oh. I see." She nodded, smiled, acceptingly. "And you'd like to bring him to the party? Fine with me."

"And nobody'd make any cracks. See, they'd know it was okay with you so it would have to be okay with . . . anybody else."

The street crew had plowed the driveway shut. Leah lunged through the snowbank, arms loaded with book bag, grocery sacks, and her briefcase, muttering imprecations as she lost one boot and then the other in the hip-deep snow. "Sonofabitch!" she crabbed. "I'll have to get some help with that or we'll be stuck until spring." She looked around for Ben's car, but didn't see it. The driveway and sidewalk were virginal; nothing had passed that snowblock in the driveway since morning. She kicked the back door open and dropped the grocery sacks on the laundry-room counter, her books dribbling lumpenly onto the floor.

Psi, yawning, came out of the silverware drawer and meowed for supper. "I know, I'm late." Leah shivered, her wool socks sopping wet, her pant legs making her skin bunch up into goosebumps. "Here, eat this and be still a minute." She fed the cat and put the teakettle on the back burner. "Din-din. What can I fix that's fast and good?" She dug two lamb chops out of the freezer and set them in water to defrost. She rushed through salad-making, set the broccoli into the steamer, preheated the broiler, made a small pot of coffee for Ben, changed out of her wet clothes, and sat down with a cigarette and a glass of wine. "Six o'clock. I made it. But where is he?" She pulled on another pair of boots, went out, retrieved the pair she'd lost, hunted the newspaper out of a snowdrift, and went back to the kitchen to sip wine and read. She nibbled at some salad, then gave up and ate it.

Someone was tapping at the laundry-room door. Leah opened the door to find a young man in a hooded jacket. "Yes?" she said.

"I used to plow out this driveway for the other people," he said. "Do you want me to plow you out? You'll never get that little Pinto through if I don't."

"Oh." She looked past him to the street. A jeep with a blade attached to its front end was parked behind the Pinto. "Fine. Do you show up right after every storm, or what?"

"Here's my name and telephone number." He handed Leah a business card. "I also do lawns in the summer and trees and gutters." His dark lively eyes moving up and down her body. His jacket was open at the throat.

Leah avoided his eyes, biting back the smart answers that came leaping to the tip of her tongue. "Do you want to be paid now, or what?"

"We could do it as a one-shot thing, or I could fix you up with a seasonal charge. Whatever you think."

She disliked him on principle. The dark eyes. The black hair curling out of his shirt collar. The arrogant stud, she thought. She bit her lip again. Lady Chatterley on Hawbrook Drive! "What do you charge for one driveway?"

"Well, how's twenty? I'll clear the whole thing right to the double garage doors, so you can get both your cars out. And I'll throw in your sidewalk so you can walk down to your mailbox." He placed one gloved hand on the doorjamb.

Leah felt her nape hairs stand up. "Fine. I'll have the twenty ready. D'you think fifteen minutes?"

"Depends. I won't waste any time." His jeans made a sound as his legs brushed each other. "You can watch from that window."

"Um." Leah purposefully closed the door between them. She went back to the kitchen, shaking her head. "I don't believe people like that exist. Imagine being screwed by a cliché!" She rearranged the silverware at Ben's place, took out ice cubes and made ice water. "And he wouldn't even be interested in me, he'd just be screwing for the sake of screwing. But I did react to him. Hostility is a reaction. Oh, Ben, come on home." She sat down with the newspaper again and looked at furniture advertisements. I'll go and look at living-room stuff Saturday, she resolved.

She was salting the lamb chops when she saw headlights come up the driveway. She glanced out the window and saw Ben's car. The driveway was clear and the jeep was cutting a narrow path over the sidewalk to the mailbox. Leah turned back to the range, lighted the burner under the broccoli, the chops under the broiler, and set the timer. She glanced out the window again as she poured wine into Ben's glass. He was talking to the snow digger, walking up the driveway with him. They came to the back door together. Ben kissed Leah on the forehead as he passed her. "I'll hang up my coat," he said.

Leah paid the snow digger, whose name turned out to be Chuck, almost pushing him out of the house. She was aware of his measuring look, of the animal awareness about him. Then she shook her head at herself and turned the lamb chops over.

"How was your day?" Leah asked Ben.

"Long. Some days are long and I can see where the time went. Other days, today, are long and I can't seem to pin down the time or where I spent it. But I did get one consultation done that wasn't all negative. Knowing that we caught a cancer before it went sour all the way . . . that helps." He sat down at the counter.

"I tried calling you today. It wasn't anything terribly important. But my students like to get their plans on the university calendar early. They want to have the traditional spring party here. Will that be all right?" She served the chops. Took one for herself.

"It's early for spring plans, isn't it?"

"Not really. There's commencement and all the finals and the end-of-year things. And if they can get the party date organized, that just helps them to work around everything else. It isn't such a big group. Only about thirty. And they're wonderful about cleaning up." She nibbled at the chop, put the bone down for Psi.

"Not a beer blast. I don't want to wake up and find beer cans and potato chip sacks on the lawn. Or any broken glass."

"No. Of course, they don't do things like that. You met some of them over Christmas, at my open house."

"Oh. Well. Fine. Whenever. I don't have to do the host thing, do I? I may have late call. If you won't mind my being in and out . . ."

"Well, then, I'll set the date and tell you or mark it on your calendar. Thanks." She poured coffee for Ben and took the plates to the sink. "We have some luck, anyway. I didn't have to call around to get the driveway plowed." She put the plates into the dishpan to soak, then sat down with a cigarette. "The snow digger says he also does lawns in the summer. Should I tell him to add us to his list of customers?"

"Fine. Whatever works." Ben finished his coffee. "I've got some notes to add to my paper. I'll want to get them ready for the typist." He kissed her absently and went to his study.

Leah washed the dishes, and took her cigarettes and a pot of tea to her workroom, where she wrestled with Rem Comp papers until ten. Then she took a bath and went to bed, brushing her hair down her back, smoothing lotion and Ecusson over her throat and arms.

She could never get enough of him, she thought. Or ever stop brooding over him, or stop wanting him. She watched him walk across the bedroom floor, the heat of her own desire making soft sharp pains flower in thistles, in thorns, from the clitoris yet untouched up to the heavy, almost bruised tenderness of her waiting breasts. He didn't have to touch her to start that pain blossoming, that ache between her legs, that soft quaking in the pit of her belly. And he knows it, she thought, the way he swaggers across the floor, his left hand casual at the knot of his bathrobe, the swing of his cock under the robe, the nodding knob of his cock, the winking eye of his cock, the hobbyhorse of his cock that she wanted to ride, that she wanted to suck. That she wanted.

And when they lay together, heavy, sodden, lax, she loved the way his face went: the lips full as he breathed through them; his lips, she thought, look this way only after we have made love. I'm the only one who sees them this way. I'm the only one who pleats kisses all along his chin and throat like a ruffle. And I'm the only one who puts her tongue to his philtrum, to his nostrils, to the envelope of his eye, to the thick leaf of his ear.

❧ The Hanged Man ☙

"BEN," she said, the following Saturday morning. "Would you go furniture-looking with me today? We have to start putting things in the living room and dining room and the spare bedroom or give up and just camp forever in the kitchen and bedroom." She had awakened before him, had lain in bed close enough to him to feel his body shift, his breathing, but not close enough to touch him. She had leaned over him, balancing on her hip and one elbow, had sipped his sleeping breath, had smelled the oil of his hair, the sharp salty smell of his semen, had begun a count of the freckles that spattered his tan shoulders, had marked as her own kissing spot a mole just at the nape of his neck; she had looked over his hip to the fur where his cock lay tucked, soft, vulnerable, and though she yearned to kiss it, to mouth it, she did nothing but smile and make promises to it, to sing to it, to soothe it, to keep it forever safe and secure. My cocklet, she had thought, humming contentedly; my thrusting bud, my knob, my pickle, my one-eyed beastling, my question, my riddle, my answer, how I could bite you! How I could toy with you, lip you, tease you, and how easily I could bite you off, my brussels sprout, my periwinkle! But I won't bite, no no! And she had eased out of bed carefully, chiding herself when she heard him shift, heard his breath pause.

"I have to go down to the lab today," Ben said now from the counter, where he sat buttering his toast. "I'm going down around ten and I'll grab a sandwich. I'll be tied up all afternoon."

"Saturday? Oh, Ben, you never have time off. You work too hard. Even if you don't come furniture-hunting you should take some time off and rest."

"I will, I will. I'll be home in time for dinner."

"It seems, though, that I saw more of you before we were married." She was grumbling, she heard it, so she smiled to take the whine out of the air.

Ben glanced at her. "Don't try to change me, Leah. I wouldn't be comfortable." He let the butter knife fall against the plate; it sounded of ice, brittle.

Leah felt her face prickle with heat; a tightening of her eyelids warned her that she was on the edge of tears. "I'm sorry," she said, placating. "That did sound like nagging, didn't it?" She added: "I'm embarrassed. Please excuse me."

"Mm-hm." Ben stared out the window and then pushed away from the counter. "Are you about ready to leave? I'll shower and shave now." He kissed her forehead. "Looks like you'll need your boots again. See you tonight." And he went to the bedroom to gather his fresh clothing for the shower.

Leah washed the dishes, fed the cat, made the bed, found her list of room measurements, loaded her shoulder bag with cigarettes, wallet, facial tissue, the lists, and a pad of paper for more note taking. Then she tapped a good-bye on the bathroom door and, prepared for a headache by two in the afternoon, set out in the Pinto to furniture-hunt. She steered the Pinto onto Highway 40 east, got into the proper lane for downtown Market Street, and tried to remember all the advice she'd gotten about furniture. "Don't buy new," Emily, the secretary, had said. "You'll find antiques are the best." "Don't buy used," Zulu had said. "My Bruce will help you outfit from floor to ceiling with new classy stuff." Esperanza, long distance, had said: "Sit on it. If it doesn't sit well it won't work." Leah decided Esperanza was right. I'll go park down in the basement of the mall and just sit on everything I see, she resolved.

But two that afternoon she had sat on a lot of furniture and had chosen a couch that was long and comfortable, yet, "not so deep that you can't get out once you get in," as she had told the clerk. She had ordered it in what was called umber corduroy. "And the cushion covers come off for dry cleaning," the clerk had assured her. And after the couch, Leah found two upholstered chairs that sat well and could be ordered in a color she called poison green.

She made arrangements to have the three pieces delivered late one afternoon during the week and tottered out of that, the fifth, store. "Now what?" She dug out her list. "Draperies." Oh. She was standing in the doorway of Herbie's Bar and Grill, so she walked in and sat at a small table.

"A glass of white wine. And do you have anything like a small salad or a sandwich?"

The waiter handed her a menu, then disappeared to return with a glass of white wine.

Leah sipped at it, made a face. It tasted like varnish. "Could I have something else, not this? A Masson Chablis?"

She was brought the Masson, sipped it, thanked the waiter, and ordered a small chef's salad with toast and cheese. She was nibbling at the toast when someone came to the table.

"Are you Leah Knutinen?" a young man asked.

"Yes, I am."

"I'm Kevin McGuire. Barry's friend. I work here part time." He smiled at Leah and offered his hand.

"Hello! How nice of you to come over! Sit down, or can you?" She looked around. "Can you join me?"

"Yes, for a minute. We're barely open." He smiled at her and winked. "You don't usually come down here, do you?"

"No, I haven't before. I'm furniture-hunting and I just pooped out in the doorway."

"I didn't think so." He smiled at her in a way that she didn't understand.

"What did I do?" she asked, glancing around. "It isn't open and I barged in?" She looked at the bar. "It's a private club?" Why did he wait on her, then?

"No. Barry'll love this! This is a gay bar. Friday and Saturday nights you couldn't *get* in. I mean, *you* couldn't get in. But Saturday afternoons are okay."

"Oh. Oh, well. By the way, how did you know me? Have you been in one of my classes? No, I'd remember."

"No. I'm on campus, too, but I work here Fridays and Saturdays. Barry pointed you out to me about a week ago. You were walking on campus with some other professors and laughing at something. We could hear you laugh."

Leah looked around the place again. "Funny, it doesn't look like a gay bar. Or what I thought gay bars look like. So much for prejudice. Although I will say, the house wine here is terrible."

"Yeah. But it's cheap. And a lot of people don't care what they put in their mouths." He looked at Leah and then looked at the floor. "Sorry."

She smiled at him. "Well, I guess you know you're invited to the spring party the kids and I have."

"Thanks. Barry said he'd ask. We'll be glad to help with stuff. You know, like the others."

Leah decided she liked him; he seemed open and willing to accept her on her terms as she was willing to accept him on his. She stuck out her hand. "Friends? I'm glad you and Barry have hit it off."

But. She began waking at four in the morning. And Ben would be rolled over away from her, his back turned to her, a distance between them in the middle of the bed. She'd waken for no reason that she could perceive; but even as she reminded herself that she was happy, that Ben was content, that now the furniture had arrived, draperies, sheer linen, had been made and put up, that the dining room table and chairs were . . . were a table and chairs; even though she reminded herself that the house was beginning to look like the look in Ben's eye that first day they moved in, that she had by now served the sit-down dinner he had requested, she had not disgraced him, had, indeed, been not bad as a hostess, as a wife of Dr. Ben Calloway; she was, while not as glittering as the chandelier that Ben seemed to love, rather decorative, even in her own opinion; she was finding the tune that he called, was able to pace the court dance he choreographed; even so, she still wakened at four in the morning with one ear listening, uneasy, with the blind sense that there was something askew. She lay staring up at the ceiling: It's not our marriage, she thought. It's not big. It's . . . like one hair is off, the weight of one hair is off, it's that tiny. And she thought: It's not Ben. It must be me.

It's that I didn't know him as well as I'd like to, before we married, she thought. And now it's difficult to know which aspects of him are permanent or subject to change because of temperament, mood.

That was something that had surprised her: that Ben, so stoic and calm and reasoned, had another aspect: quite explosive mood shifts. The first "incident"—for that was what Leah called it—was still very much on her mind. She didn't, of course, discuss it with Ben, perceiving immediately that the incident was not to be mentioned or discussed. Ever. But she thought about it, because it alarmed her. They had gone to the symphony, a program of Beethoven and a brass fanfare selection that she had always liked. And the evening had run partway through, to the intermission, when Ben and she had gone out to stand near the tall windows and have a cigarette. She had been thinking how comfortable they were with each other, standing turned three quarters to each other, talking in a desultory way, and she had thought of something funny from one of her classes and touched Ben's arm. She hadn't clutched him, she hadn't been attempting to establish property rights, squatter's rights. But he had jerked away from her, a frown of impatience blackening his eyes; he had abruptly stubbed his cigarette out and walked away from her. He walked back to their seats. She followed, her knees shaking, her breath knotting painfully in her chest. He stood back so that she could precede him to their seats, not meeting her eyes, still frowning. She seated herself and made a business of looking at the program, her hands shaking minutely, the cold sweat of apprehension, alarm, springing out under her dress. She listened to the rest of the program, the brass section, clenched with misery and bafflement.

They had walked to the car afterward in silence, and only when they were on Highway 40 west did she venture to ask him: "Did I say something wrong?"

"No."

She tentatively touched his hand, drew back when he did not respond. "Are you feeling all right? You seemed all right when we left the house. And then . . ."

"Leave it. I am fine. I don't choose to discuss it. If you can't discuss something else you'll make me uncomfortable."

She hunted around in her head for something to say, a change of subject. I feel like Psi, ratting around and coming up with cobwebs, she thought. She said, "Shall I get tickets for the conservatory this Saturday? They're doing another Rabe play: *Streamers*. I've heard from my kids that it's terrific."

"Whatever. As long as we're not going to be rushed. I've got a rough week coming. I have that paper to finish —and you do remember I'll be off to Toronto?"

They drove up the gravel driveway, the headlights making a black-and-white jungle of their lawn and the spring-budding hedge. Psi, fire-eyed, came bounding out of the blackness to roll in front of the garage doors until Ben opened the car window and called to him.

"That cat has no sense of danger," Ben said as the garage door opened and Psi strolled ahead of the car. "He doesn't care how close the car comes, he thinks he's safe."

"He trusts you." Leah got out of the car. "Will you want something to eat?" She caught Psi and cuddled him under her chin. "Cocoa? Tea?"

"Cocoa. I'll be in in a minute. I want to check if my left front tire is developing a slow leak."

Leah went into the house, kicked her shoes off, padded stocking-footed around the kitchen while she heated milk in a saucepan and mixed the cocoa, sugar, salt, vanilla, and butter together in a cup with hot water from the faucet. Psi sat on top of the range and washed his face, gargling at Leah when she passed.

She was stirring the cocoa in the saucepan, the burner turned to low medium, when Ben came into the kitchen. He came up behind her, sliding his hands under her dress, taking her pantyhose away from her with one long sweep down her legs, and before she could react, he had begun to stroke her clitoris with his thumb, was holding her buttocks apart and rubbing the head of his cock around her anus, a wetness from his cock coming hot and thick into her anus, into the folds of her labia and being rubbed by his thumb over her clitoris. Leah gasped and dropped the spoon, half turning to Ben, but he caught her in his arms and held her, half-carried her, half-dragged her from the kitchen to the bedroom, where he swept pillows up under her so that she lay face down, her buttocks up in the air, and he pinned her that way, his body heavy upon her, his breath in her ear, his insistent thumb stroking the clitoris, his cock rubbing a demand on her anus, and she struggled with him, against him, moaning with the suddenness of this almost-attack, this lightning-sharp lovemaking that made the hot thrusts of pain and desire burn along her thighs and belly. She wanted to turn to put her arms around him, she wanted to clasp him between her legs, to wrap herself around him, to be pinned to him. But he held her down, his face and mouth pressed to her neck, his hands moving her body, pulling her buttocks open, the cock demanding entry at her anus then at her vagina until she began to moan, began to beg him to please, please. And he did, coming sharply with great painful thrusts into her vagina, almost lifting her from the bed, so great were the thrusts; so deep were the thrusts of his cock that she imagined, deep in her well of sensation, that he was thrusting up at her heart, he was going to climax in her throat, that when the first tremors of climax came he would split her completely.

She moved under him, wanting him, not wanting him; she was unable to relax into the lovemaking. Instead, even as she was aroused almost to climax, she felt alarm, heard a wounded, alarmed cry from her sea self. She fell back from climax; she tried to turn in his arms to see his face, to read his face; she did not understand this silent assault, this savage lovemaking, this not sharing of pleasure but a taking by him. She did not know him at all, she thought. And with that thought she went cold. She didn't know what to do, turning in his arms, unable to read him. She clenched against him, made her body stiff, closed, flattening out under him so that he was pushed away. "No, Ben," she said. "Please."

She heard his breathing change, heard him gasp sharply: knew that he had come within her just as she had stiffened against him.

He fell away from her, lay next to her, his eyes closed, his face closed to her.

"Ben," she said tentatively. "I'm sorry. But I don't understand." She was sorry. Guilt wrenched the back of her throat. She reached out to touch him.

But he rolled away from her to his side of the bed, out of reach. He found a pack of cigarettes, took one out and lighted it. Still without looking at her, he sat up on the edge of the bed and began to unbutton his shirt, taking his tie off, beginning the ritual of getting ready for bed.

"Ben," Leah said. "What happened? What changed you? You changed. . . ."

He looked at her, his eyes bleak. "I'm not unfeeling, you know, Leah. I'm not a monster. What did happen? You shut me off. I can't just overlook that. I have my sensitivities too." He dropped his shirt and undershirt into the laundry hamper and strode to the bathroom.

"Ben! Can't we talk about it? I didn't mean to shut you off or to hurt you. But you changed. I don't understand what happened."

He talked to her through the closing bathroom door: "Leah, I have to be up early tomorrow. I work very hard, you know." He closed the bathroom door with a definite, sharp click.

She sat on the bed. She wanted to say: "Ben, I know you work hard. And you're a sensitive, even difficult man and I want to understand you. But I don't understand what just happened. Was I wrong? Wasn't *I* being hurt? Why did I panic? Tell me what you want!" She said nothing and heard only the rush of the shower from the bathroom, and from her sea self that small moan of bewilderment and pain.

She went to the kitchen, walking around to ease the pain, shaking her head at the saucepan of cocoa that had been forgotten on the range. She put the pan in the sink and ran water into it. She found her own cigarettes and sat down in the window seat, stared out at the black, frosty lawn, at the moonless sky, at the stars. She felt sore, cold. The cold began at her sex, his semen now seeping down from inside her to chill her. She bunched her muscles under her and sat upright on her bones, trying to draw herself back together, to knot herself back to her own center, to close herself away from the cold she felt all around her now. She sat smoking her cigarettes, watching the sky, listening to the silence within her, finally hearing Ben step out of the bathroom.

He had gotten into bed and rolled over onto his right side, turned away from the middle of the bed.

"Ben, please. I really am sorry. But we need to talk. I need to talk about it."

He put a hand over his eyes. "Leah, I have to get up early."

"Please. I won't sleep a wink if we don't at least try to sort it out, what happened."

"Nothing important happened. I'm still here. You're still here. We have a life together. If you'd allow it to go on. Please, Leah. Don't brood. Just let me sleep."

Finally, she accepted it. She sighed and went to the bathroom, showered, and put on her nightgown. She knew he'd be asleep, or pretending to be asleep, when she returned to the bedroom. She wasn't surprised to find the bedroom lights out and Ben curled into a knot on his side of the bed.

April Fool's Day. Leah stood at her desk reading her calendar. "See Harold. His request." She knew what that was about. Harold, the chairman of the department, wanted an interview with her about her current status, her publishing history and future, and tenure. "Or the refusal of it," she muttered aloud. She rummaged around in a desk drawer for her file, her vita. The thin volume of haiku in its jacket: her pride. "He'll want to alert me that next November first is Death Day. And I must, must *must* collect everything I have ever done to not fall through the holes of this fabric, this—where did I put my pub list? I know, Harold," she grumbled. "More articles, more criticism, more poems. Not just one done and one coming. And get the book of *How to Teach Rem Eng* done and to the publisher. Ech." She sat down at her desk and began sorting through the mail. Her knees ached, her hips felt heavy, lumpen. She was mildly depressed, fighting the flurry of harpies that nagged and yattered at the back of her thoughts.

She felt sensitive, precarious, waterlogged; felt like a sack of water on stilts. I'm not pregnant, too, and that . . . well, it's stoic and philosophical I must be. "We won't take heroic measures," Ben says. "To get pregnant." So I must keep practicing. And perhaps we don't want a baby this soon. Before we are accustomed to each other. But still. I wonder if God is being witty. "Take what you want," God said. "And pay for it." I didn't want a baby once. And now, God's wit, I pay for it. I won't think about it. I won't think about that, if the abortion has made me so that I can't get pregnant. I *won't* think about it. Not in the daytime. Not in the nighttime. Not at four in the morning and not in April and not in August.

She hated it, this tendency of hers to think about things that could not be changed, things that slipped from their shadows and pursued her from four o'clock in the morning through the day, things that came sighing out of the dark weeds of her mind to whisper, to drag their weight against her.

The telephone rang. "Hello, Leah Calloway speaking."

"What are you doing for lunch?" It was Ben.

Surprised, Leah looked at her wristwatch and then at her calendar. "Nothing, why?"

"Come home for lunch today. You have time. Your next class isn't until one."

"Come home? Aren't you at the lab?" She looked at the calendar. "It is Tuesday, isn't it?"

"Yes. Come home for lunch." He laughed and she heard the telephone click down.

Mystified, Leah pushed her mail and a batch of blue books into her book bag. She made a note to herself to call Emily for an appointment tomorrow. Then she went home.

Ben's black Ford LTD was in the driveway, but Ben was not in the house. Leah walked from the front door through the living room and the dining room to their bedroom, calling him. Then she saw him in the back yard talking to Chuck.

"Hi!" Leah said, walking out into the sunlight, shading her eyes with one hand. Then, as she rounded the corner of the house, she saw lawn furniture—a table with an umbrella, chairs, benches, and a brightly cushioned chaise lounge. "Ah! That's the reason you're home." She hugged Ben and nodded to Chuck.

Ben grinned at her. "Do you like it?" He smelled of beer. "I saw it last week and thought you'd need some stuff for your student party."

"It's grand! How did you ever keep it such a secret? Delivery people usually make a point of spoiling surprises."

"Do you like it? It's all wrought iron, so it won't fall apart. And the cushions are covered with waterproof fabric. Here, come sit down and see if you like it." Ben led her to the lounge and sat her down. "How's that?"

"The height of posh! Oh, thank you, I really love it all!" She smiled at him. "Do you want to have lunch out here? You managed a perfect day. I'll go make sandwiches. Or just some cold chicken from last night, and cheese and . . ." She looked at Ben, then turned to Chuck. "Would you like to stay for lunch? You must've helped unload all this. *Would* you like to stay for lunch?"

"I'd like to, thanks. But I can't today. I have lawns to get organized. I start now and by summer you all have beautiful lawns. This is certainly a nice set." He ran one hand over the top of the table. He grinned at Leah and flashed a look at Ben, then grinned even more brightly at Leah. "I'll come by next week. I'll take care of you." He let his hand linger on the table top, then he nodded to them and walked away.

Leah was momentarily annoyed. But then the pleasure over Ben's surprise swept the annoyance away. "Come on," she said, taking Ben's hand. "I'll dig up some lunch for us. Let's eat out here today." She hugged him as they walked into the kitchen. "Oh, thank you. You really are the *best!*" She hugged him and kissed him; his lips were warm. From the sun, she thought. And kissed him again. She leaned back in his arms and looked fondly at him, thinking: He smells of beer and his mouth is warm from the sun, almost like after lovemaking. Delicious! She felt her own lips become full, warm, and that heat filled her breasts and made them heavy, the heat melted along her body so that she pressed herself against Ben, wanting him; gently wanting him. She thought; Now why am I lubricious about him; it's the taste of his mouth, some kissing fullness of his mouth.

But he put her away from him. "I've got to get back to the lab. I'll just take some chicken and a glass of milk."

Disappointed, she said, "Oh, must you? Okay, sit down and I'll get the chicken out. Can't I make a cup of coffee? Salad? There's that chocolate cake?"

"No, thanks. Just the chicken and the milk." He tapped his fingers on the counter, waited for her to set the plate of chicken before him.

"I can't get over how thoughtful you are," she said, pouring milk into a glass. "When did you see the set? I don't remember your mentioning that you'd even been looking around."

"Mm. I was downtown one Saturday and saw it in a display window." He drank some milk. "I thought it would be nice for your party. And for any other casual entertaining you may choose to do this summer."

"I wish I'd known you liked looking at furniture. Or even just browsing around, we could do that together." She saw a frown flicker around his lips momentarily, but went on. "Well, if the weather's nice we can have the party outside. And if the weather is rotten we can have it indoors. Shall I invite some of your colleagues? Like the couples that came to dinner? Do you think they'd enjoy a supper party with my zanies?"

"Whatever you think is best." He wiped his mouth with a paper napkin. "I'm going to be late." He kissed her, took his jacket from the back of a chair and walked out the kitchen door. "See you at the regular time," he said.

She made a pot of tea for herself and sat at the kitchen counter, staring out the window, thinking: He really is thoughtful. What a very nice man he is. He does unexpected nice things. She heard a motor, harsh, crackling, explosive, from the side of the house and saw Chuck drive a lawn-mowing machine around the conrer of the house; he sat loose-legged astride the machine, shirtless, a bandanna around his head; he sat, Leah thought, cockalacious. He is cockalacious, she thought. Like Psi. He even walks like Psi, a kind of arrogant ramble, the rolling cock-conscious walk of a stud animal. He's like Psi, too, he'd jump anything. She remembered the time when Psi had jumped a female poodle, looking like a tiny jockey riding a big furry horse, humping away with his rear end and his eyes crazy with lust. Just the instinctive jump and hump. She watched Chuck's progress around the front and side lawns. Had Ben hired him for the summer?

She drank the last of her tea and lighted a cigarette, glancing at the kitchen clock. Time to go back to the campus. She stopped in mid-stride. Right after this spring semester would be perfect for her and Ben to get away. She'd make the reservations and get the tickets as a surprise, just as Ben had surprised her today. She'd call Mrs. Mack at his office and get her to help arrange Ben's schedule to allow four or five days free. He relied on her for his appointments, she could do it and he'd never know until the last minute! Almost skipping, Leah grabbed her handbag and car keys and went back to campus.

"Yes, I can do that," Mrs. Mack said on the telephone. Leah had called her the next day from campus. "He's out of the office now and I can just arrange his appointments around that week. I'm glad you gave me so much notice. Now, you know if he gets an emergency that's something I can't handle for you."

"Yes, I know that. But isn't there someone who covers for him? I know he's always doing that for the other pathologists at the hospital."

"Indeed he does. Well, I'll organize that, but I can't guarantee they'll keep the secret. We'll just plan as if everything is going to work out."

"Thanks a lot!"

Leah placed the telephone in its cradle and gnawed on her lower lip for a moment. "Now to see Harold. She gathered her folder and handbag together and purposefully strode down the hall to the English Department office and her interview with Harold Rawlings, her boss.

Leah always felt intellectually nude with Harold. She sat outside his office now, hearing her hairpins rattle, listening to sweat begin to run down her spine, the nausea roiling at the bottom of her stomach. "And a brain gone bad," she muttered under her breath. A sea creature out of its depth, I am, slogging, gurgling, beached. Damn and damn, I am never going to grow up. It is beyond me. Here I sit, a folder of publications, my own damned collection of haiku, some valid credentials as a teacher and . . . and . . . I am as vulnerable as a cow whale, rolling one eye skyward, belly up in too shallow water. Exposed. And nude. She groaned. Then blushed, aware that she had groaned aloud and that Emily had glanced up from her typewriter.

"This won't hurt at all," Harold said, ushering Leah into the big office. "It's for your own good, you needn't look so harrowed." He propelled her to a large upholstered chair near his desk. "Sit down. Here, have a cigarette. How have you been? I don't see enough of my favorite people."

He was always impeccably hospitable, kind, observant. Leah sat down and gratefully lit a cigarette. She placed her folder on his desk, aware of the sweat on the palms of her hands, the faint smudges on the folder.

He took the folder and looked through it. "I'll need time to assess this, of course. And if you don't mind parting with it for a few weeks, I'll need it for the staffing committee. You no doubt know that we've had budget cuts. The first step we've taken is not to replace those who left us this last year. But sad to say, that wasn't enough. And now we will perhaps be . . . not renewing some of our staff. Not that you need to feel threatened. But." He glanced up at her face, then down at the folder. "I know that you have established yourself with us as an excellent teacher. He smiled gently at her, then opened the book of haiku she had included in the folder. "Yes, I see they did a creditable job for you. I understand you are bringing out another collection?"

"Um, yes. I listed that under pubs."

"And you know that I will need anything else that comes in, copies of any of your articles, any criticism you've done." He smiled again. "The Remedial English text. I want to make the best impression for you."

"Thank you. I *know* you are being extraordinarily kind to me with all this personal aid."

"Because, from past experience with you, I know I must. Or lose you by default. I warn you that this is the last time I shall coddle you." He smiled at her and pretended to frown. "You must train yourself to be more assertive. Now." He tapped his finger on the folder. "I thank you for your time and for these aids. The staffing committee will meet and consider. And, as you know, there are those who will speak on your behalf as well as the naysayers, who *are* necessary. And then the dean must have his say. Don't worry, I think I am safe in saying that you stand a good chance to be renewed. Tenure, of course, is something we must consider carefully." He stood up and walked around his desk. "Now see, it was not at all painful, was it?"

"Thank you." She stood up, shakily. She wanted to throw herself on the floor in front of him and put his foot on the back of her head so that she could pledge fealty, loyalty, anything, but please let her go on teaching. But she knew he knew that she loved teaching; she could see that knowledge twinkling at the back of his eye.

He ushered her toward the door. "We don't see enough of you at the faculty hours." These were the biweekly or monthly four-in-the-afternoon meetings of the faculty over sherry and biscuits to hear one of the department read a paper or article that would soon be in print. "One would almost think you like your students better than your peers, your colleagues." He was needling her, she knew.

She nodded. "I do always plan to come. But somehow there's always a student with a problem."

"Ah, well. But I needn't remind you that these faculty hours are useful." He had his hand on the doorknob. "We may appear to be pompous, Leah. But there is a kind of courtly dance, an etiquette, to climbing this particular ladder, if I may mix, dreadfully, two metaphors. You take my meaning, I am sure." He smiled again and turned the doorknob, letting her bolt past him.

"But I can't dance," she heard herself half-whisper.

"Can't. Or won't?" He shook his head at her. "We would be so pleased if you would read at one of the hours. You did read for us your first year if I recall? May I tell Emily to schedule you?"

"Oh, please, no!" She blushed. She felt the red patches spring up along her neck right to her hairline. "Thank you. Perhaps I'll read next fall if there is a time." Her shyness was strangling her; she cleared her throat. "Please, the others are so comfortable and at ease. And . . ." she stopped, wordless.

"We'll see. Rosalind will be reading this Thursday at four. Perhaps you'd care to come and give support to the other female on the staff. Can I appeal to your female chauvinism?"

"Ah, but Rosalind was to the manor born! You know she was breast-fed by a PhD! She has all the patina and gloss right from the cradle."

"Do I hear envy?"

"Yes. Of course, you do. She's bright, attractive, went to the right schools out east, got her PhD at the right school, and taught at a glamour school in the Midwest. And she writes elegant little poems." Leah grinned. "I am ferociously jealous of anyone that good and that visible. You know that." She looked at Harold. "I understand you. Devious! Yes, I'll go and hear Rosalind read.

You are Machiavellian, d'you know that?" She shook her head at him. "The fair Rosalind."

As she walked back to her own office she thought: It could be that I won't be renewed. If the staffing committee has set up a competition between Roz and me . . ." She stamped into her office and slammed the door. Well, damn, she muttered to herself. I thought I'd grow up one of these days, but I haven't. Damn and blast. I should have been going to all those "hours" and I should have gone to lunch with the right people. She looked through her calendar at the months and days that had gone by; and she, heedless of the dance, had her four o'clocks scheduled with Insalaco, Robinson, Wiesel, DeWitt, Nicholson, Barry; not one faculty member to bless her. Soberly she sat down at her desk. "I've had too much fun teaching," she said aloud. She paged through the rest of the spring calendar. No, it was too late. She could read at every "hour" and buy drinks from now until graduation and it wouldn't begin to dent. Damn my shyness! she thought. I should have, at the very least, gone into the faculty coffee lounge every morning and sat around and nodded intelligently. But one look at those Byronic brows, those white-streaked beards, those elbow patches, those deep and droning voices, those literati! and I go calf-shy and awkward. And could I change now, they'd not know why I was changing, and they'd be right to resent me. No. I can't change. All this time I should've been, like Rosalind, nodding and yipping "Cogent!" like a goddamned peahen at any utterance from the beards. Ah, no. Leah, lumpen, unrepentant, unruly, is not smart, crafty, nor has she ever the wit to be expedient, and so she'll sulk along, have her little cry, and pursue her one-way path to unrenewedness!"

She lighted a cigarette. That's it, she thought. And that isn't it. Exhaling smoke through her nose, she could feel one of her better crying fits coming on. This one would include wounded pride (because she knew she should have overcome her shyness and hadn't), insulted sea creatureness (that's what she called any insult to her bashfulness), waywardness (because she *was* being wayward and could not force herself out of it), and the hateful admission of jealousy toward Rosalind the fair. "Ow! Don't start now," she scolded herself, twitching her nose, blowing it, wiping away the grapefruit-sized tears. "You don't have time for this. You've had reminders of all kinds, from Harold, from your good friend Jesse, from Emily, from Bill Gilman. But no. Is there such a creature who is shy *and* arrogant *and* stubborn? Yes. Well, go home and mope. And make dinner and behave."

She stubbed the cigarette out, grabbed her book bag and handbag, checked the window and walked out of her office, locking the door behind her. I'll make dinner and be cheerful, she resolved. Ben will come home and we'll sit on the lawn furniture and watch the moon come up.

He came home half an hour late that night; she saw the car turn up the driveway and jumped up from the window seat to put the steaks under the broiler and to pour the water and the chilled wine into glasses. She met him at the doorway and hugged him; he turned his cheek for her kiss and put her away from him. She clung to his arm for a moment; he smelled of hair oil, she noticed, and thought: He must've stood really close to someone in an elevator. Leah noticed with half her attention that his shirt was loosened from his trousers around the waist, his tie was slightly askew. The rest of her mind was on rib eye steaks and the bearnaise sauce she had left on the top of the range. "How was your day?" she asked, turning the steaks, closing the oven door.

"Long, warm. I have some work to do in my study tonight. I have that Toronto seminar coming up the end of the week." He passed through the kitchen, and she heard him walking along the carpeted hallway to his study. "I'll be ready for dinner in a minute. Where's the mail?"

She always placed his mail on the refectory table in the hall, and glanced up now to see him take it. "Toronto?" she asked. "But will you be home for the party?"

"It doesn't matter if I am."

"Yes, it does! I invited some of the people from the lab and the hospital. And Mrs. Mack."

"Well, I suppose I'll be home, in any case." He went into his study for a moment, then came out to the kitchen and helped Leah to carry the steaks and vegetables to the dining-room table.

During dinner, as she talked about her day, the interview with Harold, she noticed he tapped his fingers on the tablecloth, seemed preoccupied. "Is something wrong?" she asked. She poured coffee for him.

"Ah, no. Did you have any plans for tonight?"

"No. I was just telling you about Harold and how I have to get busy with that book on Rem Eng. . . ."

"I see. I'm a bit edgy, Leah. If you . . . think I'll go for a drive."

"Oh." She waited for him to invite her along.

He finished his coffee, dabbed the napkins to his lips, and sat back in the chair.

"Something is wrong? Did I do or say something? What?"

"No. I . . . I'm going to stop at the lab for a few minutes." He rose from the table, kissed her forehead, and went through the kitchen to the garage.

Leah did the dishes, fed the cat, worked on student papers, and dug through her rough draft of the Remedial English Composition book. With half her mind she worked over her old notes, listened to the radio, found herself lighting fresh cigarettes while other cigarettes still burned less than half-smoked in the ashtray, found herself staring out of the window sightlessly, her hands idle on the desk top, found herself peering through cigarette smoke at the Tarot cards that she shuffled and laid into a pattern, found herself listening to the stillness in the house, listening past the lute on the radio to the shifting of night air in the empty rooms.

At eleven she had no more reason to wait up. She put the notes and student papers away, emptied the loaded ashtray, and, hating the silence that followed her through the house, turned the radio on in the bedroom while she showered and put on her nightdress. The silence was implacable. It pressed against her back as she walked around the big bed to remove the spread; it brushed against her hair as she took it down from the topknot; it breathed along her bare arms and stirred the hairs along the back of her neck; it took possession of the white expanse of bed, shared the bed with her, breathing cold upon her, breathing distance upon her, chilling her so that her hands became cold, so that she became cold. So that she sat on the bed and was herself silent.

ঌ The Moon ଞ

THE party was a success. Leah had spent the days before the party roasting, slicing and making salad out of a turkey, baking and slicing a ham, deviling eggs, boiling, broiling, frying, stewing, brewing all kinds of edibles. "You have enough for a threshing crew," Zulu told her just as the guests began arriving.

"I know. I love cooking for crowds. About twice a year. I don't think I ever recovered from growing up on the farm."

"Ben's home, I see," Zulu croaked. She had a cold and was coaxing her throat with what she called a toddy: rum and lemon juice and sugar, steaming hot. "I'm gonna ask him to look down my throat."

"Ask. He hasn't done that kind of doctoring in years."

"With a houseful of doctors you'd think I could get *some* advice!" Zulu moved away, looking for someone to examine her throat.

"Can I do anything to help?" Barry asked. He had a bagel loaded with cream cheese and strawberry jam in one hand and a small plate heavy with ham, turkey, eggs, meatballs, cheeses, and potato salad.

"No, thanks. Did Kevin say he could make it?"

"Um. Ah, yes. But he won't be with me." Barry blushed. Before Leah could question him he'd moved away from her, and she saw him looking at Chuck over the heads of Mrs. Mack and Miss Insalaco.

Leah stared for a moment. "What a nervy bastard," she muttered. "Crashing a party. Hmm. Well, what can it hurt?"

But when Ben passed her at the serving table, she said: "Did you invite Chuck?"

"No. I may have mentioned the party to him. Surely you don't object."

215

She shook her head. "I don't think so. Not on . . . I don't know. Am I seeing things or is he . . . uh . . . making a play for Barry? Why would Barry even be interested, when he and Kevin have been . . . serious for so long?"

"There aren't enough kinks with just one person."

Leah had been talking to herself. She was surprised that Ben had answered her. She looked at him.

He shrugged his shoulders. "I see Mack coming. You really were thoughtful to invite her." He walked away to greet Mrs. Mack, who twinkled and smiled up at him.

"Leah?" Kevin touched Leah's arm shyly. "I didn't know if I should come. Is it okay?"

"Of course! I'm glad you did come. Come over here and let me feed you." She steered Kevin around so that his back was turned to Barry and Chuck. "Here, have some punch. Or would you like beer?" She babbled at him, loading a plate, pouring punch into a cup. She thought: Damn that Chuck! And damn Barry! She felt her smile become forced, but continued to jabber at Kevin. "Would you like to have the grand tour of the house? My students have all been out here at one time or another. Anyway, I need to refill the punch bowl." She herded Kevin inside. "We thought we'd keep the door open and people could wander around. . . . Yeah, I like the fireplace. I know it's crazy to have a fire going but . . . Do you need anything?" She saw Kevin glance around the living room. "This is my husband's study." She opened the door to let Kevin glance in.

"He's got a lot of matches." Kevin put his plate down for a moment, sifted the matchbooks through his fingers and back into the large pewter bowl on Ben's desk. "Is that your husband out there? The tall man with the wavy hair?"

"Yes, it is. I'll introduce you when we go back outside."

"I thought I'd seen him around. You really have a nice home, Leah. Where do you do your schoolwork? In here, too?"

"No, my workroom is on the other side of the living room. Not as posh as this, though. Come on, I'll show you."

Kevin glanced at the matchbooks. "Herbie's. I'll bet he has matchbooks from all over."

"He does. From the cities where he's been. Toronto. Cincinnati. San Francisco. There's even a couple from New Orleans. Did you want one?"

"No. It's just interesting."

Psi came in from the dining room. He stood on his hind legs and patted at Kevin's knee.

"He thinks he can beg some turkey salad from you," Leah said.

"He certainly can! He's terrific. I didn't know Siamese were friendly."

"He's devious. I should've named him Iago, he's so clever. Or Machiavelli. Look out, if you feed him you'll be stuck with him all afternoon."

Kevin let Psi take some turkey salad from his plate. "I like him."

"Well, let's get him out of here. Ben's study is pretty much off-limits. Psi eats papers, especially important ones." Leah carried the cat out of the study and closed the door. "Now, on to the rest of the house."

"Leah," Kevin said. "You don't have to do this. I know what's going on. Barry, I mean."

"Oh."

"I'm okay. I mean . . . well, I understand him."

Leah felt herself blushing, wanted to *not* discuss any of it, Barry or Kevin. Or their behavior. "Okay. Fine. Would you like to go outside, or would you like to see if you know anyone in the living room? I could introduce you to some of the other guests . . . anyone look interesting?" She felt herself blush again. Goddammit, she snarled at herself. A yenta for the . . . star-crossed, the double-crossed. She saw Kevin watching her, understanding her.

"I'll go back outside with you and help you with the punch bowl, how about that?" he said. "You don't understand, do you? Barry *wants* to be faithful. But he's cock-happy right now. He hasn't stopped being Barry. I know you care a lot about him. He's still Barry, but he's got this cock hunger." He grinned at her. "I know all about it. I went through it. He'll outgrow it."

"I'm glad. He's fortunate to have you for a friend."

"Yeah. The guy he was with before, the craphead, was cock-hungry. But he won't change, he'll be cock-hungry all his life. And that hurt Barry, you know? To love someone who's always going to be looking for new cocks, new kicks. You can't take yourself very seriously if your lover doesn't take you seriously." Kevin spoke softly now: "It must take a lot of strength and trust to let the other person go on that way."

Leah saw Ben coming toward them and smiled. "Ben, come and meet Kevin."

"Hello." Ben nodded to Kevin. "Leah, the punch is running out. Where did you put the reserves?"

"Oh! That's why I came in. Here, I'll get it. It's in the back of the refrigerator in those gallon jugs." Leah smiled at Kevin. "Excuse me, duty calls."

"Let me help. Can't I carry something for you?" Kevin set his plate on the kitchen counter. "See, empty hands."

Ben said, "Thanks. I'll go outside and check the rest of the stuff. Oh, we need some more forks. The plastic ones ran out." He went to the silver drawer. Psi was lying on the silverware when the drawer was pulled open. "Damn! Get out of there, Psi," Ben said.

"He gets around, doesn't he?" Kevin asked. "He was just eating some of my turkey salad a minute ago."

"We won't tell anyone the cat was sleeping on their forks and knives," Leah said, handing Kevin a gallon jug of punch. "Here. Would you pour this into the punch bowl? I'll bring the ice. Should I lock Psi in my workroom? People might not like having a cat walk around on their dishes."

"I say the hell with 'em," Ben said. "If they don't like our cat they can go home." He grinned at Kevin. "You don't mind a cat sitting in your salad, do you?"

"I like Siamese in my salad," Kevin said, following Leah out to the buffet she'd set up on the lawn.

Zulu joined them there. "Nice party, Leah," she said. She watched Kevin pour the punch. "I don't know you yet," she said to him.

"Oh," Kevin introduced himself. "I'll pour you some punch, if you like," he said.

"Thanks. Say, Leah, who's that stud over there? The one talking to your student." Zulu pointed the punch cup at Chuck's back.

"Oh. He's the man who does our lawns. Chuck. I don't know his last name."

"Hmm." As Zulu put the punch cup down, Leah could see the flicker of lust move in her cat-green eyes. Leah and Kevin smiled at each other and then turned away to add ice to the punch.

The last guests were leaving; Leah waved good-bye from the driveway, part of her attention on the departing guests, part trying to think where she had put the large trash can liners. "No, go ahead," she heard Ben saying. "Take the whole case."

"Are you sure you won't want some yourself?" Barry was allowing Ben to load a case of beer into his arms.

"No. I don't drink beer. It will just hang around."

"I won't let it go to waste!" Chuck said. He took the case from Barry. "Come on. Thanks for the great party!" he said. His shirt was open, revealing his well-developed chest and flat belly.

Leah muttered between her teeth: "Thanks for not dressing." But she smiled and waved as she hunted under the tables for stray silverware. Kevin had been among the first guests to leave, thanking Leah: "I did enjoy myself. Don't worry about me, I'll be okay. Barry just has to get it out of his system."

🦢 Ace of Pentacles 🦢

CLOUDS and a ship. Leah turned the Ace of Pentacles between her fingers. Travel. "That's true: Ben flies, flew, still flies." She closed her eyes against the thoughts that pressed for her attention. Impatient with herself, she sat down at the desk. She had come back from pacing the hallway, the dark house, had come to her study to close the door against the silence in the hall, the moving shapes that slipped along at her heels and fingered the hairs at the nape of her neck.

She had gotten the airplane tickets, had called ahead to reserve a suite at the resort called Tara, had checked and double-checked with Mrs. Mack that Ben's schedule was clear for five whole days and nights. Then, a week before their departure, she had rushed home from more furniture shopping, had brought champagne, and artichokes, which he loved and which she did not, had prepared a candlelight dinner for two, and then had waited.

She had run out of matches and her lighter was dry, so she had gone into his study to mooch a book from the large pewter bowl, was still standing there when he came in.

"Hi, love," she'd said. "I didn't hear the car." She moved toward him for a kiss. "How was your day?"

"What are you doing in here?"

"I needed a match." She held up a matchbook.

"You aren't using my matches! Oh, Leah. I know you used them at the party and I didn't say anything. But this is going to stop." He stalked past her. "Do not use these matches."

"I'm sorry. I didn't know they weren't for use. I'll replace them." She spoke softly, glancing at the matchbook in her hand, reading it. "Herbie's."

He took the matchbook from her and tossed it into the bowl. "Leah, don't I have any rights to privacy?"

"Of course you do. I'm sorry. I didn't know the matches were important. I didn't mean to intrude."

But he turned away from her and frowned into the empty fireplace.

"Ben, let's have dinner. I have a surprise for you, come on." She touched his sleeve lightly, supplicating.

He did not speak.

She said, "Ben, I didn't know the matchbooks were important. I thought they were around, like the matchbooks that collect in the bottom of my handbag. I thought they were like the matchbooks you pick up in passing through places. I have matchbooks in the Pinto, in my desk drawer, coat pockets, and I don't even know where they came from or how they got into my possession, except I must've picked them up."

He still said nothing, but continued to frown into the fireplace, his face averted.

"I do apologize," Leah said.

He waved the words away.

"Oh, Ben. Please. Look, I got tickets and reservations for Tara for next week for us." She took the tickets out of her sweater pocket and held the bright papers out to him.

Something moved behind his obsidian eyes, then stopped. "Don't. Don't placate me. Don't bribe me."

"Bribe! It's a present to both of us! I thought we could take five days and go away together over this spring break."

"No. I can't. I don't have the time. I'm working my balls off. Forget it." He glared at her.

She couldn't understand. She pored over his face, searched his eyes, seeking something that made an answer.

"You use the tickets," he said. "Go away yourself. You need the time alone."

"I don't want to be alone. I'm alone enough. Anyway, I already set it up with Mrs. Mack. You do have five days clear."

"Don't bribe me! Don't smother me. For Christ's sake,

Leah, don't smother me!" He pushed her away and strode out of the study, down the hall and out of the house.

"What? What?" Leah gawped after him.

He left, the big car skidding down the driveway, its taillights blinking as he made the turn out into the street.

Leah felt herself blushing with rage. "Bribe! Smother!" Something lethal had come to life in the house. Leah walked back to the kitchen, cuddling the thing to her breasts, letting it sip the unhealthy juices of her rage and resentment.

She didn't know what to do with herself. She lit a cigarette and poured a glass of wine. She paced. She cleared the unused dishes from the dining room table and folded the tablecloth. She jerked the silverware drawer open and Psi came sliding out. "Why don't you ever sleep where cats are supposed to sleep? Like the laundry basket?" She said: "I'm fit to burst." She hauled the vacuum cleaner out and attacked the house, vacuuming the carpets, the draperies, the ceiling, the corners where dust and cobwebs had not even been thought of yet; she vacuumed the fireplaces, sucked up the ashes, changed the bag inside the vacuum, viciously attacked the couch, the chairs, the lampshades, tops of doors, banging, clanging, rattling; she was killing the house. Now she was limbered up. She tore the bed apart, changed the sheets, threw sheets, shirts, underwear at the washing machine, hauled out the plastic bucket, scorched her hands with boiling-hot water and scrubbers, kneed her way across the kitchen and bathroom floors, rinsed, waxed, swore, fussed, bitched, eased the rage in her heart. No, she thought: Not eased. Just wore it down a bit. The lethal bloodless thing was there, waiting.

She put everything away and took a shower. Wineglass in one hand, cigarette in the other, she walked through the house, her freshly washed hair hanging down her back, her cotton nightgown soft against her skin. It was after midnight. She listened for the bells to sound the quarter hour, stood in the open window of her study for a moment, then went back to the bedroom. She heard Ben's car on the gravel, saw the headlights briefly.

He came into the bedroom.

She watched him step across the carpet, tried to read his face even as she held hers up for his kiss. "Will you want a sandwich?" she asked. But his lips moved to her neck, warm; his breath stirred the hairs at the place behind her ears. He drew her close and held her, kissed her. She leaned back to look at him, somehow to get past his face to his feelings, but he kissed again, those warm lips parting hers, that way he had of taking her breath away from her. And she could feel him, that tender hot thing between them, moving along her thigh; and his arms kept her there, his mouth opening hers, his hands opening spaces in her that required him, his cock, to fill her. And, the anger retreating, she opened to him; even unwilling as she was, even as her sea self retreated, she opened to him and let his fingers touch the sensitive inner lips of her body, held her breath in dread and heat as he, standing with her against the window ledge, held the head of his cock to her flesh and strained with her to move, to convulse together. Not joining him, but struggling, she felt herself falling backward away from the window to the bed, where his clothes were shifted aside; and when she faltered, to recover herself, to move away from him, he lay heavily upon her, cupping her breasts, breathing with his wet open mouth upon a breast, his naked legs horribly wonderfully between hers, his long hot cock dripping along her thighs, touching, burning until her traitor-bitch body moved to suck him in; and even while she ground her teeth and glared, she wanted him. "This is better than a sandwich, isn't it?" he asked. She blushed in rage, in heat, in lust, bucking under him to receive him, to be impaled by him, to, if she only could! kill him. "I won't come," she grunted, steeling herself to only clasp him with her thighs and move against him, to let him move inside her. My anger will keep me from coming, she thought, and shuddered with each sucking thrust; she moved, tightened, and grinned like a poisoned dog at him. But he could always take her will away from her, tonguing it from her mouth, cupping her buttocks, somehow finding and thumbing the most delicious tremors along her vagina, so that even as she mumbled "Technician" she moaned "Please!" and felt the awful consummation begin.

And she heard herself saying: Yes. And wished even as she came that she could stop this, could remain so deep within herself that she would not lose herself in what she knew might well be a loveless fuck.

Then they lay clasped together, staring at each other, he with that look of achievement, and then he moved again inside her, buried his face in her neck, and she felt the sharp tattooing of flesh, the abrupt buck and thrust as he allowed himself to come, as he took power over her.

The clock. She squinted at it in the dark. Four o'clock, she thought. She slipped out of bed quietly so that Ben would not be disturbed. She saw him turned on his side away from her, far on the other edge of the big bed. He was sleeping hard, she could hear his breath; he seemed to tug at sleep, greedy for it; his lips and jaw moved as if he were sucking sleep from the breast of night.

But she could not sleep, would not sleep, she knew. She walked through the dark house to her study and sat down on the Icelandic daybed to chain-smoke and to stare out at the glittering black lawn. She found herself shaking her head; tears moved slowly from her eyes. We have to talk. But what could I say to him? It sounds like the wailing of the wimp to say: There is no comfort here in this house, in this bed. In that bed. In that polar ice cap of a bed. In that ice field. There is no calm or comfort or taking of time to browse contentedly along the silences and the thoughts we might share. Which we don't share. We don't comfort each other, even in sex, which should be comforting as well as what it already is. If what I wanted was only what we had tonight, fucking, distance, I need not have married. Nor should I have married. No, nor he. He need not have married me for this. But the distances he puts between us are increasing, so that even in the tightest clasp I stare across the void he has placed between us.

Or am I wrong, Ben? Point it out to me, show me. I will put my nose dutifully between my paws and study the matter, con it, and where I have been wrong I will put it right. What my eyes will not tell me, surely my nose will. Or my ears. I am a sensible creature, water mammal that I am, I can learn, I can be educated. She sighed. No, that won't do. He feels smothered; his privacy has been invaded, his space intruded upon. And I am the intruder.

But how can that be? He invited me here, asked me to be here. I have come here to be with him, and find that I am intruding. A tear ran along her cheek to her lips. She tasted the salt, dabbed it away with a tissue. But there I go, she thought, lucubrating. If truth is a bitch, I'll coax her from the kennel. It may be she'll mother the other bitch, hope. She blew her nose. We'll talk, she resolved. We'll go on the vacation, Ben and I, and we'll talk. And I'll listen for what goes between and under his words.

She brightened and vowed: We'll solve it.

But they didn't go on the vacation. "I cannot go out of town right now," he said. And said no more about it, merely calling Leah from his office to tell her that he would be late for dinner that night.

"Oh, Ben, we really need the time together. We need to talk. We are having problems and we need to talk, to clear them up." She hated the sound of her voice, it had gone high, had gotten nasal, plaintive.

"I don't think this is an appropriate time, do you? On the *telephone?*"

"But it's the only time I can talk to you. Right now."

"Leah," he sighed.

She could hear the aggravation, the subtext of annoyance and resignation under the sigh.

"Do I have to make an appointment with you? Ben, our marriage is in trouble."

"I don't know why you say that. I'm content. People take time to settle into a life together, to adjust, to . . . accept."

Fleetingly, she wondered if it was that simple. "No. There's more than that," she said. "I really do need to talk to you about this marriage."

"Leah, I don't think there is anything to talk about. Unless, of course, you are unhappy enough to . . . discontinue." He sighed again. "Leah, it is unpleasant, this kind of talk. Do you see why I dodge? I find it less than pleasant to come home to a wife who clamors for painful discussions. For confrontations about matters that I, frankly, do not intend to change." She could hear him shift his weight in the leather chair. "No, I do not intend to change. I thought you understood that long ago. And that you married me with that understanding." She heard him say something away from the telephone. "I must go now. I will see you tonight." He hung up.

She placed the receiver in its cradle. Anxiety made her gasp in pain with each breath. "I don't know what we were talking about," she said aloud. "Have I been clamoring, yapping at his heels? Do I meet him at the door with a list of complaints? Do I proclaim dissatisfaction with each breath? Have I been a geyser of gabble? Have I stood over him with a litany of faults and accusations? What? Do I turn a cold ass to him at night? Do I roll my eyes in boredom when he talks about his work? Do I belittle him?" Anxiety twisted into anger.

She went to her desk and began sorting through the final exams she was writing for her Dramatic Lit class. Well, I'll sneak up on him, she decided. He doesn't like confrontations, so I'll have to try another way to get him to talk. But dammit, never talk to him on the telephone, never talk to him at dinner, never talk to him in bed, or at breakfast, or on the way home from the symphony or a play; never talk to him about our marriage . . . well, I did call through the bathroom door a couple of times, but that wasn't satisfactory. He just turns the shower on. Is it me? Am I imagining we have a problem when we don't? She lit a cigarette and stared at it for a moment. No. Something is wrong.

She worked at her exam writing, typed the exam on ditto masters, and prepared her final lecture notes. Then she went out to the kitchen, fed the cat, tossed the salad for dinner, sliced ham, prepared broccoli, sat in the window seat and looked out across the lawn. "I won't even try to talk to him tonight. I'll find a better time. Anyhow, he knows I'm not happy; he'll be concerned, he'll want to sort things out too."

"I'm going to Toronto Friday," he said that night. "I've been asked to read a paper. We might even get that funding for early detection."

He came back from Toronto, and they did not talk because he was rushing to prepare another paper for Cincinnati.

"I'll talk to you, Leah, let me get some rest," he'd say over dinner, tapping his fingers on the damasked table, glancing at his watch. "Is it *so* serious that I must constantly be up against a wall of accusations?"

"I didn't mean to accuse you. Of what would I accuse you? I do, badly, need some time with you, to talk. I feel we are losing each other. Or I'm losing you."

"Leah," he sighed. He let his coffee cup rattle in the saucer. "Hardly world-shaking, is it? That I'm busy. People do have marital anxieties, but the world doesn't stop."

"No, but it's important to me. To us, I'd think. If one of us is hurting, shouldn't that be important?"

"Of course." He left the table, brushed her forehead with his lips. "I promise you, we will talk. You aren't losing me." But he escaped her outstretched hand, striding from the room, tossing that kind smile, that detached smile, that relieved smile at her. "Get some rest. I'll come to bed early too."

And she'd waken at four o'clock, slip out of bed to pace the dark, waiting house. She knew that she did not pace alone, but that the apparition, the creation of her rage and resentment, paced with her, no longer sipping from her breasts, but full grown in blood and carnality, slouching in the dark with her, touching the hair at the back of her neck with cold sighs.

Then one night while Ben was in Cincinnati, she moved out of the bedroom, out of the big bed, to the Icelandic daybed in her study. "I can't sleep in that bed anymore," she told Psi. "I can't find a comfortable place in it. I feel I need a rope and pitons to scale it, I could go ice fishing in it, I could yodel and get an ice echo."

"I didn't buy it to sleep in alone," Ben said when he came back. "Are you punishing me?"

"No. I just . . . got too lonely in it."

He looked at her, turning her face up to confront her eyes. "Oh, Leah," he sighed. He held her close for a moment. "I'm home now. Let's just have a nice dinner and listen to some records and go to bed early. No tension, no big confrontations. Okay?" He kissed her. "I know. But I have important work to do. So just go along with me."

She allowed herself to be muted, muzzled. She fell into a kind of subdued misery, aware that he was eluding her and that, short of some kind of explosive outburst, she would not be able to bring herself to force the issue.

"I assumed you knew," he had said. "There's been someone all along."

"Assumed I knew," Leah said aloud now, pacing the long hall, "Ben in California assumed I knew!" She clenched her hands together until the fingers cut into each other. "Assumed I knew. You . . . sexualist! Like Bernstein and his black eye that he assumed would notify Clara. The cuts on his back from rolling in glass. So he assumed Clara would read the tracks, a bloody map of his sexual excursions! You, Ben! Did I not see the matchbooks? How many times did I look blankly at them in the pewter bowl and never once, not once did they tell me anything. Ben the sexualist lighting matches in corners, parking the car in alleys for a quickie. Is that it?" She walked to his study, the shadows running ahead of her, chittering silently and creeping into the crevices between the bricks of the fireplace as she turned on the light. The pewter bowl glinted silver, the matchbooks heaped to overflowing. "Jim's Place. Herbie's. Continental Bus Depot. The Anvil, that's in New York. First Wheat Bank. Left Bank, that's Toronto. Grenouille, New Orleans. The Truck Stop, Wyoming." She shook her head. "He's had a love affair for each of these matchbooks? What's he done, met them in banks, gas stations? He must have some little catalogue of girls. Or one girl?" Suddenly sick with rage, she had to close her eyes. The oil of nausea slid up her throat, gagging her. She had instant visions of a thousand mouths kissing his, of tens of thousands of lips sucking at his cock, of millions of fingers touching him in all the places she had thought were hers alone to touch. "You . . . whore!" The matchbooks seemed to shift minutely in the bowl. She took the bowl over to the fireplace, dumped the matches into the hearth, and lighted several. She sat back on her heels to watch as each matchbook sparked and flared, in turn lighting others until the whole pile flamed and smoked. "I'd like to toast your balls, on a long thin steel fork." She glared around the study. Her photograph smiled at her from the desk. "That goes too, smiling ninny!" She broke the picture frame and glass across a corner of the desk and threw the whole thing into the fire. She felt a crazed satisfaction as her own image twisted and turned black. Did I ever exist? she wondered. No, I must be a fantasy. Or he married a figment of our imagination.

"Oh, make sense," she demanded of herself aloud. "If you go crazy, at least be logical about it. 'I assumed you knew,' " she mocked She made fists and battered the wall for a moment, trying to find a hurt outside herself to divert her from the pain that had harpooned her so that she felt she trailed knots of blood with every move. And now that dreadful total recall began, the damned truth-seeing part of her mind that could be closed over no longer began its thousand illuminations:

"I think we should be married." Not: "I love you."

"Would you like to go inside?" Not: "I want you."

And all the careful considerate planned *choreographed* lovemakings: How she had adored the care, the sedulousness of his kisses, his watchful eye and attention to her progressions, as always shamefully quick, so quick and desirous; and now she was ashamed of how much she wanted him, now that she must face how like a gracious host he had been about feeding her his body.

How many times had he turned his face away from her, hiding, she thought, some disappointment with her, while she had lain there, trying to propitiate him, excite him, tantalize him into his own climax, even while he lay on his back and smoked and she licked and oh God what a whore she had been!

And how gently and firmly he could and did put her away from him, kiss her chastely on the forehead and turn away from her, his back a barrier to any prayers, any supplications. Was she not the good wife, the dog wife who would have lain on the floor and licked his treacherous feet on the way to someone else's feet!

"The road maps!" she wailed aloud. "And all the trips we didn't take together." How like the busy bee going from flower to flower you are, Ben! A kiss here, a suck there, is it? Is it motels, hotels, parked cars, vacant lots, directions to her place, directions to the apartment, the house? 'If the porch light is on it's okay.' But what could you do in a bank lobby? An introduction? A chance meeting? Continental Bus Depot in Kansas City. What could you do there? Tête-à-tête over the dirty book? The double-crossing star-crossed lovers, were you? And Ben, you whore, you folded this matchbook into your pocket, and wistfully held the good-bye face in front of your lying eyes and turned your high arched feet homeward?

"The maps!" You marathon sexualist, where *is* home to you? The cup of your shorts, the joint in your crotch, the knob (so easily turned) of your sex. I have a new fantasy now, Lover, about that knob, that hobbyhorse, that one-eyed steed that knows its way in the dark.

Medical conventions. Time alone to yourself; you always said you needed that time alone to rest, to recuperate from carcinomas that pretended to be pregnancies. 'I am not what I seem'; who said that?

Toronto, Quebec, Montreal, New York, Atlantic City, New Orleans, San Diego, San Francisco are only the cities I remember from the matchbooks. But let's see, the bloody maps, the blood thread that you wound—wound, ow, wounded, bloody wounds, blood and tattoos and pain as this "I assumed you knew" pains me.

Leah hauled a desk drawer out all the way, spilling its contents heedlessly on the floor. She pawed through the various maps: Mobile, Texaco, Road and Track, Greyhound, Continental Trailways, United, TWA, Eastern, Ozark Trailways. "He never went anywhere on a bus, *did* he?" she asked the four walls. It must be car trips he took, too. His girlfriends hop around like grasshoppers. What are they? A pride of prostitutes? A caravan of chorus girls? A stampede of stewardi? But what are they doing at truck stops? Bus depots in Kansas City? A truck stop in Nebraska? A motel near the Lincoln, Nebraska, airport? A truck stop in Everglades, Florida? Didn't he perhaps fuck a croc there? I'm going mad. But him. It must be more than one body, he must have sexual hyperesthesia, at least? How does he do it? A phone call from a telephone booth: "Meet me at the truck stop on Highway 71." Or a postcard: "I'll be in Cheyenne at the Hot Rocks Motel on July 10." But what a book of numbers he must have. Or does he take his chances on what is staggering around; "Maybe tonight I'll meet a veritable tartar of a tart," he says to himself, oiling his fly, smoothing his goddamned cock to the left side of his trousers. And does he give that look of mastery to the one he selects, almost arching his neck, that look I thought was mine?

But give him his due, he has never slipped. Not a smirch of lipstick on any handkerchief or shirt. No telltale long hairs on his jackets. Never any female scents, and I would have sniffed 'em out. The nose knows what the eye is blind to.

She had been opening maps and throwing them on the

floor after a glance: "I love pain. I am sexually morbid, this fondling of a corpse not quite dead. What now, you apparitions?" I go on breeding frights, here in this study, fondling a love gone bad. I babble and gibber, mad as any cock-ridden hag. Hag. Hecate, Hecuba, hags, widows, witches, what are they to me, those classy dames? "Witch, shaman, I wish I were! To dabble a finger in the juice of his left eye, to keep him breathless at my breast." Not Medea crying for death offstage, I want to maul him with my great hairy knuckled paws and to bruise him with my horned knees as I ride. "I, cacodemon, ride him high and dry, rendered sexless." Oh, I wish! Ride *him* as he has ridden countless cunts.

But *not* render him sexless; only faithful as I have been doggy faithful, faithful to the shit I have eaten thinking it was love's fastidiousness. No, I want a silver ring, finely wrought, that will fit his head, the head of his cock, just behind it, do you see, witch, sea witch, it will fit snug when erect and loosely when flaccid. And to that silver ring, shaman, fasten a fine light golden chain. One end attach to the ring. I will hold the other end of the golden chain. And when his eye roams, that one eye that I keep ringed and chained, and his little head lifts, I will say: "Hup!" and bring him docile, bring him dame-ridden, hag-ridden, to nod and neigh to my little finger, to my middle finger, to the thumb and forefinger of that hand that holds the golden chain and we will have such a faithful steed, such a happy hobbyhorse, you and I, Ben.

"Ride a cock horse to Banbury Cross!" Leah said, her nightgown swirling around her ankles. "And I will buy a tiny whip with a black handle and red leather tongues to cut the air around you, my one-eyed horse, to touch you up, one-eyed cock horse, keep you stepping to the tunes *I* call. Come to come and come to go, you and I, my cock horse, collared as you are to my ring finger. And where to go?" Follow the road maps in blood on Bernstein's back, follow the road maps that Barry splashed on his bedroom wall, follow the cartography that you have drawn on the inside of my thighs.

Leah lit a cigarette and poked through the silver ashes in the fireplace. The road maps fell together into a pile of leaves, whispering names: Cheyenne, Chicago, Tallahassee, Cincinnati, San Francisco. A penciled word on the margin of one map—"Cowboy"—meant nothing to her, but created a chitter, a stutter, a cough in the back of her mind, a cough from the center of the maze. And I ride, ride, ride the cock horse of obsession and pain, she thought. Battering my griefs under the hooves of the daymare, the dawn mare, the sea mare that sinks moaning under the weight of this chain of tears that now I wind around me.

Cowboy. Cheyenne. Something in the dust of a suitcase. A scent of aftershave. Aftershave! Leah closed her eyes, dizzy, fainting, clammy with sudden vicious chills and sweat. Beer cans in the back seat of that meticulous car, when Ben doesn't ever drink beer.

"It isn't just women," Leah said aloud. "It's worse. And he said into my deaf ear, 'There aren't enough kinks.' He said: "There aren't enough kinks with one person.'" And now I hear what he said, she thought, his words dropping through the distances of my sea world, dropping around me with sounds like knives cutting the water. And I did not, *would not,* hear.

Leah's neck hairs bristled. The apparitions, unwanted, always before brushed aside, now came glaring and powerful, demanding recognition.

And now we are at the center of the maze, she thought, the dead eye of the labyrinth; I see the beasts that have led me here. Hatred. Where I thought I was safely in love, I was snug as the grave in hate. Is it you I hate only, Ben? The fact of you, you sexualist. And which of your sex thrusts do I hate the most? Women? I'm arrogant enough to think I could cope. But men. For that I hate you even more. Because who did you have in our bed, that ice cap? Have I names I haven't known? Cowboy? Who else?

Ah, I had to know. And there is nothing I can do. I hate you because you have loved men and so have escaped me—my rage, even my love.

And left me with the succubus, suspicion. When ever again could I watch you leave and not think: "Ah, who's he going to now?" Or see you return and not wonder: "Who has he just left? Whose spoor will I find upon his flesh, whose seed? Who am I licking when I suck there?"

How, in hindsight, I love Earl, who left me so that his wife might not whelp suspicion!

O Ben. We didn't have children. But we have issue. There is more than one kind of abortion. Barren as I am now of natural children, the knots of blood have trailed me all these years, deep in my mind, stitching me together in this pattern of anger and unspoken rage. I have arranged this pattern. Suspicion, treachery, the will never to forgive, a deformed spirit, these succubi; and I am the unmother of them all, for they come from what is worst in me.

And self-pity. Who is to blame? This pattern I have traced, cut, and pinned to fit? Oh, my mother who loved her boys better than me? At my age I think that no longer is valid; that rage swallowed long ago now has no place, no substance. But I still look for doors to close before me, still wait to be put gently aside. As you put me aside, Ben, I see now, to clasp your other lovers. Like the crayfish of the Tarot, I still wave from the water, and slide back to roll my stalky eyes and tear at the water and clatter my claws in a jangle of self-pity.

No, I am to blame. Not my mother, not my father. Not dear play-doctor Mike. No witch waved over my crib, no shaman fixed entrails to my kitchen door. I, the mother of these incubi, the nurse of these succubi, I am responsible.

And I see that we are all compound/complex. There is not a simple, straightforward rendering to be had here. For as there is the undersea self, the distant eye that stares out from the water world of my consciousness, I know that I do not move alone in the sea world. That eye is not only turning outward to look at the sentient world, it is forever, inalterably turned back and inward to what has happened, to the shipwreck of the past, the drifting bones of the dead that will not lie peacefully at the bottom of my memories, but insist on gazing empty-eyed at me; and I am left here, with the wash of sea water dragging me back to struggle again.

The Unnumbered Card

LEAH turned the last card. She looked at it for a moment, then set it aside. She gathered the rest of the cards, shuffled them, and wrapped them in the back cloth. Carrying the card, she went to the kitchen and put the teakettle on to boil. Then she walked outside to watch the moon tack across the western edge of the sky, to watch the stars, and Orion, tip toward the dark horizon. The toadstools sprang up, silvery cocks amid the wet grasses; Leah stepped around them, heard the wind shaking the trees, felt it press her nightgown, saw it move through the casement cloth in the study window.

The unnumbered card, she thought. The Magus. Again. Completing one cycle, an eye on the sky, the Fool looks over his shoulder even while he steps off the edge of what is known. Is that me? Or you, Ben? You, the riddle. You who diddled with truths. Or I, fool, still to be morbid with love for you. To know that my flesh craves your touch as I crave the suck and sound of you.

But I am unchangeable, she thought, sea creature that I am. I cannot learn your dances, your riddles, Ben. I bruise. I am afraid of deeper cuts, that I may begin to like the thousand cuts, the little hurts; worse, that I might give suck to those incubi and succubi, that I might like them tearing at my nipples, might, indeed, offer them the substance of my life. I have the taste for it, I could live with self-mortification, run to lick your cum from the face of any truck-stop fuck you find.

My flesh yearns for you, Ben. But more than flesh, there is a part of me that is worth loving, and that part of me, my sea self, truly likes you, loves your constellation for virtues; and that part of me I must keep whole.

She heard the teakettle whistle and went back to the kitchen.

She sipped the hot tea and smoked a cigarette. She found a pencil and a pad of paper. She began a list: "The cat carrier. Newspaper." Her hands trembled so that she had to rest her arm on the counter to hold the pencil. As she looked out the window she saw the sky brighten with dawn, turn watery, clear. She heard the wind make its sea sounds in the trees. She wrote: "Packing cartons. Pinto tune-up." And part of her mind thought: Against our will we sometimes find truth. She wrote: "Cat food. His shots."

She almost didn't hear the telephone when it rang.

"Leah? This is Ben. I really need to talk to you."